## "FIRE GOD, LOOK AT THAT!"

Luke looked up where his Messenger pointed. Overhead, a star was falling. Luke squinted against the light, his gaze caught on the ever growing flare.

At first a point, then a hard-edged oblong structure, and then, finally, with ponderous slowness, the shape of the vessel became clear: a capital ship, layer upon layer of armor, plexsteel, shielded glass. It seemed impossible that something so huge—the shadow of it covered the vast parade ground entirely, and even blotted out ranks of barracks on either side—that something that gigantic, could ever become airborne. And as Luke watched, it fell, a city of death, toppling. . . .

# ROC BRINGS THE FUTURE TO YOU

# CHAINS OF LIGHT

## Quentin Thomas

A ROC BOOK

ROC
Published by the Penguin Group
Penguin Books USA Inc., 375 Hudson Street,
New York, New York 10014, U.S.A.
Penguin Books Ltd, 27 Wrights Lane,
London W8 5TZ, England
Penguin Books Australia Ltd, Ringwood,
Victoria, Australia
Penguin Books Canada Ltd, 10 Alcorn Avenue,
Toronto, Ontario, Canada M4V 3B2
Penguin Books (N.Z.) Ltd, 182–190 Wairau Road,
Auckland 10, New Zealand

Penguin Books Ltd, Registered Offices:
Harmondsworth, Middlesex, England

First published by Roc, an imprint of New American Library,
a division of Penguin Books USA Inc.

First Printing, August, 1992
10  9  8  7  6  5  4  3  2  1

 REGISTERED TRADEMARK—MARCA REGISTRADA

Printed in the United States of America

1

## THE WEB

Midday meal approached, and already the Emperor had murdered three of his Chamberlains. The first two were dispatched cleanly, without pain, but the third High Chamberlain died messily. Luke stared at the pool of blood and scattered flesh. He wondered if he wasn't overloading a bit.

"Somebody clean that up," he mumbled absently, and sank back onto the body form cushions of his throne. It was the third Chamberlain he'd murdered, and the day wasn't yet half done.

*Am I overdoing it?*

It was a touchy question. He could never surrender control, but lately his temper had begun to explode for the most trivial reasons. Not that there was any danger. He could slaughter Icons by the billions and never run out. Icons were—well—*Icons*, and as such, inexhaustible. But the symbols of his violence made real could become a problem.

And what, after all, had the Chamberlain done? Already the offense was fading from his awareness.

He sat up straighter and blinked. Time did a tricky two-step, bowed to the Emperor's whim, and the whole scene began to replay—and since the Emperor's location was a matter of personal choice, he chose to be in two places at once.

Luke watched the High Chamberlain approach the throne, but this time, his point of view was from high in the rafters. He glanced at his own body and saw that he wore the form of a lowly slave, ragged and dirty, perched like a scrawny bird in a barely visible niche near the gilded ceiling of the formal audience chamber.

Nice detail, Luke thought to himself. Then he turned back to examine the scene below.

The chamber loomed as a huge space enclosed by gilt, by hanging crystal, by tall, mullioned windows, by ancient-dressed stones, by silk banners, and by intricately patterned marble floor blocks that gleamed oily beneath the warm illumination. Smells of pepper, of sweat, of overheated perfume wafted to his aerie. The low, continuous murmurs of courtiers, ambassadors, supplicants, and even ragged beggars filled the air with a sound like bees. And so they were, Luke thought, bees come to the greatest hive, where the source of all honey ruled with absolute power.

The Chamberlain reached the lowest of the Three Steps, which guarded the throne, and bowed three times. His rich jewelry glittered in the hazy light. Dark blue robes shifted like the scales of a great fish. He advanced to the Second Step and bowed twice and then, finally, mounted the Third Step. He bowed one last time. He stood, touched his chin, and said, "Greatest One, I beg your mighty ear."

Luke could hear the soft words as if he were only inches away. Though his present body listened from a distance, it heard what Luke wished to hear, simply because he desired it. So far, so good, Luke thought. Everything according to protocol. Nothing to piss me off.

"Speak . . . Chamberlain," the Emperor replied. He had forgotten this new Chamberlain's name.

The Chamberlain dipped his head slightly and said, "Oh, Mighty One, the Empire is under attack. The news is grievous. Vast armies assault the Outer Marches—"

The Emperor leaned forward, his green eyes flashing. "I don't want to hear this," he said.

The Chamberlain paused. "But . . . Highness. The Empire itself is threatened—"

The Emperor raised one slim hand, and the Chamberlain *screamed*!

From his vantage point, it seemed to Luke that a haze sprang up around the Chamberlain. The functionary's shape blurred, swayed this way and that. The air about him turned white, then misty red. Luke knew what it was. Invisible knives flayed the Chamberlain, each one slicing a tiny bit of flesh from his bones. Within moments, nothing remained but a viscous puddle of blood garnished with shredded flesh and, in the center, a single gold-chased ruby ring, its stone winking like a reproachful eye.

Luke blinked once again. Now, as he sat on his throne and watched a horde of slaves scrub the offending mess from the Third Step, he understood. It wasn't the Chamberlain. It was the news he brought. The thought of attack on the Empire made him feel both queasily frightened and filled with unreasoning rage.

Attack!

How could it be? It was impossible. The Chamberlain must have been lying.

But *all* of them? He remembered. Each of the three who had died this morning had carried the same message.

He sighed, and glanced at the shimmering denizens of his court moodily. Wherever his gaze passed, others looked down or away. It was not safe to meet the glance of the Greatest Emperor, not on a day when his humor was so unsettled.

He sighed. "Bring my Generals," he said.

A fourth Chamberlain approached. He looked exactly like his three predecessors. He completed the Ritual for Approaching the Throne and said, "Mightiest One, you have no Generals."

Luke felt his irritation begin to boil over yet again, and forced restraint upon his natural urge to deep-fry the Chamberlain into a smoking fritter.

"Well, then," he said, keeping his words soft and reasonable. "I'd better make some, hadn't I?"

## THE HEGEMONY: CITY

In the chamber where the template lay in supposedly perfect stasis, an attendant named Charlie noticed a curious thing. He was a good-looking young man with a high, clear forehead, eyes framed in premature laugh lines, good bones, white teeth, and brown, curly hair—very much a young man of his time and place. He was intelligent and thought himself cosmopolitan, but now he paused and stared in surprise. His youthful face broke into a grin. He was just out of the Imperial College, fully trained in the convolutions of modern nanobiology, and still young enough to empathize with the event he observed.

But was it a first? He'd only been on this job a few months, and so he sat at a terminal and jacked in. A few moments later he jacked out, after reviewing the history of this template. His grin was wider. He checked to make sure the cameras that watched the template with unblinking electronic eyes were properly focused, and made a short note of description in the daily log.

Two hours later his relief appeared, and Charlie, still grinning, told the young woman what he'd seen.

The woman, whose name was Eileen, chuckled. "You're sure it's the first time?"

"I checked."

"Well, isn't that nice?"

Charlie, who possessed a masculine understanding of just how nice it was, nodded. "Yeah. I still remember my first one."

"The first time you had sex?"

Charlie shook his head. "Nope. My first wet dream."

She eyed him dubiously. "Really? You remember something that trivial?"

"It's not trivial. Not if you're a boy."

She glanced at the template that rested, nude and unmoving, within its crystal shroud. "That's not a boy."

"Of course it—he—is."

She had never been trained to think of the template as human. The thought, to her surprise, mildly disconcerted her. "And it dreams?"

"It must," he replied. "Look. There he goes again."

Both stared, as before them, the template's penis began to grow erect.

"I wonder what its dreams are like?" Eileen mused.

Charlie, who had a fair comprehension of how the Web functioned and what role the template enjoyed there, smiled sadly, almost enviously. The template would be spared the sorrows, but also the joys, of human adolescence.

"Wonderful dreams," he said. "Wonderful . . ."

## THE WEB: EMPIRE

Normally the process by which Blanks were programmed into Icons was carried out automatically by the legions of Teachers, which swarmed in their Universities, but in this case, the Emperor decided to take a personal hand. After all, this would be the creation of a whole new class of Icons, and one which the Emperor had never anticipated.

Moving his personal Court was always a complicated process. Normally he went nowhere without a vast retinue of slaves, courtiers, and advisers. The Empire was an incredibly complex creation, and the Emperor preferred to follow its day-to-day rules exactly. He found comfort in the rituals that allowed him control over the trillion subjects within his domain. But now he determined time was of the essence. He dispensed with the usual massive preparations and simply appeared in the Great Hall of Learning at the heart of the University, which occupied a large part of his capital.

He stood a moment, observing silently. All around him bustled and rustled black-robed Teachers, their faces intent upon their myriad tasks. Many were followed by small groups of Blanks, who wore white robes and empty expressions. That would change, the Emperor knew, as each Blank received its training and eventually, fully programmed, joined one of the millions of classes that made up the fully realized society of the Empire.

His sudden appearance caused a stir. The Teachers glanced at him, uncertain of what to do with an Imperial apparition. In the end they did nothing, but their ranks parted as the Deans of the University appeared in a crow-colored phalanx and swept across the wide stone floors toward their master.

The Chancellor reached him first and bowed three times. Ritual was more relaxed in the halls of learning, and since the Emperor had not come with a full retinue, perhaps this was an informal visit.

"Chancellor, what do you know of Generals?" the Emperor asked without preamble.

The Chancellor drew himself up. His eyebrows arched. "Generals, Mightiest One?" He turned and glanced at the Deans, who mostly shrugged, but one stepped forward and bowed.

"Highness, my department is interfaced with the Librarians on this subject. We have no use for the knowledge in a practical sense, but the question has come up in some of the work we do."

The Emperor nodded. The work of the Empire was endless, and reached into dark corners of which Luke himself was ignorant. Well, not entirely ignorant. Luke could know, if he so desired, the most minute detail of the Empire. Generally he didn't so desire, and the work went on automatically, tended by Librarians and Teachers and Administrators who oversaw the unceasing flood of Icons and their connections.

"Go on," Luke said.

The Dean, startled at this unexpected attention to his own rather obscure discipline, stood taller. Personal interest from the Emperor! His department need no longer lurk in moldy disrepute, but could hold its collective head high, even as the Dean now did.

"Does the Mightiest One wish programming?" the Dean asked formally.

"The Emperor does," Luke replied.

"Ah . . ." sighed the Dean. His future was assured.

The Chancellor stood aside and motioned the Dean impatiently forward. "Go on, man," he hissed. "You know the drill."

The Emperor smiled slightly.

"Uh, ah, yes," the Dean spluttered. He did know the drill. He had just never expected to use it. He hesitated one final second, then bowed again, this time more deeply. "If the Emperor will accompany me to the Hall of Programming?"

Luke nodded. "Lead on . . . Dean."

He wondered what this one's name was. Damn. Even an Emperor couldn't know everything.

The thought startled him, and he examined it as he followed the Dean. Couldn't know everything?

But of course he could.

It was his job, wasn't it?

## THE HEGEMONY: CITY

When he arrived in the template chamber for his next watch, Charlie reviewed the history of the preceding day. There had been no repetition of yesterday's wet dream, but there had been several erections. He noted the number, and then ran a comparison scan for the life of the template. After he saw the results, he grinned again.

No doubt about it. The rate of frequency was definitely increasing, particularly in the last few months. His interest grew more engaged. It was easy to forget—or suppress, as Eileen did—the knowledge that the templates were human. But Charlie had not grown jaded about his charges, and this template intrigued him. He tried to draw parallels between his own experience and what was occurring with the template now. He couldn't quite do it, but the idea excited him. There were so few templates, and most of them were very old. This was, to his best knowledge, the only one of this particular age.

A template approaching puberty. Perhaps there might be a paper in it.

On a hunch, he checked another figure.

The result made him smile even wider. He ambled over to the shroud and stared down at the template. "Hey, kid," he said. "You know you're only two days away from your thirteenth birthday?"

He stopped. "Maybe we ought to throw you a party. What do you think of that?"

Charlie, for all his knowledge of nanobiology, had only a smattering of learning about the ins and outs of the Web, or of the potential inherent in the vast technological infrastructure that bound the worlds together. He had, for instance, never heard of the Twisten except as a fairy tale used to frighten children. That the Twisten actually existed was something he'd never considered. That the Twisten might be interested in *him* was an idea beyond his wildest dreams.

But an odd—to him it seemed humorous—idea began to grow. It started just after his most recent autonomous pleasure-therapy session. He didn't notice the idea wasn't entirely his. All he knew was that it appealed to him. And maybe the template would enjoy it.

After all, the template's birthday was only two days off. Charlie wished somebody had thought to give him such a gift on *his* thirteenth birthday.

## THE WEB

Luke and the Dean who followed him reached a smaller chamber just off the main hall, where Luke seated himself in a low, leather-covered chair that immediately molded itself to his shape. It was like sitting in a warm, comfortable hand. The Dean knelt and placed his fingers on Luke's forehead. Luke stared down into the Dean's eyes.

It was a strange feeling. Like looking into a mirror. Not hard to understand, because the Dean, like all of Luke's subjects, looked exactly like himself. The Dean was an Icon, and all Icons in the Empire were precise duplicates of the Emperor. There were ways to introduce differences, and more than a few times Luke had done so—but the results had been disappointing. Differences made for control difficulties. It was simpler to let the Icons remain what they were—trillions of versions of himself, each with differing capabilities, but overall structural identity.

The Dean's fingertips lightly caressed his temples. He could smell the Icon's warm breath in his face. Normally it would be *lese majesty* of the worst sort for an Icon to approach this close, but the ritual of imparting demanded it. What would shortly occur was at the very heart of the structure of the Empire—a Dean, an emperor of information in his own right, would interface with the Emperor, impart his knowledge, and participate in the creation of a new class of Icon. Within nanoseconds, Luke would know everything this Dean knew about Generals—more than enough to format countless stacks of Blanks that would eventually become Iconic Generals.

"Sire, are you ready?" the Dean whispered softly, his words soft caresses on Luke's cheeks.

Luke felt a flash of irritation. Why did he put up with all this flimflam Imperial bullshit?

He calmed himself. The answer was simple. He put up with it because he had decreed it. The Empire itself was an Icon, a structural illusion by which he controlled the data-handling capabilities of his part of the Web.

And the Web—

He pushed the thought away. Something had begun to bother him about the Web, too, but now was not the time. "Proceed . . . Dean," he said. *I really should try to learn their names.*

The room where the ritual took place was small because it didn't need to be any larger. It was plain because it would soon vanish. And it would vanish because, like the Empire and everything in it but the Emperor, it was an illusion of very high order.

The winds began and illusions fell away. All that remained was the Web. The Emperor, Lucifer, who called himself Luke and would soon be thirteen years old, experienced the truth of his environment.

The truth was the Web, and the Web was chaos.


## THE HEGEMONY: CITY

When the technician, Charlie, got off-shift, he left the vast building that sheltered his charges and hurried to a sidewalk. He didn't glance at the inscription embossed upon the arch of the great doorway through which he jogged. He'd seen it thousands of times, beginning when he'd first decided to spend his life's work here, and then on a daily basis after he'd finally received his degrees and qualified for the task.

*"The Hegemony Is Bound in Chains of Light."*

Taken of itself, it was a curious thought, but to a ten-year-old boy still searching for a vocation, the image had been seductive. He'd been able to visualize it then, the great sweep of the million planets, all meshed into cohesion by gossamer wings of pure brightness. And here, in the ancient heart, in this very building, was the center of it all—the Hegemon's Web, by which all the matrices were ordered and governed in the endlessly multiplied brains of a few hundred strange, almost holy, beings.

The magic had endured for years, long enough for him to attend the Imperial University and graduate with the highest marks in his class, but now, after six months in that building, the cynicism of reality had done its work. He tried to conceal it from himself, but Charlie understood what he was—a glorified babysitter for hyper-powered infants who would grow old before his eyes, but would never, ever wake.

Some of the awe remained, though, and would only

pass with the passage of his own youth. They were *his* babes, and he still cared about them, about what they *were*, and about the incredible power contained in their sleeping forms.

To him, they were human. He liked to imagine they had human needs. And this particular template, the one called Lucifer, was young enough to strike empathetic chords in his own humanity. Or so he thought, as he agilely dodged through the hordes of the City With No Name, which coated the skin of World, from which the Hegemony and everything in it began and ended.

He was a denizen of City on World, and no other identification was needed. The concept was as much a part of him as the inexorable messages locked within his genes. He would have been surprised to find that others regarded him with cold amusement. For Charlie, the Hegemony existed within the crushing weight of eternity—but for the Twisten, it was but the passing whim of one who showed every sign of going renegade. Thus, in the small perversity of an insignificant technician's errand, did the first kiss of conflict between the True Powers occur.

History being what it is—lies told by victors—one side or the other should have embellished the moment with trumpets. Instead, Charlie tripped as he stepped onto the people mover headed for the Scarlet Sector, and bumped his elbow.

"Shit fire," he said, rubbing the tingly spot. He wondered if he could accomplish his self-imposed mission and still get home in time for his regularly scheduled autonomous therapy session.

## THE WEB: THE DEEP BENEATH

Illusion fell away like crumpled tissue into darkness. Then, at first barely visible and filmy, the chains began to appear. An invisible wind howled, filling space with a long and lonely cry. It was the quantum lament, down where the particles rubbed and scraped and crashed against each other in ceaseless atomic dance. As electrons shrieked, the chains grew brighter. Each chain represented a stack of Icons, millions or billions of them. Dancing before him like an incandescent dervish was the glowing chain of the Dean and his School. He was surprised to note it wasn't large at all; but the art of war, and the knowledge of Generals who pursued the art, was not one of Luke's specialties. Now that would change.

He smelled damp, burned wood, and tasted rusty iron. The wind howled in his ears. His Empire, reduced to essentials, stretched out around him like the universe which, in fact, it was.

He had no sense of his own form, nor did he care. The means by which he still heard, and tasted, and smelled the inputs of this place had no consequence. He was Emperor, but he couldn't know the limitations imposed on him, and those like him. Stunted self-knowledge was one of those limitations. The Emperor was—but he didn't know *what* he was.

The snakelike chain of the Dean bowed toward him, and Luke spread figurative arms. Then darkness and light coalesced, and the wind screeched furiously as a river of electrons lurched and flowed between them.

It never occurred to the Emperor that the process might be painful—in this context he didn't understand such concepts. The exchange was what he was, and what he did; it was his essential function. Thus, he could not know—another imposed limitation—that in a place very near, but very far away, a technician noted a transitory blood pressure spike, and machines monitoring brain function recorded a short episode of increased activity within the template duplication nodes.

What Luke felt was exhilaration, as knowledge flowed into him and power flowed out. It was the power of creation—and when he was done, the chain before him was vastly thicker and longer, swollen with newly created Icons.

The Illusion returned, and the Emperor stared at a much larger Dean, one now bloated with the potential to birth Blanks by the billions.

Now the Dean was great among his kind, for the Emperor had remade him into a principle Icon. The Dean sank to his belly and placed his forehead on the stony floor. "Majesty, I thank you," he said simply.

"Rise . . . Dean."

The man climbed to his feet. His green eyes flashed with a new fire. Luke regarded him thoughtfully.

"Make me some Generals, Dean. And whatever else is necessary."

"Yes, Lord." The Dean paused, waiting.

Luke remembered. "Oh, you can go."

Relieved—had the Emperor seemed a bit . . . absentminded? Unthinkable!—the Dean bowed a final time and turned.

"Oh, Dean?"

"Yes, Majesty?"

"What's your name?"

## THE HEGEMONY: CITY/SCARLET SECTOR

City on World was precisely that. World, occupied by the Expansion of Man in such long-ago antiquity that even its original name was lost, had become a monument to the never-ceasing urge of government to expand into all available space. Even the near-surface orbits were packed with whirling, glittering shapes. World's system had once possessed a ring of asteroids. The circling rocks no longer existed, or at least not in their original forms. Gigantic chunks of nickel and iron and heavier metals had been smelted for their metal or burned for their power, transformed into the thin rime of metal and ceramic that coated World in a seamless cover, or remade into different satellites orbiting a stranger core. Even World's sun, carefully husbanded, was dimmer than it once had been, after eons of careful energy sucking which had, no doubt, significantly shortened its life.

Sixty-five billion humans inhabited the skin of World, from five-mile towers to force-bubbles, which floated barely above the magma layer.

The Scarlet Sector consisted of two hundred levels. Each level was approximately fifty miles on a side. The sum added up to half a million square miles devoted only, and entirely, to every sensation of all the worlds and times of man. Although a minuscule fraction of the total area of World, the Scarlet Sector enjoyed vastly disproportionate patronage. All humans, at one time or another, itched. The Scarlet Sector existed to scratch. Any itch, any time.

Charlie took the slide away to the nearest T-feed center, a matter of five minutes. The T-center, a time-stained, echoing place, swiftly took his codes, stuffed him into a booth, and blasted him into atoms. Thirty seconds later—the time lag was due to processing, not transmission—other machines in a distant T-center slapped him together in a procedure that bore more than passing resemblance to that which operated within the templates themselves.

Charlie thought nothing of it. He barely noticed either center. For him, it was a matter of *stepping in* and *stepping out*. The only difference he noted was that in the place of his arrival the light was more artfully dimmed, and there seemed to be a lot of sweaty movement going on in the shadows. He shrugged and passed on, and a moment later entered the Sector proper.

A soft weight landed on his shoulder and a rumbling voice whispered in his ear, "Something, my darling?"

Charlie turned, squinting against the crimson flare of light that cast this part of the Scarlet Sector into harsh, unforgiving shades of black and gray. A bear of a man towered over him, his massive paw still resting lightly next to Charlie's neck. The bear-man smiled, revealing teeth that ended in points. *How does he eat?* Charlie wondered, and then, *What* does he eat? A thick pelt of gleaming fur covered the bear-man's body. His face was hidden with wide, silvery goggles. At first Charlie thought his accoster navigated by infrared, but then the man lifted one lens to reveal nothing but blank fur beneath. No eyes at all.

"Well?" the bear-man rumbled hopefully.

For a moment Charlie actually considered the proposition. The bear-man was certainly exotic enough. It would be like fucking a rug, he thought. But then his self-possession reasserted itself. The signs were ominous. Those who haunted the exits that debouched into Scarlet Sector did so because of age, taste, or criminal tendencies. They were allowed no other place.

And that mouthful of needle-teeth was *scary*.

"No, thanks," Charlie said politely, shrugging away the paw. "Another time, perhaps."

The bear stepped back, his blank silver stare focused on him like a silent searchlight. "Ah. Something else, then? I know many things, many places, young man."

Charlie shook his head one more time, then reconsidered. "No, wait a minute." He held out his hand. "Credit check?"

The bear nodded and extended his own shaggy paw.

Their palms touched, and the tiny computers that resided just beneath the skin of every citizen held short
conversation. Satisfied, the bear-man withdrew and
said, "What do you have in mind, pal, if not me?"

Charlie told him, and the bear-man laughed. "That's a
good one, friend. Kind of tame, but good. And easy
enough to find. I know just the one."

"What's the fee?" Charlie didn't frequent the Scarlet Sector often, but he wasn't entirely a fool.

Bear-man shrugged. "Not much. Ten percent, for
finders."

Charlie knew that his would-be guide would steer
him to someone whose price was already inflated to
cover the bear-man's surcharge, so that he would pay
the bear-man twice, but he didn't care. What he
sought was mundane, and therefore cheap.

"Good enough," Charlie said.

The bear-man shifted out of seductive mode. Charlie didn't notice until he realized the man had turned
off his pheromone broadcasters. So that was what was
under all that hair. Once again his interest was
piqued—pheromones, properly handled, were always
a trip—but then remembered he had a job to take
care of. Nevertheless, he reminded himself to record
the bear's codes for later reference. It might be nice,
on a slow night, even with those teeth . . .

"Right this way."

Charlie followed.


## THE WEB: EMPIRE

Luke had never consciously lived in the Hegemony
of which he was such a vital part, but he had modeled
his own Empire on it, as much as he was capable. He
tapped into all data transmission as a matter of course.
Whole countries of Icons were dedicated to nothing

else. They fed their data to the Librarians, who made it available to all who needed it. In his Empire, everybody had a function. Sometimes it was confusing—for his Empire was an Icon as well, although he lived in it and thought of it as real. Yet he knew it wasn't real, and this gave rise to the welter of indecision that assaulted him now.

He had returned to his private chambers, where servants had already prepared a meal. The table on which his meal was served in a seemingly endless succession of courses—he liked to pick and taste—was made of ruby-encrusted pearl onyx, its perfect black surface swirled with pools of embedded milk. It was an exact copy of one on which the Hegemon himself dined. Luke understood that the Hegemon existed in the World, and was his master, although he didn't understand how or why.

He stared down at a chased silver tray that overflowed with exotic fruit, then glanced up vacantly, the food forgotten. The ugly memories of the day returned. Murdering an Icon was not, precisely, murder. The Icon was, after all, only a duplicate of himself, and so erasing the pattern, no matter how violently he did so, was not a crime—at least, not in any sense of the word he understood. He suspected the whole concept of crime—or of any other moral axiom accepted in the Real World—had little validity in his own Empire.

His Empire existed only for him, for the simple reason that it *was* him. No more, and no less. He recognized the concept of masturbation in an empirical sense, and was even able to leap to the idea of mental masturbation.

"I wonder if the Makers . . ." he spoke aloud, "know what they have made."

Makers was his own term for those shadowy, nameless inhabitants of the Real World who had been responsible for his own creation. He knew so little about their purpose, or his own. It bothered him. He sensed great changes coming, upheavals for which he had small comprehension or understanding.

These attacks, for instance.

Attacks? Who would want to attack him? It was a personal attack, of course, for he was the Empire, and any assault on it was equally on him.

There were other Empires. He had commerce with them. They traded information. One of those Empires specialized in Generals and Soldiers, and occasionally hired out its armies as mercenaries to those who needed them. He'd never felt the need, for he'd never been attacked. But, obviously, others had, or why the necessity of an Empire of Soldiers?

"Chamberlain," he said softly.

A moment later the most recent incarnation of that Icon appeared. Luke examined his face and saw his own features, albeit with a different hairstyle—his normally short, black, curly ringlets had been allowed to grow, and were heavily greased and encrusted with small, glittering blue crystals—and wondered why he never got bored with so many copies of himself. In theory, at least, it should grow tiresome—but narcissism on the scale he experienced was only a word in his vast vocabulary.

"My Lord?"

"Have other Empires been attacked in ways similar to our current crisis?"

The Chamberlain blinked. He'd been afraid the Emperor might still be in a killing rage. He knew the fate of his three immediate predecessors and was, in his own way, no less a fully integrated personality than the Emperor himself. He didn't want to die. Now the Greatest Ruler was calling it a crisis.

He trod carefully. He was fully programmed with all information relating to the assaults, after a session with the Librarians and the Deans. It was a normal part of his job, which was to act as adviser, deputy commander in chief, and general conduit for any wish the Emperor might conceive.

"Other Empires have been attacked, Highness," he said slowly. "But not in the precise manner we have been."

Luke's green eyes grew sharper, more penetrating. Something was hidden here. "Explain, Lord Chamberlain. What are the differences?"

"In the other cases I'm familiar with, the attacks have come from the outside. That is, forces alien to an Empire attack it, and must be repelled or destroyed."

"Yes," Luke said impatiently, "I understand that." The idea of others warring on the Empires of the Web was repulsive, but not unheard of. He knew what such things meant in the Real World, as well—somebody attempting to break into or otherwise corrupt the Web itself. These forays were always detected and, he supposed, punished in some Real World way. Maybe by the Hegemon himself.

"Is that happening now? Is somebody trying to invade our Empire, perhaps take Icons prisoner?" The Real World analog of this was data theft.

The Chamberlain shook his head. "No, my Lord. The invaders don't come from beyond the Empire."

Luke shook his head slightly. Now he was completely confused. "Not from outside? Then where?"

The Chamberlain sighed, and resolved to die as quietly as he could. "From inside, Highness. The invaders are Icons like myself. They are *you*, Your Majesty."

## THE HEGEMONY: CITY/SCARLET SECTOR

Charlie paused and stared at a woman whose skin was made of tiny snakes. The snakes, small green things with sapphire eyes, grew directly from her flesh, and darted tiny, pointed tongues at him. The woman reclined on a velvet lounge behind a brightly lit window on the Street of Whores. He thought that a mild conceit—in Scarlet Sector, there must be thousands of such streets, and each called itself *the* street—but she did look interesting. He wondered what she could make those snakes do.

"Come, Master," the bear-man said gently. "The one you want is just down here."

Reluctantly, Charlie turned his gaze from the snake-lady. He had never been in this part of the Sector before. It was ill lit and shadowy, and the sanitation machines must have been damaged or—more likely—reprogrammed. He found himself unexpectedly responding to the general air of decay, to the truly bizarre creations who waddled and snuffed and lurched on by, bound on indecipherable errands of lust. He nodded at the bear-man. "Yes, I'm coming."

But that was what Sector was for, wasn't it? Almost a therapeutic place, where a human could plumb whatever cricks and corners existed in the bowels of his psyche. He felt weirdly exhilarated—he would have to return soon, on his own account, and spend some time. This looked a lot more interesting than his autonomous therapy sessions, and was probably cheaper in the long run.

A few moments later they reached a window that fronted a cubicle filled with gray mist. The fog within eddied and whirled in interesting oily patterns, but he could see nothing else.

"This? Is this all?"

The bear-man must have been used to such initial disappointment, for he merely raised one massive paw and said, "Wait." He reached forward and rapped sharply on the plexwindow pane.

For a moment nothing happened. Then the mist, as if responding to his signal, suddenly turned the color of blood. Star-shot fragments of black light began to dance within the crimson flow.

"Pretty," Charlie murmured.

The motes moved faster and faster, until the blood roiled and foamed, and the dots became hard, brittle lines of vibration. Charlie had seen such hallucinations before, under the effect of certain tailored varieties of amphetamine, but he understood this vision was not a product of his own neurochemical factories.

"Now . . ." the bear-man breathed softly.

The blood sank with a swirling motion into the bottom of the cubicle, swirling out like water from a tub. The lines of vibration remained, hanging in the air like small brush strokes. Then Charlie saw it. A pattern began to form, as if an invisible artist were sketching a figure with only the most delicate movement of his tools.

Hair first, dark, gleaming and long—but oddly cut, crude, chopped off. Then lips curved in a cool smile. A face took form, then a body, long, lean, hard-muscled. When the figure was nearly complete, she looked down and smiled at him, as if she were aware of his presence beyond the plex. Perhaps she was.

But Charlie felt a small, cold nugget grow in his gut. She was beautiful, oh yes, but inset above a slightly crooked nose were two blank holes. Something red danced within, like tiny perfect fires.

Then, the final apparition made her complete. Two spinning crackles of aching, emerald-shot green burst into flame on either side of her skull, looped around her head like planets, and dived finally into the deserted, burning sockets.

The effect was more than startling. Her gaze pierced him, beckoned him, knew him in ways he hadn't thought possible.

She was terrifying.

He wanted her desperately.

The bear-man watched his charge. Now he smiled. He knew when the mark was hooked.

"Nice, eh?" he grunted.

Charlie licked lips suddenly gone dry as sandpaper. He was painfully conscious of the working of his body, and the sound of tongue on flesh was a sharp, desiccated rasp in his ears.

He knew his erection was completely obvious, and didn't care.

"She's . . ."

"I know," the bear-man agreed.

"I . . . I'd like—"

"Of course you would. Have to test things out, first, right? To make sure she's okay for your little plan?" His voice was rancid with spurious jolliness.

"Uh, yes. That's right. A test—"

Charlie moved toward the window, but stopped as the bear-man's paw caught his shoulder again. "Not so fast, my darling one."

"What? What do you—"

"Your palm, sir. Give me your palm."

Sudden relief. "Oh. Of course."

When the transaction was sealed, the woman behind the glass moved forward slightly, her eyes ensnaring Charlie's attention like snags of barbed wire.

Unthinking, he moved again, but the bear-man turned him slightly and said, "This way. You can't do anything through that plex."

A door opened on darkness. "Right in there," the bear-man said.

The hole was open, but seemed impenetrable. Yet was that the faintest flash of emerald, there in the dark?

"What's her name?" Charlie asked.

The bear-man laughed. "Naomia."

"What's so funny?"

"I thought everybody knew Naomia."


## THE WEB: EMPIRE

"I don't understand this," the Emperor said.

The Chamberlain, who had tensed his body in expectation of invisibly flaying knives, a wash of burning oil, or something even worse, relaxed at the unforeseen mildness of the reply.

"I don't, either, Majesty."

The Emperor looked up at his Chamberlain. Under normal circumstances, no subject of the Empire was allowed to force the Emperor to look up, but Luke permitted such things in the privacy of his quarters.

"How can I attack myself?"

The Chamberlain's duty was to answer any question the Emperor asked, or show him where to find the answer, but he was stumped. "Majesty, I have spent much time with the Librarians and the Deans. None of them have ever heard of such a thing." It was not a strictly true answer. The Chamberlain's predecessors had done the research, but since the new Chamberlain encompassed all the experience of every Chamberlain who had gone before him—and there were thousands—blurring the truth was understandable.

"The Deans know nothing? The Librarians have no records?"

"Not of something like this, Sire."

Luke thought about it. He gnawed on his thumbnail, then shook his head. "Do they have any ideas?"

The Chamberlain wasn't precisely sure what the Emperor asked, but he recalled something one of the Deans of Science had mentioned. He had passed over it, though this Dean—whose school wrote Icons for the Administration classes—was one of the greatest. But his theory was so inconceivable!

Yet the Emperor demanded ideas. Perhaps this insane theory would qualify.

"Yes, Sire. One of them." He paused.

"Go on."

Thoughts of knives and oil began to percolate within the Chamberlain once again, but he pressed on. "There is the possibility of corrupted chains, Sire."

Luke raised his head sharply. "What!"

The Chamberlain noted the dangerous tone, but there was nothing he could do. He was the Chamberlain. His function was to handle questions. "The theory goes that it is possible for an Emperor to make mistakes. To created flawed Blanks and corrupted chains."

Luke half rose from his chair, his knuckles whitely outlined where his fingers gripped the carved mahogany arms.

"Impossible!"

The Chamberlain blinked. Still alive. So far, good enough. "Yes, Sire. It is impossible, of course."

But Luke sank back down, shaking his head slowly. He took one hand from the chair and stared at the thin bones that fanned across its back. Then he did what he'd been designed to do, although he couldn't know just how thorough those design parameters had been. He was Emperor. His true function was to rule his Empire. Now he did so.

"Of course it's possible, Chamberlain. It's happening."

The Chamberlain bowed slightly. Amazing. The Emperor was evidently not going to kill him. Two such escapes in less than an hour.

"What are your orders, Sire?"

This was the other principle function of the Chamberlain. As he channeled input to the Emperor, he also routed the Emperor's output to the appropriate receptors.

"My orders? I'll have to take a look for myself, I suppose. But first, I need to know more. Have we requested help from other Empires?"

"Not yet, Sire."

"Do so."

There was a note of finality that the Chamberlain didn't miss, and this time his bow was deep. "Yes, Majesty." He began to withdraw.

"Chamberlain?"

"Yes, Sire?"

"Do it quietly. And carefully."

"Of course, Sire."

The Emperor nodded, and the Chamberlain withdrew. In the silence, Luke stared at nothing, and wondered what was happening to him. The Empires of the Web could communicate with each other, but what he had requested was the equivalent of a Search. Such things were almost unheard of. He might have to go himself, and he found it hard to imagine the changes he would have to make.

His Empire was his own. It was an Icon he had created. He allowed no other Icons' presence here, unless properly translated into pseudo-Icons that duplicated—and were as controlled—as his own subjects.

He supposed the other Empires were no different. But what was it for an Emperor to become . . . something else? Or, more chilling, for an Emperor to submit to the power of another? His problem was becoming more deadly, more defined. He was somehow attacking his own Empire, and might have to leave it in order to save it.

Would he do it?

Could he do it?

*Did he have a choice?*

# 2

## THE HEGEMONY: CITY/SCARLET SECTOR

"Mother of God!" Charlie gasped.

The bear-man came up behind him and hoisted him up by his armpits. "I don't think so," he said mildly. "It just feels like it."

Charlie stared at the dim, shifting light of the Street of Whores and shook his head in disbelief. His knees buckled again, but the bear-man held him firmly. A raw, raging heat still burned in his crotch. He couldn't think clearly. It felt as if his brains had been sucked out through his penis. Savage waves of fever, then jittering chills rampaged through his body. He breathed in harsh, strangled rasps.

He had never felt better in his life.

After a few moments, his legs began to show signs they might support him.

"Better?" rumbled the bear-man softly. "Don't feel bad. Everyone's like this, after a session with . . . her."

Charlie staggered back and propped himself against the cold blankness of the plexwindow. Nothing showed behind the vacant glass, not even shifting fog. The plex had gone mirror-mode and when he turned, only his red-rimmed eyes stared back at him, wide and wild.

"You going to be okay?" the bear-man asked.

". . . Think so," Charlie said. He swiped at his forehead. His fingers slid across a film of cold sweat.

He closed his eyes, and an unbidden montage burned furiously in the darkness of his skull. The scenes were fragmentary. The only thing he remembered fully were her eyes. Those molten green sockets were seared into the folds of his brain.

He inhaled raggedly, grateful for the conditioned coolness of the street air. At least the ventilation systems were working properly. "God . . ." he muttered again.

"I'll walk you back up," the bear-man said.

Charlie forced himself to stand straight. The logical part of his mind told him she was only a whore, no matter how good, just a prostitute. The other part, that knew its kin was closer to reptile than human, didn't think anything at all. It only desired, and right now, what it wanted more than anything was for Charlie to put out his palm, shake with the bear-man, and go back into that green-shot darkness.

"Can I . . . I mean—"

"No. Sorry." The bear-man knew what he wanted, too, but he shook his head. "Only one to a customer. That's why I laughed, you know?"

"What?"

"When you asked what her name was. You'll never forget it now, will you?"

"Naomia." *Naomia!*

"Right. You okay to walk now?"

"I think so."

The bear-man led him gently, almost solicitously,

back to the T-center. Just outside the entrance, he paused. "Will she do?"

"For what?"

"Your little plan. The one you told me about. Or was that a lie?"

Charlie had completely forgotten. "Oh. God, yes. She's fine." Then doubt assailed him. Naomia—what would she do to the kid? His first time? Burning Gods, she was enough to wake the dead. But that was, after all, more or less what he had in mind.

"How can I get in touch with her?" He was pleased that his voice sounded brisk, businesslike.

"You can't. But I'm here every night, and I'm easy to find." The bear-man moved closer and said, "I'll give you my code."

Charlie took the paw. His chine's receptor node obediently copied the bear-man's comm codes. "You want mine?"

The bear-man squeezed his hand gently. His phero-mone broadcasters were going full blast. "Sure, darling thing."

But after what he'd just experienced, the bear-man no longer had the slightest attraction. He transmitted his codes anyway. The bear-man was the only connection he had with . . . Naomia.

"They call you Charlie," the bear-man boomed affably.

Charlie summoned a reply. His chine smoothly provided it.

"And your name's Grog."

"That's it," the bear-man agreed. He flashed a mouthful of bony white needles. Somehow the effect was cheerful—but after Naomia, not inviting. Nor were the pleasure machines he'd always used before in the privacy of his home. For one shaking, terrible moment, he wondered if anything would ever be. Anything but *her*.

# THE WEB

Luke held audience in the Privy Council chamber, a much smaller, more intimate affair than the formal audience chamber. The room was dominated by a long table intricately carved of rose quartz, shot through with veins of black and silver. His throne dominated one end of the table, from a raised dais. Light scattered from two huge chandeliers shaped to resemble willows, although their drooping leaves were made of hammered gold. Tall mirrors along the walls reflected the anxious expressions of those gathered to advise their master; the High Chamberlain, the Chancellor of the University, the Head Librarian, the Chief Executive Officer and his assistant, the COO, and one strange, but traditional participant in these proceedings—an unimprinted Icon, chosen at random. A Blank. The Blank's simple white pants and shirt looked out of place among the finery of the rest.

Luke stared down at his closest advisers. Nobody seemed willing to return his gaze. He took it as a bad sign. "Gentlemen," he said at last, "what have you got for me?"

For a moment he thought nobody was going to reply. The Chamberlain cleared his throat. "Majesty, we have interfaced with other Empires. The CEO has a report."

Luke nodded. "Very well. Go on."

The CEO, who wore dark, richly tailored robes, seemed unhappy. But he leaned back in his chair and raised one hand. "Majesty, I had the communications people initiate interface with ten Empires. We chose them carefully, after a search through our own Libraries. All of them have been attacked, at one time or another. Some of the details were shadowy enough that we hoped they'd experienced a situation similar to our own." He glanced at his hand as if surprised to see it there, then placed it palm down on the tabletop.

"What was the result?"

The CEO shook his head. "Unless they were all lying, nothing, Sire. All the attacks they experienced were from the outside. Standard cases of data theft or intrusion for other reasons."

Luke considered. "What about the Empire of Ice?"

The CEO shifted uncomfortably in his seat. "We were unable to interface, Majesty."

"Why?" The Empire of Ice specialized in Generals and Soldiers. If anybody would have experience in fending off attacks on other Empires, they would be the ones.

"Their Librarians said they had no records of such things. That's all they would say. Then they broke the interface. Very abruptly."

Luke was puzzled. Relations between the various Empires were supposed to be, within limits, open. This refusal of cooperation was bizarre.

"Is that suspicious, CEO? Could the Empire of Ice have something to do with our problems?"

To Luke, it seemed a legitimate question, but it obviously unsettled the advisers around the table. If the attacks on their own Empire were frightening, the idea that other Empires might war on them was inconceivable. It had never happened. The injunction against fraternal warfare was formatted into their very patterns at birth, before any other imprinting was done to a nascent Blank. The Empires made up the Web, and the Web was more than the sum of its parts. No individual Empire could be allowed to alter that truth.

As Luke waited for a reply, he realized how their limitations hampered their ability to advise him on this problem. Only he, of all of them, had no specific formatting or imprinting. Perhaps only he would be able to advise himself.

There was another, though. "Blank," Luke said sharply.

The Blank, who had remained silent at the far end of the table, looked up now. His expression was empty. Not unnatural, for the Blank was a tabula rasa, a raw pattern yet to be written on. No Blank ever, in Luke's memory, contributed anything to these discussions, but tradition dictated the presence of one such. Luke tried to recall the reason for the tradition, but could not. That was, in itself, odd.

"Yes, Sire," the Blank said.

"Do you have any ideas about all this?"

The others at the table regarded the Blank with interest. The Chamberlain smiled encouragingly. "Go on, man. Answer the Emperor."

The Blank's lips moved slightly, but nothing came out. Finally, the Blank nodded. "In this Empire," he said slowly, "the Emperor rules everything. So if something is wrong, then it must be the Emperor's fault."

The Head Librarian gasped. The CEO scowled and shook his head. The Chamberlain half rose from his seat and growled, "You forget yourself!"

"No," the Emperor said softly. "He's right." He searched his memory for an ancient phrase. "The Emperor has no clothes."

Only the Head Librarian smiled faintly at the phrase. The others looked puzzled.

"It means, gentlemen, that only this Blank sees the truth and isn't afraid to tell me. He's absolutely correct. This Empire, everything in it, even *you*, is under my absolute control. If we rule out attack from beyond the Empire, then it comes from the inside. Which means it comes from me."

Luke exhaled tiredly. "And that means only I can solve it." He spoke slowly. "And I don't know how to do that. You will have to help me."

A ripple of shock oozed down the table. Imprinted on each one's most basic pattern was the understanding that the Emperor was all powerful. To witness Luke admitting his helplessness was deeply upsetting to them, for it threatened the most basic tenets on which the Empire was constructed.

Luke watched their discomfort with something almost like amusement, for he understood a further truth. Their precious Empire was an Icon, too, no stronger or less vulnerable than they were. It could all be wiped away in the blink of an Imperial eye. They couldn't remember, for when their reality changed, their memories of it changed as well. But Luke's function was different, and he recalled everything. The Empire had worn different Icons. Luke himself had been different. He remembered a time of infancy, when the Empire had been much smaller, and not an Empire at all, merely an ever-growing collection of tiny children who played mindlessly in a sun-dappled afternoon. The Empire Icon changed even now, although the Emperor was the only one who knew it. At times, he wondered where it all would lead—what the Empire would become in the future, as he changed it in response to—what?

He gnawed on one thumbnail and considered the surprising thought. *Why* did he constantly change the Icon? There must be reasons . . . but for the life of him, he couldn't find them.

Was that what these attacks represented? Some new change, for reasons of which he had no awareness?

If this was the case, then the situation was far worse than he'd guessed. The Empire was at risk, and even the Emperor was powerless. But there were still things to try before he faced this final awful possibility. He spoke sharply. "Why wouldn't the Empire of Ice interface with us fully?"

He looked down at the CEO and waited. That worthy finally said, "We don't know, Sire. They wouldn't tell us."

Luke nodded. "Then I will go and ask. They can't refuse me."

Everybody, even the Blank, exchanged relieved glances. Luke smiled at them all, and hoped what he'd just told them was true.


## THE HEGEMONY: CITY

Charlie returned to his home, a neat three-room apartment situated on a broad street only fifteen levels beneath the surface not far from the Hall of the Web. He immediately went to the kitchen. "Food," he said loudly.

A screen on the far wall lit up. The computer that controlled his environment began casting up five-second panoramas of gorgeous meals. Charlie stared at each one, his mouth dry, his stomach grumbling. Why so hungry? He couldn't guess. Maybe something to do with Naomia. The fulfillment—no, the devastation of one basic urge might be the trigger for others. He didn't care. He was starving.

"Fine," he said as a particularly inviting repast glowed on the screen. At his words, the picture blanked off and a menu appeared. Roast Tsien-tsien duckling, orange marmalade, crispy oyster salad, three-jewel noodles. "Yes," he said impatiently, "just cook the damned thing."

His kitchen made soft, sighing sounds as hidden machines ordered, received, and began to prepare the meal. He paid no more attention, but wandered into his living area and collapsed on a form cushion. The warm feel of it as it clasped his body lightly reminded him of her, of her all-encompassing technique, of the way every nerve in his skin had been massaged, stroked, teased to unbearable ecstasy.

He shook his head. Think of something else. He realized that he felt hot, sweaty, and that a sharp, pungent odor filled the room. He sniffed, puzzled. Then he realized the smell came from his own glands, harsh, animalistic, and infinitely arousing.

"A shower," he muttered. He rolled off the cushion and headed for the bath. Maybe he could *wash* the memories away.

Maybe the Hegemon would drop in for tea, too.

Two hours later, bathed, fed, and almost able to ignore the insistent hunger that had settled in his groin, he looked up in surprise as his door watch chimed.

"Yes?"

The large wall screen in his living room flashed on to reveal a full shot of Eileen Michelson standing in front of his door, her palm slapping impatiently against the lock plate.

"Sound," he said. Then, "Eileen . . . ?"

"Charlie, let me in."

"Sure. Open up, door," he said. The screen flicked off and looked just like a wall again, while a tall rectangle slid open to reveal his coworker.

"Eileen—what brings you out?"

She was an oversized girl, skinny, bony, with broad shoulders and long, straight blond hair of that peculiar color that only looks golden in certain light. Now it looked almost brown. Her eyes were her best feature, wide and faintly almond-shaped, filled with an indefinable color that reminded him of filmed golden mirrors. They were the first thing Charlie had noticed about her when they'd met, and on the few occasions he thought of her, they were what he remembered.

He didn't think of her often. They hadn't really hit it off, even though their shifts often overlapped, and they saw more of each other than Charlie really cared for. It was that air about her, now very much in evidence—something between disdain and irritation, as if Miss Michelson was more or less generally pissed off with everybody in the world who wasn't lucky enough to be her.

"Charlie, what is this shit?"

She stalked across the room and held up a tiny chip between her thumb and forefinger. Charlie noticed for the first time her fingers were quite long, with big, reddened knuckles and bitten-off fingernails. The hands of some kind of laborer. Charlie had never seen a real laborer, but this was what he guessed their hands would look like. The chip was another matter.

"Where did you get that?"

"Out of your chine, of course."

"God damn it, what were you doing fucking around in my stuff?"

A long, nasty look of triumph suffused her features. "That's not *your* chine, Charlie. Not really. Any tech can access anything."

He stared at the chip. Had she read it? No doubt, he thought with a sinking feeling. Otherwise, why was she here?

"You read it," he said flatly.

"Of course. I, uh—" She faltered slightly, then recovered. "I thought it had something to do with that nasty template you've been so concerned about. Something came up—"

"I bet it did," Charlie interjected, as venomously as he could.

She caught the joke and scowled. "Charlie, you're

a grown man. This is a job, not some kind of game. If you won't show any responsibility, somebody has to."

"And you're it?"

She nodded. "It looks like it, doesn't it."

He sagged back against the form cushion. "How much did you read?"

"Can I sit down?"

"Sure," he said. "Go ahead. Floor's free."

She glared at him. He turned away, motioned at the floor. "Go on, sit down."

She wore conservative black glitter paint on her legs and a businesslike miniskirt beneath a billowy white top that accentuated her overall storky impression. As she seated herself, the image grew more intense. For all her defiant arrogance, there was something pitiable about the way she hunkered down, all bony knees and stringy flyaway hair, like some kind of weird bird settling into a nest.

"So you did read my chip."

"Not your chip. Besides, Charlie, what a goddamn fucking stupid thing to do. I mean besides your juvenile plan, to *write it down* and leave it where somebody else could find it—what were you *thinking* about?"

He felt heat rise into his cheeks. She was absolutely right, and he sometimes forgot just how stupid he could be. But it was only a fucking prank, right? And now she was no doubt going to piss all over his parade.

"You going to turn me in?" he said sullenly.

"No. I'm going to help you."

Slowly he turned to face her full on. "What did you say?"

Her smile was not at all pleasant. "You heard me. I'm going to help you."

He considered. Either he was crazy, or she was. Most likely both. "Why?"

"Because," she said, and now a nasty edge shivered along her words, "you don't have any choice."

"Huh?" He was lost.

"Just sit there and shut up, and let me explain."

He nodded. It felt like something large, slimy, and cold had gotten stuck in his throat.

"So explain."

She nodded. "I made a copy of your chip."

The slimy, cold thing in his throat dropped like a stone into his stomach. He'd thought what he had planned was only a prank, generated out of a combination of curiosity, misplaced compassion, and boredom, but he doubted his superiors would view it that way. To mess with a template was, he now realized, *dangerous*. The templates were the Web, and the Web was the most important thing in the Hegemony. And this awkward, inimical woman had *proof* of what he'd planned to do. It could mean his career at the very least, perhaps even greater punishment. Jail, or personality reprogramming.

The room suddenly seemed hot, stifling. His sudden terror must have shown on his face, because Eileen's almond eyes narrowed in recognition.

"That's right," she said slowly. "A copy. Which is in a nice, safe place." She paused, but he had nothing to say. Only a generalized and terrible understanding that he was completely in her power.

"You can go ahead with your plan. Find a"—her wide, thin lips twitched slightly in distaste—"woman to do the thing."

"Prostitute," he interjected dully. How could she be such a prude, in this day and age? He saw that things were seriously fucked up with Eileen Michelson, and wondered how he'd missed something so obvious before. She couldn't even force herself to describe the act he'd planned for the template. *Blow job*, he wanted to shout. *Gonna get that kid's dick sucked for him!*

It had seemed funny at the time. Now it was a disaster. *How could he have been so stupid?*

"I already have," he told her as, unbidden, twisted emerald memories of Naomia flashed through his thoughts.

Her eyebrows shot up. "Oh? How . . . convenient."

He nodded miserably.

"Well, good. Then set everything up, and let me know when it's ready to go."

He looked down at his toes, then up at her cold, set expression.

"Eileen, why?"

"What do you mean?"

"This gets you involved, too. You won't have leverage any more. And it's dangerous. Why are you doing this?"

Now her smile went even wider. "But don't you see, Charlie? I'm not doing it. You are."

And he saw that it was true. He was utterly trapped. If he didn't go ahead with it, she would expose his plan with her copy of his chip. And if he did, she would have even greater power over him. *Why?*

"Why?" he repeated, this time aloud.

The wide, flat grin stayed on her face, but her eyes went dead as scuffed marbles. "Because I'm a spy, Charlie. And now, you are, too."


## THE WEB: EMPIRE

Luke had never physically visited another Empire, but his Icons had, and now he searched his collective memory for clues on how to prepare for the trip.

Commerce went on between the Empires constantly—the information trade never ceased. There was even an entire class of Icons—the Messengers—whose job consisted of nothing more than carrying messages out, and bringing data back from the hundreds of Empires that occupied Web-space. From the opulence of his own quarters, Luke summoned the Chief Messenger. The Icon—whose name was Durward, and whose appearance was bizarre in the lush richness of the Imperial Chambers—arrived almost immediately.

"Greatest Majesty," Durward began, performing the opening move in the extended ritual of greeting.

Luke raised one hand. "Can the shit, Durward," he said. "Just you and me, and we're private here, okay?"

Durward bowed smoothly. "Whatever the Emperor wants," he said.

Luke stared at him. Of all his subjects, the Messengers, although identical to him in form, resembled him the least—and the Chief Messenger, epitome of his Icons, was the most bizarre of all. The Chief Messenger was, of course, precisely his own height and weight and body image, but any resemblance beyond this basic configuration was hard to discern. Durward's black hair flowed long and wavy to the base of his spine, caught at the nape of his slender neck in a ring of beaten silver. Further constraining the hairy explosion was a similar band made of smooth gold and set with emeralds that encircled his skull and crossed his smooth forehead. The sparkling gemstones picked up the green glitter of his gaze.

He wore black pants that came to his knees made of thin, shimmering material that might as well have been paint. A tattered leather shirt covered his narrow chest and shoulders, but ended above his navel, which was painted red. Long hanks of dirty white fur studded the shirt in places, so that Durward seemed to be molting. On his feet were huge, clunky black boots inset with intricate patterns of chrome studs. Around his wrist dangled and jangled a host of brass, silver, gold, and crystal bracelets, and from his right ear dropped a bangle made of bright green feathers and golden fishhooks.

"I have never personally visited any of the other Empires," Luke began slowly. "And you have."

"Yes, Majesty." Durward's lips twitched slightly. His green eyes seemed to laugh at his Emperor's ignorance. Of all the classes of Icons, the Messengers were the most impish, the most disrespectful. Luke supposed it had something to do with their wider exposure to the other Empires of the Web. They knew that his Empire wasn't the only one, and that there were other ways of living and doing business. What, he wondered, do they think of me?

Then he realized it was a stupid question for, in many ways, the Messengers, like all other Icons, *were* him. Yet, because they struck an answering chord of *rebellion?* in his own personality, he tolerated their disrespect and cherished their flamboyant differences.

"What can you tell me," Luke asked, smiling in return, "that I should know?"

"Well, first—" and now, the Chief Messenger almost openly grinned—"you probably shouldn't ride a bike."

The Messengers traveled by bicycle on their ceaseless journeys. They were so ubiquitous, they were barely noticed, unless they ran down some hapless Icon on the streets or sidewalks of the Empire. And even between the Empires, Luke's Messengers rode their strange contraptions. It seemed a point of pride with each Messenger that no two bicycles could be alike. Some rode small, buzzing machines, while others perched atop high, awkward things with tires as thick as their thighs. Each bike was personally decorated by its owner, and their individual creativity expressed itself in leather, stone, precious and very unprecious metals, things that rang and clanked and made odd sighing noises, Sirens that cut the space before them like razors, or lights. The lights! Some bikes glowed, while others flared, blinked, or strobed in patterns that confused the eye and disoriented the brain.

It was strange, Luke reflected, that this class of Icons should strive so hard for visibility, yet still remain an unremarked, barely noticed grace-note on the Empire's daily life.

Luke hadn't given any thought at all as to how he would travel. He had supposed he would move with his normal grandeur, surrounded by his retinue, the air full of the sound of beating drums and shuffling feet. But now, examining his Chief Messenger's elf-like grin, he thought, why not? Why *not* go a different way.

"Why can't I ride a bike?" he said.

"Because you don't know how, Majesty."

He considered. "I could learn."

Durward bowed slightly. "Of course, Majesty. You can do anything you want to do."

It wasn't precisely wholehearted agreement. "Tell me of the Empire of Ice," he said at last.

"Ah. Yes, Sire. It is a strange place. Doesn't look anything at all like our Empire. Much colder. Or hotter. Much . . . smoother."

Luke had trouble conceiving of a complete Empire different from his own. He was so totally master of his own environment that the thought of a place where he had *no* control was unsettling, even frightening.

Shit, he thought to himself. I haven't even got this off the ground, and already I'm having second thoughts.

"What are their people like?"

"Of Ice?" Durward shrugged. He didn't seem terribly concerned by this vision of otherness. "They don't look like us. They are very fierce. They kill." He rolled the last words out with a slow, doomsday rhythm, although the faint smile on his face didn't change.

"Kill?" This concept was even more alien to Luke. He knew that Icons could be destroyed—he did so himself constantly—but the idea that Icons could be destroyed by other than their Emperors was extremely disturbing.

"Yes, Majesty," Durward repeated. "They kill. They are trained that way, in the Empire of Ice."

Luke closed his eyes, felt the soothing dark inside his skull, and tried to assimilate the idea. "Have they ever killed any of our Icons? Any of your people?"

"Occasionally."

*"What?"* This was the most shocking of all. Why had he never heard of it? Or had he? No, of course not. If some force destroyed his own Icons, it must be like killing a part of himself. How could he overlook such a thing?

But he couldn't recall anything like this. Why?

"Durward, think carefully. Tell me what you know of this."

"Certainly, Sire." The Chief Messenger placed one slender finger alongside his nose and squinted through his left eye. The effect was so droll and mocking, so overdone, that Luke smiled involuntarily. But what Durward said wasn't amusing at all.

"Sometimes they waylay us. They set up traps or ambushes. Occasionally we come upon their Icons when they are moving out to other Empires—as hired mercenaries. They are most warlike at such times, and will kill for any reason, or no reason at all. When we visit the Empire of Ice, we have to be on guard all the time."

"But why do they do this, Durward?"

Another shrug. "I don't know, Majesty. It is a different Empire, is all. They must have different ways of doing things. Different rules. But the Icons of Ice are fiercer than any others. I know that to be true."

"I see," Luke said slowly. "Do you think they would attack . . . me?"

Durward glanced at the floor. "I don't know, Sire. I don't know what they might do."

Luke nodded. He had never realized just how ignorant he was of certain things, certain situations. "I see." He pursed his lips, then said, "Bring me a General."

Durward looked up quizzically. He knew the instruction was not directed at him, but he was curious to see the result. If the word General was new to him, though, he made no sign.

A low rumble, as of some powerful engine, sounded just outside the window of the small chamber. Luke stepped over and peered out. At first he simply stared. Then he motioned Durward over. "Come here. You've got to see this."

Durward pushed in next to him, seemingly oblivious to the fact that he had actually *touched* the Emperor— and since the Emperor himself didn't take notice, nothing at all was said. Instead, they stared out the window, down at the small courtyard that fronted the rear of this wing of the palace.

"Holy Burning Gods," Durward whispered. "That sure isn't no fucking bike . . ."

"But what the hell *is* it?" Luke breathed in reply.

"I've seen things like it, in Ice," Durward said.

"They call them battle mods, or tanks, something. I don't remember exactly . . ."

The General below had just finished disembarking from a vehicle that stretched half the length of the courtyard. From above it resembled a gigantic beetle; from its sides extended three pairs of thick, armored legs that ended in massive, clawed feet. Short, ugly tubes protruded from the top of it. Their snouts were scarred and blackened, as if barely controlled energies had ravaged the metal there. The skin of the thing was pitted and black—it looked as if the tank had rolled in acid. Its engines, even idling, sent deep, thrumming vibrations through the palace walls.

The General stepped away from the tank and glanced up. Luke could tell nothing about his features, which were covered by a white helmet and black face plate. A smaller bug hidden in a bigger one, he thought.

The General saw the Emperor watching him and snapped off a flawlessly rigid salute. His uniform, unlike his vehicle, was all starched angles and tailored seams. Several rows of jeweled decorations encrusted his chest.

Durward chuckled.

"What's funny?" Luke asked.

"Get out the rubber gloves," Durward replied. "Here comes a perfect asshole."

Luke's lips twitched as he watched a line of smaller, but equally unattractive vehicles disgorge a swarm of copies of the General. Some sort of assistants, he supposed, and found it remarkable that one man needed so many flunkies. Of course, he reflected, it was the man's first visit to his Emperor. Perhaps he was nervous.

A few moments later he heard the heavy tramp of booted heels outside his chambers, and then, with an almost audible flourish, the General and his minions presented themselves.

"Highness, I am Hendrickson, your Chief of Staff."

Luke had returned to his comfortable seat—not quite a throne—and nodded in reply. "Welcome, General Hendrickson. My Chief of Staff, eh?" Even as he spoke, he searched his mind for the information he knew would come. Ah. Chief of Staff. So this man oversaw his entire military establishment, new though it was. A lot had evidently been done in a short time. That wasn't unusual. Once the Emperor made his will known, things tended to move right along.

"General, have a seat." Luke gestured to another chair across from him, next to where Durward half sat, half reclined with one leg sprawled casually over the arm of his own chair. The General glanced at the Chief Messenger. His expression remained blank. He had removed his helmet, but his eyes were still shielded by chromed mirror-glasses, which gave his short-trimmed skull the hidden expression of a hungry insect.

"Thank you, Sire." General Hendrickson turned to his entourage and said, "At ease, gentlemen." Then he seated himself and explained to the Emperor. "These people are my staff. We are prepared to answer any questions you might have."

Luke nodded. His mind tossed to the surface of his attention explanations for each unfamiliar concept. As the automatic mechanism did its work, he began to understand just what he'd created when he'd shifted a part of his normal production to "Generals, and whatever else is necessary." Evidently quite a lot was necessary.

"General, we are informal here. What can you tell me about the"—he had to search again—"military situation?"

General Hendrickson nodded briskly, and looked over his shoulder. One of his staff—equally bedizened with medals—stepped smartly forward with two assistants. Everybody seemed to have clusters of golden stars on their shoulders. The two assistants swiftly set up electronic map boards. The leader of the trio took out a light-pointer and gestured at the first map.

"Here," he said, "is the principle area of invasion."

Luke stared at the map. Even Durward leaned forward slightly, his dancing eyes alive with interest. A long, curving line stretched the length of the screen. Near the center of the line, it curved sharply inward, like a pocket.

"Very large forces have appeared in this sector, Majesty," the staff man said, pointing to the pocket. "They are poorly armed, but they make up for their lack with numbers. The sheer weight of their armies has destroyed large areas here, and more of them are appearing all the time."

Luke shook his head. He couldn't understand this. Where were these invaders coming from? If his theory was correct, he was creating them himself. But he couldn't imagine how.

"Have we taken steps to push them back?"

General Hendrickson nodded. "My forces have counterattacked in several places. The situation was worse only a short time ago—that bulge you see was much larger recently. However, we don't seem to be able to score a decisive victory. The problem is, as I said, numbers. We destroy the invaders by the thousands, but ten thousand spring up to replace them."

Luke stared at the map. He couldn't imagine what the lines there represented. Thousands—tens of thousand—of Icons fighting, dying. Pieces of the Empire actually *destroyed*. And somehow he was the cause. As he studied the map, a conviction began to grow—

no matter how many Generals or Soldiers he created, no matter how vigorously his forces prosecuted the war, he was doomed to fail. For he was fighting himself, and that was a battle he couldn't win. He wondered if this General, his Chief of Staff, understood.

"Majesty," Hendrickson said slowly. "The situation is very dangerous. I have to confess, I'm at a loss. I don't understand where these—rebels, for lack of a better word—are coming from. If it were an invasion from the outside, from another Empire, we could cope with it. But it isn't. These Icons are no different from our own. In fact, they appear to *be* our own. I . . ." His voice trailed off helplessly.

Strange, Luke thought. I'd always heard that military people were arrogant, totally self-assured.

He sighed. "I know, General. Tell me this; can your forces hold the line? I mean, for a time, at least."

The General nodded. "Yes, Sire. If the situation remains relatively static—that is, no sudden increase in the number of rebels, or breakouts in new sectors of the Empire. We are stretched somewhat thin right now, even with the continuing creation of new military Icons. Perhaps Your Majesty could speed the process—?"

"I could, General, but I agree with you. More soldiers aren't the answer—not a final answer, at least. In all your experience, have you ever heard of a situation like this? A rebellion within an Empire?"

The General, who had only been created a short time before, shook his head. His ignorance wasn't due to his recent creation—for he had received every bit of knowledge available to the Empire as a whole relating to things military. He was the head of a stack and, as such, was an ultimate expert, an adviser to the Emperor himself.

"No, Sire. I haven't," he said simply.

"I was afraid of that," Luke said. But he wasn't surprised. If he himself didn't have any answers, how could his subjects?

"General, please have your staff leave us. I would speak to you in private."

"Of course, Sire."

They waited while the small mob folded up its displays, adjusted its uniforms, and tramped out amidst a flurry of salutes and bows. When the room had gone silent, Luke said to Durward, "So. What do you think?"

Durward glanced at General Hendrickson. "You get to do it yourself."

"Yes," Luke said. "Tell me, General. What Empire has the most experience, the most knowledge of things like our . . . problem?"

Hendrickson didn't hesitate. "The Empire of Ice, Sire. They have defended against every kind of intrusion. I haven't heard of anything like this, but perhaps they have."

"They aren't responding to our queries," Luke told him.

The General shook his head, puzzled. "Why not?"

"I don't know. I guess I'm going to have to find out myself."

Now Hendrickson raised his head and stared directly at the Emperor. It was hard to tell, since his eyes were hidden by the mirror-glasses, but he seemed shocked. "Yourself, Majesty? But that is horribly dangerous. I couldn't guarantee your safety, not even with an entire army. We are Soldiers, but Ice—they are war."

Luke shook his head. "I'm not taking an army."

Durward winced. He knew whose fate was about to get sealed.

"Majesty, you can't go alone! Anything might happen."

"Oh, I'm not going alone. Durward, here, will accompany me."

Hendrickson turned in his seat and stared at the Chief Messenger, aghast. "Sire, you would entrust your safety—the safety of the Empire itself—to this . . . this . . ."

"Fuck you, General," Durward said happily.

"Sire!"

"Well, General, do you have a better idea?"

Hendrickson went silent for a moment. "Are you absolutely determined to do this thing? Go to Ice yourself?"

"I am, General. What else can I do?"

"Then you must allow me to provide an escort."

"No armies, General. We couldn't defeat Ice anyway."

"Yes. But perhaps a single man."

"One man, General? What difference could one man make?"

And now the General smiled. It was a startling expression, beneath the glassy blankness of his eyes. "A very special man, Majesty," he said. "We can do that, at least. A *very* special man."

Luke glanced at Durward, who shrugged slightly. "Very well, General. Show me this . . . very special man."

## THE HEGEMONY: K'MILL

Karl Hayden glanced at the screens and stopped dead in his tracks. "Jesus . . ." he muttered, an imprecation to a God far older than he imagined.

He slid into one of the form chairs that fronted on the display wall and lowered an interface ring over his skull. He closed his eyes. There was a moment of darkness, and then his vision cleared, as the interface established itself between his human brain and the machines that occupied heavily guarded chambers beneath the room.

His awareness was altered, heightened by the powers of those machines. Now he examined the alarms that had activated the initial warning systems. The problem was . . . there! Yes. In nanoseconds of real time he was in the area, observing from hundreds of robot sensors that dotted that region of space on the outskirts of the K'Mill System.

The robots saw with electronic eyes, and what they observed was a particular sort of curdling in real space that signaled the presence of activity in underlying Twistor Space.

Visitors were coming, and by the look of things, a *lot* of visitors. A part of him checked the incoming logs, but nothing was listed of this size—only the normal comings and goings of the small amount of trade K'Mill carried on with the rest of the Hegemony.

Now data was flowing into his skull, hip-hopping back and forth between the machines and his own awareness. Two—ten—a *hundred* ships—and big ones, too. He couldn't imagine what was going on, but there was definitely a problem. Yet, even as he suddenly withdrew from interface and glanced around the watch room, the truth of the matter was beyond him.

The Hegemony had been at peace since the Agorn Wars almost fifteen centuries before. Hayden knew his history, but to him, that was all it was. Just dead history. That he was witnessing the beginning of an attack on the Hegemony itself, even with the evidence before his eyes, was completely outside his calculations.

Some sort of huge trade caravan gone awry, he guessed. Or some kind of mistake in the switching systems.

Two of his screens flared bright red, and he ducked back under the interface ring. For some reason, he couldn't immediately establish contact with the defensive monitor satellites, but when he finally did, the reason became obvious.

Vast swatches of the tiny machines no longer existed. His view from the remainder was constricted, but not so much that he couldn't make out, with his augmented sensorium, the horrible apparitions vomiting out of T-space, one ponderous shape after another.

The ships were the size of small asteroids, great, blackened spindly constructions that resembled skyscraper buildings without the skin. T-space itself was a shambles here, so packed with the intruders that real space boiled with the collapse and re-creation of the channel. He brought two of the planet brains on line and snapped a fast request.

"Analysis."

The gigantic computers buried in the crust of K'Mill itself observed, considered, and issued their opinion.

Hayden broke interface and stared into the flashing silence of his station. "Invasion?" he muttered. "Who the fuck would want to invade K'Mill?"

Later, when the clear blue atmosphere of the planet began to bubble away, seared into plasma by weapons of incalculable power, he would recall his question and curse his stupidity.

The ships hadn't come to invade.

They had come to kill.

# 3

## THE WEB

Just outside the Imperial Capital, sheltered at the base of a low ridge of foothills called The Giant Steps, the new camp sprawled for almost ten miles along the banks of the Suwanee River. The ground here was either marshy or stony, and only a few stunted pines grew in the maze of narrow canyons and sheer cliffs that led up into the Steps themselves. The first thing Luke noticed was the wind. It blew constantly and steadily, scouring tiny grains of quartz from the humping granite of the hills and flinging the fine grit in biting clouds the length of the camp. Luke shivered as he stepped down from the big, armored gunship that had brought him to this newest part of his realm. General Hendrickson reached out and caught his arm, lest he stumble on the final step.

"Thank you, General." He stopped, conscious of the great rotor blades above his head slowly whop-whopping down into silence. The wind gusted in his ears, then filled his nose with the dark green smell of hidden pines. His ears echoed from the noise of the trip—a battle chopper was not his usual mode of travel, though he judged it a more comfortable way to journey than the General's initial invitation to accompany him in his tank.

Durward hit the ground behind him, leaping from the copter's doorway, ignoring the steps entirely. He bounced once, looked around, and said, "What a fucking pit."

Luke hid his answering smile, but he had to agree—the camp was desolate. Their small party stood at the edge of a huge, gravel-covered parade ground. In the distance, several small groups of men were marching back and forth. The harsh, barking sound of their instructor's orders echoed thinly in the chilly air. Beyond the parade ground were row upon row of unpainted wooden barracks. Evanescent streams of pale gray smoke issued from tiny chimneys atop the structures, quickly snatched away by the ceaseless gusting wind.

Luke watched his breath curl in a silver cloud before his face. "Have you got someplace warmer, General?" he said.

General Hendrickson, seeming a bit discomfited by the Imperial presence, snapped a quick salute and said, "Of course, sir. Right this way."

The General led them quickly toward a much larger building fronting the parade ground behind them. This structure, unlike the barracks, was constructed of ten stories of pre-stressed concrete. Ordered rows of black-glassed windows stared blindly at the camp.

An extraordinarily ugly structure, Luke thought as the General marched quickly toward the main entrance, which was guarded by two spit-shined troopers bearing strange, ungainly weapons.

Hendrickson returned both guards' salutes as another pair of men opened the doors from the inside.

His boot steps made sharp popping sounds on the naked, polished concrete of the floor.

"Right in here, Majesty," he said, and pointed to a door that bore the sign: "WAR ROOM—RESTRICTED."

Two more guards, armed as heavily as the first pair, stood at the back of a clerk whose purpose was to check identification—although for this party, the clerk leaped to his feet and executed a rigid, perfect salute.

"At ease, Soldier," Hendrickson grunted. The guardian relaxed slightly, but seemed anything but at ease as he pushed a button that caused the armored door behind him to slide open.

The room inside was huge. Great screens filled two walls, beneath which sat technicians who worked silently at wide consoles, their fingers flying over touchpads or their lips moving quickly as they replied to messages piped into their ears through the white, round helmets they wore.

The General led them to a row of padded seats atop a raised dais in the middle of the room. From this vantage point—the chairs swiveled—they could easily observe anything. When they were settled, the General said, "These are temporary quarters, but our permanent HQ won't be ready for at least another two weeks." He shrugged. "We control the defensive efforts from here." He pointed. "That screen"—he stopped, shook his head, then continued—"is monitoring the progress of the Battle of Twin Rivers."

Luke stared at the screen with great interest. It was his first view of the actual fighting.

"Burning Gods . . ." Durward muttered.

The view was of a vast panorama of destruction. The landscape stretched flat from the confluence of two wide rivers across a broad, burning valley that slowly rose to a rampart of scarred hills. There was no green visible. The foliage here had either been burned brown or reduced to wide blackened scars. Their viewpoint was from high in the sky, too far above the battlefield to make out individual figures; but the tracks of destruction were evident, and faint, silvery lines betrayed the presence of columns of loyalist forces. Parts of the area were obscured beneath shifting clouds of smoke. Even as they watched, a sudden series of scarlet dots speckled the landscape.

"Artillery. Fire missions along the front lines. We're shelling our own positions," General Hendrickson grunted sourly. The tiny match points flared out, and a new line appeared, somewhat to the rear of the first. "And retreating," the General added, his voice even more troubled.

Luke forced himself to turn away from the carnage. "General, I'm an amateur, but it looks like we are losing."

The General nodded, not trusting himself to speak. Like all high advisers, he knew of the frequent fate suffered by minions bearing bad news to the Emperor.

But the Emperor merely nodded. "I don't understand. You said that these—invaders—are poorly armed. How can they be defeating our own armies, with all their equipment and training?"

The General sighed. "Numbers, Sire. They are inexhaustible. We kill one, and two spring up in his place."

Luke considered this. What was going on? Why was he doing this to himself?

Or was he?

He simply didn't know. But it was obvious he would have to find out. The scenes before him told a simple, horrible story. The Empire—he himself—was at terrible risk. And time was slipping away.

A thought tugged at his attention. "General, what do these invaders look like?"

Hendrickson cleared his throat. "Like, uh, myself, Majesty."

"You mean like me."

"Yes, Sire."

"Do you have any pictures? I mean, close-ups?"

The General nodded reluctantly. "Yes, Sire."

"Good. Show me."

Hendrickson made a slight hand motion, and the vista on one of the main screens disappeared, to be replaced by a still picture of a charging figure.

Luke stared in openmouthed dismay.

This warrior was primitive in the extreme. It did bear a resemblance to himself, but only slight, and in the usual way; same body structure, same hair color, same green eyes. Beyond that, the marauder was like nothing ever seen in the Empire before.

Nearly naked, the figure brandished a crude, stone-tipped spear. A necklace of claws rested around its slender neck. Its hair was tangled and bushy, braided here and there into long, bead-garnished snakes. It wore crude leather moccasins and, around its narrow waist, a leather belt, from which were suspended a small pack, a stone knife, and an equally primitive ax. The belt also cinched in place a thigh-length leather skirt—and here, Luke's eyes widened at a curious sight. The flaps of the skirt did not meet in front, so that the renegade's genitals were exposed, to reveal a very large erection.

Luke glanced at the General. "Are they all like that?"

"Yes, Sire. Very primitive."

"I mean . . . the physical condition."

The General nodded slowly. "Yes. All of them."

"But what does it mean?"

Hendrickson shook his head. "Sire, I don't have the faintest idea."

Durward spoke up. "They're horny. That's what it means."

The Emperor and the General stared at the Chief Messenger. Finally Hendrickson broke the silence. "What," he said, his voice choked with disgust, "does that have to do with war?"

Durward chuckled. "Beats the hell out of me. But it's obviously got something to do with *this* war."

The General was still scowling at Durward's reply when a sudden commotion near the main doors signaled a new arrival. The General glanced over, then turned back to the Emperor. "Sire? You're still determined to go ahead with this—unwise visit to Ice?"

Luke's lips narrowed. He nodded sharply and said, "Now, more than ever, General."

The General exhaled slowly. "Very well. I told you I would give you a very special man. He is here. Would you like to meet him now?"

Luke watched the small group approaching their vantage point. Most wore the usual military garb he'd already seen, but one seemed different. He couldn't quite catch the difference yet.

"Yes," Luke said. "Please have him come up."

A moment later a slender figure approached the Emperor and bowed, once.

"Sire," Hendrickson said simply, "this is Stone."

Luke stared at the youth who stood before him. Stone's black hair was cut very short, almost a buzz. His young face was unlined, but somehow hardened, as if the muscles beneath his fair skin were tougher, more full of tension than normal flesh. His eyes were the clear green of perfect emeralds. He neither smiled nor frowned—in fact, his lack of expression was striking, as if his usual thought processes were in suspension, waiting.

And he did not bow.

They stared at each other for a long moment. Then Luke stood. Before the uncompromising regard of this subject, he felt a sudden, uncomfortable need for the reassurance of his own power.

He said, "I am Lucifer, the Morningstar. I am your Emperor. Kneel before me."

He heard General Hendrickson gasp softly behind him, and what might have been the faintest chuckle from Durward.

Slowly, then, almost solemnly, Stone dropped to one knee, never removing his gemstone gaze from Luke's. Finally, his head bobbed once, and he replied, "I am Stone. I kneel before my Emperor."

Suddenly Luke felt ridiculous. He stepped back, shook his head slightly, and said, "Rise, Stone. Welcome."

Stone stood up. "Thank you, Sire."

General Hendrickson whispered softly into Luke's ear, "I'm sorry, Sire. I didn't explain precisely *how* Stone is different."

Luke waved him away. His attention was riveted on the form of this newest and most strange of his subjects.

"Stone," he said. "Are you loyal to me?"

Stone regarded him. There was an almost imperceptible pause before he replied, "In all ways and things, Sire."

A nagging uncertainty began to prick uneasily into Luke's thoughts. Everything was said, and said correctly, but somehow it was *wrong*. He wondered what the General meant, but was too absorbed by Stone's presence to pursue the question. There were legions of rebels out there destroying his Empire, and he had created them. Was this man something new, and even more deadly, in the strange tricks he seemed to be playing on himself?

"Would you protect me?" Luke asked.

This time the answer came with no hesitation at all. "With my life, Sire."

Better. Much better. But Stone was only one man. "How?" Luke asked.

"In many ways, Sire. Very many ways."

It was all so puzzling—and Luke suddenly realized that he didn't entirely trust this man. In fact, he understood with a sinking feeling, he didn't even trust *himself*. He turned to Hendrickson. "I would speak privately now."

Hendrickson nodded. His eyes were troubled as he dismissed Stone and his coterie. Stone bowed before withdrawing, this time unbidden, as if he had already proved whatever point it was he had to make. Or is it only me, Luke wondered, who feels uneasy?

When Stone had gone, Luke said, "All right, General. What is so different about Stone?"

The General scratched at the corner of his mouth before replying, obviously searching for words.

Can't anybody tell me anything straight out? Luke wondered.

"Go on, General, say your piece!" His irritation must have burned through his words, because Hendrickson jumped slightly and began talking immediately.

"Stone is different, Sire. He is the ultimate individual warrior. His pattern was imprinted with everything we know about war and its practice. He has been specially formed in the physical sense, as well, with powers far beyond a normal soldier. He is a killer. It is his genius to be a weapon." Suddenly the General looked confused, as if he just now understood the full import of what he had said.

An ominous expression playing around his eyes—Durward had seen it before, and unobtrusively edged away from the Emperor—Luke said tightly, "And was this done without my permission, General? The creation of such a dangerous Icon?"

The General swiped across his forehead at the shining beads of sweat that had suddenly appeared. "Sire, he is not just a weapon. He is *your* weapon."

"And what, precisely, does that mean?"

"He was designed only, and solely, to be your protector. You noticed he didn't hesitate when you asked him about it?"

So the General had picked up on the oddness of Stone's responses. Luke nodded. "I also noticed that he *did* hesitate when I asked him if he was completely loyal to me."

"Yes, Sire. It is a part of his programming."

"*What* is a part of his programming?"

"He is not entirely under your control." As soon as he said this, Hendrickson cringed, as if expecting a blow. But Luke merely regarded him thoughtfully, remembering his own unsuccessful experiments with similar Icons.

"And why is that, General?"

Hendrickson lipped his lips. "Sire, what do you think would happen if you ordered me to kill you?"

Luke stared at him. Finally, "I don't know. You tell me."

Looking most unhappy, the General said, "I would try, Sire. I don't know if I'd succeed, but I would surely try. I wouldn't have a choice. I'm unable to resist a direct command from you."

Luke began to have a glimmer. A faint smile suddenly flickered on his lips. "And Stone? What would he do?"

"He would refuse, Sire. You don't control him completely, and that is one of the areas in which he would be able to disobey you."

"I see. And the . . . other areas?"

"Anything similar, Sire. His prime directive is your survival. Even you cannot countermand it."

"Whose idea was all this?"

The General stepped forward, ready for whatever punishment his Emperor desired. "Mine, Sire."

The men on the dais stood frozen, waiting in the moment.

"Good job, General. Well done."

Durward laughed aloud at the expression on Hendrickson's face, but the General only bowed slightly, stepped back, and said, "Thank you, Sire. Thank you."

In his rooms later—there were always rooms for the Emperor, wherever he went in his Empire—Luke finally relaxed against a pile of cushions and picked idly at a tray of food that had been brought in. The quarters were smaller, more rough-hewn than he was used to—plain white walls, harsh angles, a deep blue form carpet scattered with huge pillows—but this was, after all, a military installation. Across from him Durward sprawled haphazardly against another pile of cushions, eyes closed, humming softly. Luke stared at his Chief Messenger and wondered how he could seem so unaffected by all of this. Was it his traveling experience that gave him a kind of perspective? Or was it something else?

"Durward?"

"Mmm, Sire?"

"How come you're so calm?"

Durward shrugged. The movement brought a low cascade of tinkling sounds from his jewelry. "I dunno. It's not my problem, I guess. It's your Empire, and when you're ready, you'll fix things." The Messenger paused. "Won't you?"

Luke blinked. Of course Durward would feel this way. In some sort of dimly felt understanding, Durward knew the truth—that the Empire was the Emperor.

And what, precisely, did *that* mean?

Luke took a bite from his ham sandwich, but his thoughts swirled far away from food. Or did they? He considered. I don't need food, actually. I eat because I choose to do so, but I don't really have to. Feeding myself is only a part of the overall Icon I've constructed—but, at the bottom, what is the Icon? Merely a game I play with myself.

He eyed Durward thoughtfully. And what, he wondered, does this bizarre copy of myself think of *himself*?

"Durward, who are you?"

The Messenger glanced up, startled. "What?"

"You heard me. Who do you think you are?" For some reason, a concealed part of Luke waited breathlessly for the reply. But Durward seemed puzzled.

"I don't understand, Sire. What do you mean?"

Luke made a small, encouraging hand movement. "Go on, just say whatever."

Durward considered. "I'm your Chief Messenger."

Luke nodded. "Yes, of course. But what else?"

Durward raised his right arm and examined the host of bracelets there. "I'm a—I'm cool."

"What does that mean?"

The look in Durward's eyes spoke volumes—confusion, discovery—as if these were questions he'd never really considered. When the Messenger spoke again, his words were slow and halting. "I'm . . . I do the right thing. Shit doesn't bother me. When I'm . . . out of the Empire, it doesn't bother me. I can function. Some of us, you know—they can't."

Cool. What a strange concept. And the rest of it—

Luke didn't usually devote much thought to the mental twists and turnings of his subjects. If he thought of them at all, it was merely as extensions of himself— so that the occasional slaughter of a Chamberlain was less than the biting of his own nails. But evidently something was going on—the Icons were more than they seemed. Particularly this Icon. This *cool* Icon.

And did all the others, the rest of his trillions of subjects, have similar ideas? Were they all *different* from him, separate in their own completeness? If that was true, then what he'd done to his Chamberlains— what he did to *any* of his subjects was no more than . . .

Murder.

His mind rocked. For a moment he felt himself losing his grip on the Empire itself. The room around him faded sharply, became translucent, and he saw the swirling, chaotic bones that underlay his own reality. He saw the Web, and for the first time, felt threatened by it.

"Sire!"

He shook his head. Durward stood over him—a breach of protocol—looking down, his eyes wide and worried.

"Sire, are you all right?"

"I'm fine, Durward. Everything's fine."

But it wasn't. Somehow he knew it would never be fine again.

So why did he suddenly feel so much better?

Morning came with a slow roll of dismal fog across the vast parade ground. Hendrickson had insisted on an Imperial review of the troops. "It will do them good, Sire, to know you care about them."

Luke stood on a thin-framed metal reviewing stand hastily constructed in front of the headquarters building. The chill that clung to him, penetrating even the heavy fur coat he wore, did nothing to improve his disposition. Nor did the knowledge that the General was in error—he really didn't, despite his revelation of the night before, care much about the tiresome rank upon rank of faceless soldiers who slogged briskly through the murk before him. It was all very well to realize that Durward, one of his closest advisers, had a personality formed and shaped into something completely distant from him—but it was quite another to make a similar leap for this blank-eyed horde that served him in ways that had not even existed a short time before.

"My armies," he mumbled softly, but not softly enough.

"Beg pardon, Sire?"

"Nothing, General. Just a thought."

The General turned back, a proud smile on his face, and Luke heard a muffled comment from Durward, who hugged his own spangled leather coat to his chest and breathed small smoke rings of breath at the General's back.

"Fucking *cold*," Durward said.

Luke turned. "We'll be done soon. Then we can start on the rest."

"I'm not looking forward to that, either."

Stone had not yet made an appearance. Luke wondered about that. Was this whole effort wise? Everybody seemed to think it dangerous. He wondered what Stone thought. Or did Stone even understand danger?

There were still questions to be answered. His decision was not yet final. But, he understood as he unobtrusively moved his feet in a slow, warmth-generating dance, he had to do *something*. And soon. Those hideous battlefield scenes he'd witnessed—those were scenes of death.

Whatever was happening wasn't trivial any longer. It was murder, as surely as his own actions with the Chamberlains were murder.

Perhaps, he thought suddenly, it was even the same thing.

Something. *Soon.*

# THE HEGEMONY: CITY

The silence of his cluttered living room was strained and surreal. Charlie couldn't seem to focus on her. His eyes looked elsewhere, at rambling piles of form cushions, at the dark green carpet on which Eileen sat, her face smugly watchful.

"You're a spy," Charlie said dully. Even as he spoke the words, they seemed flat and meaningless to him, utterly insane. Eileen Michelson a spy? A prude, maybe. A confused young woman too impressed with her training and position. Even a fanatic, in this time when faith was only discredited philosophical coin.

But a spy?

"Yes," she said grimly. "I am."

"Horseshit."

"Charlie."

"Yes?"

She gestured with the tiny chip. "I have your balls, right here in my hands."

The image filled him with dark humor. "You only wish."

She stared blankly at the chip, turning it slightly so that its gold-etched surface caught shadows from the indirect lighting. "Fine." Then, with a decisive movement, she slipped it suddenly into a pocket on the front of her billowing blouse. She unfolded herself awkwardly and began to rise from her position on the floor. "I'll get it to the supervisor tonight. Probably just send it from my home terminal. Okay with you, wise guy?"

"Hey, *wait*—"

"No, you wait. I'm trying to tell you, Charlie, I'm not joking. Maybe 'spy' is too melodramatic for you. Good enough, ignore it. Just say I work for somebody—no, better, I work for some*thing*. Something I believe in. You don't need to know any more than that. All you have to do is what you were already planning to do. Is that so hard to understand?" She paused. A curious expression twisted her long features slightly. "You didn't really think you were going to pull it off without my help, did you?"

He was still sprawled on the floor against the form cushions, which now felt slick with his own sweat. "Eileen, I'll be in deep, deep shit if you turn me in."

"Ah. Now he begins to understand."

Charlie was still punchy. This sudden transformation of his coworker from annoying wallflower to crusading espionage agent had jangled his already overloaded synapses. But one thing was becoming very clear. Somehow, what had started as nothing more than a prank had become deadly serious. It wasn't just Eileen and her fantasies—if that's what they were, please let them only be bizarre daydreams—it was Naomia. Now he was being whipsawed between the two women, and the conflicting fears and lusts they engendered in him.

It was too much. All he wanted was to rest for a few hours. In the morning everything would be much clearer. He'd be able to think, to decide. Maybe it would all turn out to be a hallucination.

He stared up at her as she stood, staring down at him and waiting.

"All right," he said.

"All right, what?"

"I'll do it. What you say. But we have to talk more."

She nodded. "Yes. We will. Tomorrow?"

"You call me," he told her.

"You're off tomorrow. I'll come over."

The thought made him nauseous. "No."

She smiled a final time. It did his churning stomach no good. "Sorry, Charlie. I tell you, not the other way. Tomorrow. Ten o'clock in the morning." She turned and marched toward the door, her back rigid with triumph. Just before she left, she paused and turned. "Oh, and Charlie?"

"What?"

"I'm *not* going to go away. You be ready tomorrow. We have things to do, to decide. Understand?"

Wordlessly he nodded, but she had already disappeared into the hall. Figures she's got me wrapped up tight, he thought sourly.

And she does. She does.

## THE WEB

"We're gonna have to give you a disguise," Durward announced after breakfast, which had been an uncomfortable affair with Luke seated between his Chief Messenger and his Chief General, who amused themselves by scowling past him at each other.

Disguise? A novel thought. He hadn't even considered the mechanisms of his trip.

"Why a disguise?" he asked.

"Well." Shrug. "You can't go traveling as a Messenger and look like *that*."

They had returned to their temporary quarters. Luke wandered to the fresher room and examined himself in the tall mirror there. "Like what? What's wrong with the way I am?" He peered at his reflection. He saw a slender, well-shaped young man with clear green eyes, short dark hair, a high, unlined forehead. Entirely unexceptionable, certainly nothing to engender the undercurrent of distaste with Durward's pronouncement.

"Well, *look* at you. Then look at me."

Luke did so. "Oh," he said.

Durward nodded. "Even if you ride a bike, you don't look anything like the rest of us. Messengers of all the Empires are different, of course, but you can tell by looking right away whether they are Messengers. It's part of our . . ." He squinched his shoulders uncomfortably. "Our mystique, if you want to call it that."

Luke wondered how he'd look with a different hairstyle. Oddly, the thought wasn't unwelcome. And Durward's ragged clothes did look awfully comfortable.

"Well," he said slowly, "how about this?"

When he turned away from the mirror and saw Durward's mouth hanging open, he grinned. He'd forgotten that few understood just how widely his powers extended, even to the choice of his own form.

Durward stared at the scruffy apparition that had appeared in place of the neat form of his Emperor. "That's . . . perfect," he said. "How do you do that?"

"I'm not sure. I just do."

Durward scratched at the right edge of his nose. "Will it work outside the Empire? In Ice, for instance?"

Now it was Luke's turn to pause, shocked. He'd never even considered the question. "I don't know." In theory, he should be inviolate, even to another Empire's power. But perhaps that was only within his own Empire. And Ice? Ice *killed* Icons. Would his body image hold in that strange place?

"What happens when you travel outside the Empire?" he asked Durward.

"It depends. Some places, nothing. Others, I change a little."

"Change? What does that mean?"

Durward picked at the spot where he'd been scratching. A bright red pimple was growing there. "I dunno. I'm a Messenger, but I'm a message, as well. I sort of plug into whatever Empire I go to—pass on the imprint I'm carrying. Some Empires can handle me with no change—and so I stay myself. Others can't. So I change into something they *can* handle."

More new concepts. Luke stretched his mind to encompass them. "Change how?"

"I end up looking like their Icons. I'm still me, but I look different. I look like them."

"Does that happen with us?" He'd never thought about the day-to-day converse with other Empires. It went on constantly. He saw Messengers everywhere in his own domain, hurrying to and fro with their loads of data. And he saw his own Icons. It was discomfiting to think that some of those comfortable, familiar figures might have been something else entirely.

"Yeah, sure," Durward said. "Some we take as is, some we change. Some are really strange for us—I've seen them in their own places, but never here. Since we do communicate, I assume they change when they pass our borders." He paused and stared at his fingertip. "Damn."

"What?"

"Popped that fucking pimple. Look. It's bleeding."

Luke stared at the offending bit of waxy sebum and blood. He never got pimples.

"Look," Durward said. "You're getting one, too. In exactly the same spot."

## THE HEGEMONY: CITY/SCARLET SECTOR

"You didn't comm me you were coming," Grog said. "Naomia can't see you."

The tempo of the Scarlet Sector seemed different in

the morning. The passages were less crowded, slower, more lethargic. The few patrons who ghosted listlessly about seemed either exhausted, or obsessed, or both. Everything had a gray cast to it. Charlie and Grog stood just outside the T-center, beyond the general flow of traffic. Even Grog seemed subdued. In the washed-out light, the bear-man's eyes were filmy, translucent. He seemed to have trouble focusing on Charlie's features, and kept pawing absently at the ruff of hair that surrounded his own face.

"What do you mean, she can't see me?" Charlie said. His crotch throbbed with sick anticipation. He'd risen early, showered, flung on clothes without attention. His usual morning erection seemed more insistent, had taken longer to go flaccid, and somehow, instantly upon entering the Scarlet Sector and spotting Grog, had returned with painful splendor. Grog glanced down at the obvious indication of Charlie's physical state and showed a mouthful of needle-teeth.

"Just can't get enough, can you?" He made a low, rumbling sound that might have been laughter. "She's not my type, you know—but don't feel bad. You aren't the only one. All her clients, they get this way. It's like a disease."

If Charlie thought it odd that Grog, the pimp, should describe Naomia, his prostitute, as a sickness, he made no sign. He turned slightly away from the larger man, an effort to disguise his arousal, but Grog only chuckled again. "But I'm sorry, man, can't do nothing about it. She's like a princess, that one. Works when she wants, no more, no less. And she's done till tonight."

"I have to get a message to her."

Grog nodded equably. "Sure you do. Everybody does. She's real popular, that one. Everybody wants Naomia." He leered, an awesome sight involving bulging eyes and flashing teeth. "To, uh, talk to, of course."

Charlie shook his head. "I'm going over there."

"Where?"

"To her place."

"Sure, what you gonna do? Bang on her window? Pound your pole there in the street? Cause that's all you're gonna get, you know. I'm telling you, she don't see anybody in the mornings. Not even me."

Charlie glanced up at his face, started to speak, stopped. Began walking with great determination away from the T-center. He didn't look back, even when Grog called after him, "Good luck, man! Although it ain't gonna do you a bit of good!"

The Street of Whores sported a hang-dog veneer. In the washed out patina of the morning, the few windows that were still lit seemed vague, like comm screens tuned to static and visual white noise. Charlie looked neither right nor left as he strode mechanically down the street, searching for the remembered place.

"Hey, buddy—" a low growl, elicited by his heedless passage from a jostled wanderer, but Charlie ignored him. There. Yes, there!

He came to a halt before the window. It was empty, blank. A scarred wooden floor showed through the glass, a vacant wooden chair. Dangling from the ceiling, an unlit length of glow strip hung like ancient technological moss. Was this the place? The right window?

Frantically, Charlie placed his nose right on the plex, his heated breath making small, expanding blobs of steam on the surface. This tiny cubicle bore no resemblance to the star-shot swirling smoke that had mesmerized him the night before. It looked like a barren closet—surely no place for magic.

But—yes, there was the door. Exactly where he remembered it. This was the place. If his mind didn't remember, his balls did—and reminded him with a painful jolt that set his teeth together and brought a soft moan through his lips.

What was wrong with him? He felt loose, crazy. "Naomia," he muttered, the word hitting the plex and stopping dead. He stepped away. The door. He moved to it, raised one fist, pounded three times.

"Naomia!"

Only the hollow, booming sound of concealed emptiness.

*"Naomia!"*

He pounded with both fists, pounded and pounded, then stepped back and kicked the heavy metal barrier. Strollers halted, stared, sniggered knowingly. He never saw them. After a time he stepped back, panting, his hair in his face, his knuckles skinned and a fresh agony rising from his right big toe. Broken, maybe. He ignored it.

He began to make a soft, mewling sound, a choked cry of hopelessness.

"Naomia . . ."

The door screeched rustily and opened a few inches. Nothing beyond but darkness.

He pushed in willingly, eagerly. Into the dark. Into the empty. Without thought, without anything but a terrible, rising passion.

This is hell, he realized at last. And I want it.

## THE WEB: EMPIRE

Pimples?

Wondering, Luke turned back to the mirror. His reflection glimmered back at him. He moved closer. Sure enough, just to the right of his nose. A small, cherry-colored spot. It was a pimple. And he had not willed it there.

Had he? Perhaps he'd unconsciously copied Durward's style, right down to skin blemishes. But wasn't that taking it a bit far? He stared at the offending pustule for a moment. He blinked.

Gone.

He let an unconscious sigh of relief escape his nostrils. At least he could still control his own appearance. Which was, now that the pimple was gone, somewhat splendid.

He stepped back slightly, the better to appreciate his new creation. It wasn't, in the strictest sense, a new Icon. The Emperor could not be an Icon, for he created Icons. But it was different, no doubt about it.

His features seemed somehow changed, without being changed, as if the planes and angles of his face had altered somewhat, become sharper, more prominent. He looked . . . tougher, he decided. There was now something of Stone about him, as if unseen strengths were hidden just beneath his skin.

And the getup!

Luke was used to robes, to soft, folding things that weighed heavily around his ankles, that hid his slender form beneath layers of rich fabric and thick, heavy chains of gold and silver. Now all that was stripped away, and a more narrow, harsher form bloomed forth like a steel spike driven suddenly through soft wood.

He wore knee-length purple knickers that bagged around his knees, but hugged his thighs, snugged low on his hips with a wide, soft leather belt. His belly was exposed beneath a vest made of some dark, rich fur. Around his neck was a single chain made of steel links, from which appended a jeweled pyramid about the size of one of his thumbs. He wore ankle-high boots made of red leather, whose toes were capped with shining chrome.

His hair was longer, shaved completely away one side, and caught in a long tail on the other. The dark swatch of hair hung loosely beneath its silver catch-ring, and spread in a wave across his right shoulder and down almost to his chest. He shook his head in delight and heard the sound of the tiny bells that dangled from his left ear.

His eyes seemed brighter, more alert than he remembered. Maybe there was something beneficial to this body changing. Would it hold in other Empires?

Somehow, he thought it would. A surge of strength, of clarity roared through his mind. God damned *right* it would hold.

He turned and grinned at Durward. "How do I look?" he asked.

"You look cool," Durward said, a faintly wondering tone still suffusing his normally cynical intonations.

"Cool," Luke said softly. "I do. I do look cool."

## THE HEGEMONY: SCARLET SECTOR

The narrow hallway smelled of rust and something worse—something decayed, like a piece of meat left in a warm place too long. The floor beneath his feet was hard, ferroconcrete maybe, but his shoes were nearly silent. He looked down and, in the dim light that came from the half-opened door, saw a thick layer of dust. Something wrong about that . . . and then, with a shiver, he had it. The dust before him was undisturbed, thick and smooth, as if untouched for years. But he'd walked here only a short time before.

Hadn't he?

Indecision seized him. What if this was the wrong place? His head came up and he stared around, searching for some remembered feature. But there was nothing, and he realized he wouldn't remember anything from a previous time anyway. When he'd come here before, he'd already been in the dream of her, and had noticed nothing.

His heart beat a ragged little two-step for a moment, then calmed. He might not remember, but his body knew. His muscles twitched and moved his right foot forward a step. Dust or no dust, this was the place. Already his testicles were throbbing like a pair of boiled plums in anticipation, and his erection was a painful bar of flesh.

"Naomia!" he called sharply. There was no reply, not even the faintest of echoes. Perhaps the dust absorbed sound. Without thinking he moved forward, and in a few steps came to a right-angle turn in the hallway. Beyond was utter darkness. In another time, another place, he might have been frightened. But he didn't even pause, and didn't glance back as he turned, and the faint light from the doorway disappeared entirely.

He blinked, then put his hands out to guide himself along the corridor's walls. He stopped. He stood with both arms outstretched entirely and felt nothing. He whirled. The faint light that had guided him before the turn was completely gone. The rational part of his brain told him that some residue should remain—he hadn't gone that far after the turning.

But there was only darkness, and even the walls had gone. The sound of his own breathing seemed very loud in his ears, and then he heard another sound—a deep, slow pounding that grew in volume until it filled the dark.

Thud-a-thud. Thud-a-*thud*!

His heart. His heartbeat in the dark.

He slapped his palms over his ears, pressed hard, harder, his face twisting against the terrible noise. He'd lived with the sound all his life and never really *heard* it, and now he understood the reason. The sound of his own heart pounding away was utterly terrifying, for it revealed a truth—that the body was a machine, and the conscious mind only dimly understood just how alien that machine was.

Through his flesh, his skull, his very brain the awful thunder ratcheted, until he heard another sound, thin and high and far away.

Somebody screaming.

His own voice. He was screaming. Alone and lost in the dark, shrieking in terror, only the horrible sound of his own body for company.

His eyes rolled back in their sockets. He felt himself begin to fall. And the sound stopped. All at once. Just like that.

Silence.

In the darkness, he saw a light.

## THE WEB: BASE CAMP

Durward had wandered off somewhere, leaving Luke alone in his suite of rooms. The General had not visited all morning, and Luke found himself mildly uncomfortable with the lack of any of the attentions he normally took for granted.

He sat on a form cushion that he had dragged with his own hands to a spot before the large mirror. Doing things himself. A strange feeling. He knew he could have hordes of servants around him immediately, merely by desiring them to appear—this was an army camp, rude and crude, but it was still a part of his Empire—but he found himself relishing, in a strange way, this new solitude.

And that wasn't all of it. Not only was the isolation new, but so was much of everything else. Even the bizarre, threatening attacks on the Empire. The more he considered them, the more he was certain that the key to their solution was within him somehow. The picture of the savage attacker still burned in his memory with unsubdued ferocity. So alike, and yet so different!

He settled himself deeper into the cushion. His reflection brought a grin to his face. Just like now—his appearance was vastly changed from his usual countenance, but he was still Luke, still the Emperor. And what about that savage invader? Underneath the beads and bones and Stone Age weaponry, what was *he* like? It had been something of a shock to discover the essential differentness of Durward, whom he'd thought he knew well. How different was the barbarian, and the millions like him, who were attacking the Empire now?

Yet even in the face of all those differences, the most terrifying realization had been far worse—that the barbarians were indeed himself, indeed Icons of his own creation.

He was killing himself somehow, and the tools he used were precisely the same as he would use for any other task. Icons were Icons, and the aboriginal invaders were, in their own way, as familiar as any dusty Librarian or Administrator plugging steadily away in the myriad tasks that made up the daily life—the essential existence—of the Empire itself.

So how, he wondered suddenly, was he *doing* it? Was there somewhere a College of Savages, with a Dean of Barbarity? And if so, how had it come to be? And why couldn't he find it now?

The answer to the last question hit him with stunning simplicity.

"I haven't found it," he told his mirror reflection softly, "because I *haven't looked.*"

The wide green gaze of his reflection stared back unwinking.

Luke closed his eyes.

"This," he mumbled at last, "is a *real* piece of shit."

# 4

## THE HEGEMONY: SCARLET SECTOR

"Naomia?"

His voice sounded thin and flat. There was a soft buzzing in his ears. Somehow he understood the buzzing was within him, not external. In this place of dark, there was no sound at all. Everything he heard was only a reflection of the never-heard sounds of his own body.

"Naomia!" he called again. The light, a tiny spark that seemed a million miles away, glowed steadily. He realized that, in this yawning space, he had no idea how far away the glowing ember was. It could be right in front of his face. The thought sent a chill wave of terror rocketing up his spine. He pawed frantically at the area before his eyes. He couldn't see his hands as he did so, only feel their movement.

He floated. What had happened to the floor of the corridor? What had happened to the corridor itself?

Nausea, vertigo, and horror battled for ascendancy as he felt himself teetering on the slimy edge of madness. Where was this place? *What* was this place?

*"Naomia!"*

His despairing wail was swallowed by darkness, un-echoed, gone.

The glittering orb shifted then, lost its spark-like brilliance, took on a sheen of color. Cool turquoise, a slow wash of crimson, faded amber.

Orb?

The light had been a dot, a point. Now it had a shape.

"Closer . . ." he whispered, mesmerized by dread. Yet beneath the slow drum of panic, a tiny part of his mind stood apart, cold and unaffected. *This is crazy*, that shred of ice declaimed. *You are in the Scarlet Sector, in the City on World. You entered a door and went down a corridor. World still exists, as does City, and the Scarlet Sector, too. This is an effect. This is a sham.*

He smelled an abrupt whiff of sweat, realized it was his own, and this mundane sensory input righted him as instantly as a dash of cold water.

He felt a hard surface beneath his feet. He reached out, and his fingers slapped painfully into the walls of the corridor.

Naomia, carrying a glow lantern, crossed the last few feet to him, her light casting eerie shadows up into her face. Her eyes were obscured by the low, cool radiance she bore. Around her smooth neck was a necklace of small white beads. He looked more closely and saw that each bead was a tiny skull.

"Charlie," she said softly. "Why have you come here?"

And Charlie, without having the slightest idea why, burst into tears. But his humiliation was not complete until he thought he saw the tiniest ghost of a smile play across her full lips.

"I love you," he blubbered, knowing it was a lie, but helpless to keep silent. "I love you."

Now, her smile was real.

"Come, then," she said. "Come to me, Charlie. Come now."

His hand sought his crotch, and he realized he already had.

## THE HEGEMONY: NEAR THE HALL OF THE WEB

Eileen Michelson drummed her long, mannish fingers on the desktop next to her touchpad. "Damn," she said. The screen in front of her blinked uncompromising red letters: "NO ANSWER. NO MESSAGES RETRIEVED."

Charlie Seagrave was not taking any calls, nor had he left a message for her. She glanced at the time readout in the upper-right corner of her screen. Almost ten o'clock in the morning. She'd told him she'd be in touch, to wait for her call or visit. But he hadn't. And that was upsetting.

"Damn," she mumbled again. Didn't he understand? His job, his entire career, perhaps even his freedom was on the line, and he was fucking up already. It was obvious. She hadn't scared him enough. Not enough to be taken seriously, it would seem.

She leaned back in her padded chair, fingers idly playing with a fiber-optic cable that extended from her machine. She hadn't really planned on plugging in today, but now there was a problem that could provide an excuse. The people with whom she shared the great vision had warned her about unnecessary contact, but this was something special. She needed their advice. Surely they would understand.

Of course they would. Smiling faintly, she raised the plug at the end of the cable and inserted it beneath her left ear. A moment later her eyes rolled slowly backward, although her lids remained open.

Her long, lanky body jerked once, then went soft. Her smile remained, growing slowly wider.

## THE WEB

The huge war room at the heart of the camp was nearly empty, the lights dimmed, and only the soft sound of Luke's voice dispelled the initial impressions of desertion that made the room seem dark and abandoned.

"I've never looked, you see," Luke said to Durward. The two of them lounged easily in the chairs where previously they'd watched scenes of carnage on the giant view screens filling the walls around them. Now they were alone. Durward swung one slender leg over the arm of his chair and played idly with a long, jagged twist of steel that hung from his right earlobe.

"Is this likely to be dangerous?" he asked.

Luke paused, considering. It would mean a meld with the Web, the electronic underpinnings of his Empire, where the quantum winds blew wild through swaying stacks of his duplicates in their naked forms.

"I don't know," he said finally. "I can't find any Iconic analog here in the Empire for those savages. There is no barbarian camp, for instance, that would correspond to one of the Universities or the Library or some such—a place where Blank Icons are trained into their eventual functions."

The bits of steel at Durward's neck made small tinkling sounds. His thin face was darkly thoughtful. "You mean those . . . things are appearing out of nowhere?"

"No. It's more complicated than that." Luke paused, wondering how to explain. He knew how his Empire was constructed, and how it followed rules that he alone created. Even Durward, his double in everything but outward appearance, could not know the whole story—he simply hadn't been programmed with the necessary data. For Durward, the Empire, and all the other Empires, was the only reality he knew. And for me, Luke thought, they are only shadows. But now something is appearing in this shadow, something of my creation, but deadly inimical to the creation itself. These killers are coming from somewhere beyond shadow, and there is only one other place.

The reality that underlies us all. Where the Well of the Web fountains up. There was, he judged, no reason to try to explain that finer distinction to Durward.

"No, not really dangerous," he said. "Not in any sense that matters."

Durward's leg stopped swaying back and forth. His face came up, darkly alert. "I think you just committed a grievous act of bullshit."

His voice was so full of outrage that Luke burst out laughing. "Durward, would your Emperor bullshit you?"

"Huh. Do you ever do anything else? Listen, Highness, I may be only your humble Messenger, but I know the sound of animal crap when I hear it. What the fuck does 'not in any sense that matters' mean? Will you be in danger or not?"

Once again Luke thought of the seeming chaos of the orderly fields on which he danced. Could the Web be dangerous to him? It didn't seem possible, but then, neither did the unexplained appearance of hordes of his duplicate seem any more possible. And while he, personally, had not been attacked by those terrible invaders, millions of Icons—*extensions* of himself—had been brutally destroyed. Was there any reason to expect that he, himself, would be inviolate?

Grudgingly he said, "Perhaps. I don't think so, but perhaps. But it doesn't matter, my friend. I have to do it, and there's nothing anybody else can do to help. I have to go alone."

Durward stared at him. "Are you sure about that? I know I'd be worse than useless, but—that Stone character. There's something very weird about him. I don't like him, but he's strong. What about Stone?"

Luke's eyes slowly widened. What, indeed, about Stone?

Stone's footsteps across the polished floor of the command room were dull, muffled. He approached the raised dais where Luke and Durward waited, but paused at the bottom of the short flight of stairs and looked up. Luke stared down at him.

"May I come up, Sire?" Stone asked.

Luke examined him silently. As before, there was nothing much special about Stone. The short haircut made him seem even younger than he was, and his neat, pressed uniform was a sharp contrast to the more extravagant garb the other two wore. Yet there was something—Luke tried to put his finger on it, that essential difference, but it kept skittering away from his comprehension. Perhaps it was the eyes, steady, unblinking, almost empty. Or the way Stone carried himself—supernally balanced, his hands resting easy at his sides, palms inward, fingers curled slightly, his center balanced low above his pelvis, as if he always moved in the tiniest of crouches.

Ready. That was it. Stone was always *ready*.

"Yes. Come up," Luke said.

Stone moved his head a tiny fraction forward, then back. A bow. Luke thought that Stone would never bow to anyone except the Emperor himself, and even that would always be a struggle for him.

Ready, yes. And unconquerable. In the sense that Stone could perhaps be destroyed, but never beaten.

He could never admit defeat. It was a mildly unsettling thought, until Luke realized where the recognition had come from. It came from his own core, which was possessed of similar certainty.

*I can't be beaten either*, he thought with sudden clarity. Stone was only another aspect of himself made real. As real as an Icon could ever be.

Could I make him disappear? Make it as if he never was?

Of course I could. He's only an Icon.

For one giddy moment he felt himself summoning the forces to do precisely that—to flay the skin and grind the bones of this creation, simply to do the act and reassure himself that, for him, all things were still possible.

That he was still in *control*.

And an astonishing thing occurred. Stone placed one foot on the top step, halted, and raised both his hands, palms outward, in a warding gesture.

"Don't," he whispered. "Please."

Luke froze, the forces he'd begun to raise swirled about his mind in veils of thunder and blood. His mouth opened slightly, the words he'd meant to utter caught between his teeth. Durward, unaware, moved restlessly behind him, sensing something was wrong, but unable to detect just what it was.

Luke felt the muscles of his shoulders clench and unclench, but he remained immobile. Had everything—the Empire, the Web, even his own existence depended on it, he could not have torn his gaze away from Stone's piercing green eyes.

Finally, imperceptibly, Luke nodded. He breathed out in a rush. The power he'd almost wielded seemed to leave him at the same time, and he realized he was shaking.

"What are you—Sire, what's he talking about?" Durward's voice was querulous, uneasy.

Luke stepped back as Stone mounted the final step and sank to his knees. "Thank you, Majesty," Stone said softly.

Luke looked down at the top of his liege man's head. He could see white skin, smooth and unmarked, beneath the thin layer of dark hair. The finely formed plates of bone beneath the skin—and beneath them—so delicate, vulnerable—

*Stone had not been begging. His plea had been a warning!*

"Rise . . . Stone," Luke said, astonished to find his own words firm and strong, with no sign of his inner turbulence. What was this man?

Stone came slowly to his feet. His face serious, he repeated, "Thank you, my Lord." And he stepped away, clasped his hands behind his back in a military rest position, and waited.

"What the fuck is going on here?" Durward complained. "All this please and thank you shit. Am I missing something?"

Luke turned. "Nothing, my friend. Stone, here, is just excessively polite. Perhaps overly conscious of my position." Sardonicism pervaded his next words. "Wouldn't you say that was right, Stone?"

Stone nodded gravely. "Of course, Majesty."

"Well, then." Luke felt mildly disoriented, almost giddy. Had he just survived some terrible threat? Or was all this just wild imagining?

What to do next?

"Sit, Stone," he said, and gestured at a third chair. Without a word, Stone sank into the soft leather, and Luke began to relax. A lot of strain. No wonder he felt so . . . strange. Stone was only an Icon, utterly in his power, and it had been his self-restraint that had saved the Soldier. Some part of him had realized the folly of destroying so potent a weapon, and had stayed his hand.

Of course. That was it.

"Stone, I need your help."

"Name it, Majesty."

He started to explain, then paused a final time. He was many things, Emperor, creator, absolute ruler of his own domain. These things were givens, the foundations of his very existence.

But in order to be all these things, he possessed one other attribute. He was incapable of ignoring truth.

And the truth of the matter was quite simple. He hadn't stopped out of any altruistic urge. He had stopped because Stone had told him to.

So what did that make Stone? *And what did that make him?*


## THE HEGEMONY: SCARLET SECTOR

Charlie hadn't known what to expect. How could he? His only association with Naomia had been a single night of bone-blasting sex. She'd become his dark goddess, a *thing symbolic*, not at all human. But now, as he stared dumbly at the furnishings of her small suite of rooms—too small, really, to call an apartment—he found himself overloading once again on the contradictions she called out of him like skeins of tangled thread.

A main room no larger than a few meters square, with two smaller rooms—kitchen, sleeping alcove—extending from opposite sides of the sitting room. On one wall a large holoposter of the mountains of K'Mill, towering needle-spike peaks that glittered beneath their harsh sun like impossible diamonds. Beneath the poster a shabby brown leather couch, much worn and badly patched with white vinyl tape, like a broken, wounded beast.

Threadbare Oriental carpet, old but not antique, a

pair of battered corner tables, the single straight-backed wooden chair on which he sat and squirmed uncomfortably. Out of the corner of his eye, he saw the bed, unmade, lumpy and uncomfortable seeming. *Was that where I—?* he wanted to ask. So tired, so prosaic. Not at all what he thought he remembered.

A thick, bitter smell of boiled cabbage permeated the walls, the floor, and some other smell, sweet and harsh at the same time, tickled his nose and made him fight to repress a sneeze.

Somewhere, beyond the thin walls, someone played jittery music, the sounds full of horns and nervous strings. He looked at her, where she sprawled on the sofa, her lips blood-colored, each small movement bringing a dry, brittle answer from the bizarre necklace she wore, and tried to speak. "I, uh—" he said. He shook his head, but before he could try again, she smiled at him and replied softly, "I'm a whore, Charlie. What did you expect? A palace?" She shrugged. "And not a very expensive whore, actually. Just a cheap hooker, my friend. Are you . . . disappointed?"

He couldn't answer for a moment. He really hadn't known what he'd expected, what he'd *desired* out of this visit. Just to see her again, perhaps, or somehow re-create the maddened climax of passion that had snared him so completely before.

Led here by my dick, not my brains, he thought with sudden disgust. Here, in her drab, prosaic quarters—he couldn't bring himself to call this a *home*—the magic was gone. There was only a woman who—now that he looked closer, he could see it more closely—had gone just a bit to seed, a shade too thin, the hint of shadow beneath cynical eyes, that ludicrous necklace—and he felt a slow roll of nausea.

For *this* I put myself into hock with that bitch Eileen?

He licked his lips and said, "No. Not disappointed. Just . . . surprised."

She smiled at the lie. "Charlie, why did you come? I'm not—I don't usually receive guests this time of day. You know? And just because you decided you're in love with the idea of a competent blow job, that's no reason to let you in, either." She chuckled, a bleak sound with no humor in it whatsoever. "But I did let you in. You want to guess why?"

He raised his shoulders slightly, let them fall, feeling the shame of his own foolishness. "Why?"

"Because Papa Bear told me about your little plan. And I find it interesting."

"Papa Bear . . . ?"

Her eyes flickered in mild irritation. It was early, her sleep time. "Grog. Who brought you to me."

Suddenly he recalled the bear-man and his needle-teeth, his pheromone broadcasters. "Oh. You call him—"

"Papa Bear, yes. He's a friend. And he told me what you wanted. As I said, I'm interested. But it will cost you."

The abrupt change to a discussion of commonplace business considerations disoriented him even further. He couldn't seem to get his mind in sync with the events that had snowballed around him with such alarming rapidity.

And what the fuck was Eileen Michelson doing at this moment? He glanced at his nailtale, panic rising. *Oh my God, I was supposed to be meeting her right . . . now!*

"Uh . . . ah, I hadn't really thought—*how* much?"

"Tanstaafl," Naomia said.

"I beg your pardon." *Stupid,* he thought. *I sound stuffy, pompous.*

"Old adage, Charlie. There ain't no such thing as a

free lunch. You want to hire a blow job. Or, if it makes you feel any more uplifted, you wish to purchase fellatio stimulation for a fellow being. Either way, the operative word is buy. This is what I do for a living, youngster." She paused, glanced around at her dismal surroundings, an unreadable look on her features, and said, "And not much of a living, either, is it?"

He didn't know what to say. What had happened to those crazed fires that had so energized him before? The irresistible urges that had brought him back, seeking—what? All that remained was this room, this tired, acerbic woman who looked *much* older than he remembered, and this dreary, dragged-out discussion of money.

*What was Eileen Michelson thinking of?* What could possibly be important about any of this? But she'd said she held his balls, and no telling what the deranged bitch might be capable of doing.

Fine. She wanted it, she could pay for it. She, or those mysterious coconspirators—spies—she'd alluded to.

"Money," he said, "is no object. No object at all."

They both grinned at each other. Neither of them intended the expression to signify any kind of happiness.

## THE WEB: EMPIRE/WAR ROOM

"Stone," Luke said, turning to face the Soldier, "I need your help."

Stone seemed to gather himself, straighten slightly, become somehow larger. His voice was quick and clear. "Name it, Majesty."

"What do you know of the Empire, and the Web that underlies it?"

A faint puzzlement invaded Stone's eyes. "I'm not

sure," he said finally. "I know the Empire. But the Web? I have some small knowledge of it. Are there things there that could hurt you? Would hurt you?"

Luke shrugged. "I don't know. I didn't think so before, but . . . possibly."

Stone's expression cleared. "I can oppose them, Sire. I can protect you." His words were infused with utter certainty, so much strength that Luke, involuntarily, found himself believing them.

"Even without your body, Stone? Can you protect me then?"

Stone didn't hesitate. "Yes, Sire."

Now it was Luke's turn to pause, wondering. How could Stone be so *sure*? From what well did this incredible confidence spring?

Luke shook his head slightly. "I asked you before, I think. How do you know? What powers do you have?"

"I don't know, Sire."

"What?"

Patiently, as if explaining something quite obvious to a small child, Stone said, "I don't understand my own powers, Sire. I have been thoroughly trained in things military, in the usual ways of offense and defense, but there is more within me. How I know, I can't explain. But I do know—I have many powers, but how many, I may never understand. Until they are called upon. Then I'll know." His last few words were spoken in a low, intense undertone.

Luke stared at him, nonplussed. This was madness. His bodyguard was a lunatic.

Or was he?

He had no choice. He made up his mind in that instant, and as he did so, a small part of him gasped at the chasm he'd just leaped. He would go forward and save his Empire, save himself and all the other selves that were of his creation, or all would fall. His own fall would be the last, and longest.

Not quite right, he decided.

Even after his fall, Stone would remain, still fighting, until the destruction was complete. And then he understood. Stone was truly himself, the part he shunned, the part he'd never before let into the light.

Stone was unconquerable.

"Let's do it," Luke said.

Stone grinned.

"Let's," he replied.

Luke led Stone across the nearly deserted parade ground. As before, the gray skies overhead slowly leaked a pervasive fog of chill moisture, not thick enough for rain, but heavier than mere mist. The cold cut to the bone. Luke found himself shivering, even beneath the thick fur jacket he wore, but when he glanced over at Stone, the other man seemed entirely unaffected by the weather. The crunch of their feet on the wet gravel made a lonely, sucking sound. Far off, the muffled shouts of drill instructors floated for a moment in the morning, then vanished.

"We'll go to my quarters," Luke said. "It will be quiet there."

Stone nodded, but made no reply. His eyes, in this filmy light, had gone colorless again, like pools of clear water.

Once inside the building that housed his temporary quarters, Luke paused and said, "Do you know what you're getting into here, Stone?"

The Soldier regarded him calmly. "Not exactly, Sire. But I will protect you, while I live."

Somehow, the words seemed momentous, as if they were engraved on a contract unseen by either party, but mutually accepted. Perhaps they were, Luke thought.

Inside his chambers, Luke motioned for the other to seat himself facing him. Stone sank gracefully into a lotus position, his hands resting easily, palms up, on his thighs. Luke thought the young man was beautiful, and strangely, thought this without any realization that he was so describing a copy of himself. There was an otherness about Stone that precluded the obvious comparison.

He took a breath and began. "Beneath the Empire lies the Web . . ." he said.

Stone, his eyes bird-bright, listened intently. Later, when Luke had finished, he showed no surprise. "Perhaps I always knew," Stone said, "there was more than this." He waved one hand gently, encompassing their surroundings and, by implication, the Empire itself. "I . . . sensed it without understanding the full substance."

Stone's reaction pleased Luke. The other showed no fear, only a calm interest. Durward's suggestion had been a good one. Stone would not be intimidated by the naked reality of the Web.

*And he will see me naked, too.*

"Are you ready, Stone?"

"Yes, Sire."

Luke raised his hands, and the flimsy walls of reality fell away. An instant later, the Web burned around them with the fires of a trillion ghosts.

Luke didn't fully understand how he was able to navigate the Web so easily, while none of his subjects seemed to share the ability to do so. Then the thought faded as once again he was taken by the grandeur of the world that underlay his reality.

Once, in a younger time, he had forced himself out and away, to a place where he could view his part of the Web as a whole. He'd been astonished then to discern the true pattern of the Empire, as it glittered and swayed before him. What he'd seen then had been a tree, a great, trunk-like upwelling of light that spread into an overarching brilliance of tangled branches and leaves. Each leaf a stack, and each stack made up of tiny, card-like flares—copies of himself, perfectly tailored to the tasks for which they had been created. Here and there in the great tree were gigantic branches—thick with stacks drooping and intertwined like growths of mossy fire. These concentrations were the mighty schools and institutions of his Empire—the universities, the industries, and now the army.

But that had been long ago. He had the impression the tree had grown since last he'd observed it in this manner, although from his vantage point now, it was impossible to discern the full extent of its flowering.

"We have to move," he told Stone.

"I am with you, Sire," Stone replied. It was disconcerting. A long wind blew through the tree of light, and Stone's voice seemed to come from the wind, or the tree itself. Luke tried to bring his liege man into focus, but failed utterly. Stone was there—somewhere—but more as a force than a stacked reality.

He thought to pursue the effort, but recalled his mission with a start. Technical questions could wait. Somewhere in the tree burned a bonfire that threatened to consume all, root, branch, and leaf. He had come to find that fire, to gauge its strength and, ever hopeful, its weakness.

"Follow, then," Luke said, and wrapped himself in the winds. They began to move.

Indeed the tree had grown in his absence, he discovered. The branches, dripping a cool radiance so thick it seemed like honey, clustered thick around him, creating long, golden corridors that beckoned and turned confusingly.

He navigated with no sense of difficulty, however: this was his power, the knowledge of the tree within the Web—the foundation of his strength. Here he was master—or should be, he reminded himself. He would soon find out the truth, one way or the other.

Soon enough, he did. His first intimation was the sensation of being faintly smothered, as if someone or something had protectively enfolded him.

Stone, he thought. It is Stone. And he *is* powerful.

Then the feeling went away, and he lost all awareness of his protector. In the distance he saw the first hint of trouble. The colors of the Web began to change.

First a point, a dot, in this world of flowing sheets of light. A single speck, red and unnatural. He slowed his progress. The tiny bead of lighted blood frightened him. It was out of place—*alien*—in the wonderland of light he knew so well.

"Do you see it?" he whispered.

"Yes, Sire." Stone's slow, cool reply braced him unexpectedly. He still didn't understand the connection between himself and this Soldier-creation, but he felt it there, giving him heart and hope. Together, then, they approached the point—for lack of a better word, Luke thought of it as an *infection*. As they grew closer, the ominous shard of fire began to reveal itself. Luke pushed past a final wall of golden light and stopped, frozen by horror. It was as if a protective veil, a bandage over a wound, had been ripped aside, and for the first time, he saw the full extent of the malady that disfigured the tree in the Web.

"Burning Gods . . ." he whispered.

Stone was silent, but Luke could sense his dismay as well.

As far as he could see—seemingly endless—the very fabric of the tree groaned and heaved within the fiery cancer. He stared at the awful panorama, his gut churning with nausea. He imagined a vast field of lava, still pierced by volcanoes that cast bubbling magma into the air, and across all this, the charred bones of the tree, burning. For a moment he could do nothing, feel nothing, say nothing. *See* nothing but the destruction of the tree. Of *himself*, for it was his limbs, his body on the unholy barbecue out there. He was being burned alive even as he watched.

All at once pain seized him in a blinding vice.

He screamed.

He covered his face with his hands as sound poured between his lips, a river of agony, but try as he might, neither his terrible shrieking nor his weakened fingers could shield him from the sight of his own destruction.

*Nothing* could shield him. He was naked before his own death. The molten core of it beckoned him, pulled him forward. He felt his breath leave him in a golden cloud that turned to scalding steam. And all the time he screamed.

"No."

A voice. Deep, dark, thrumming with strength.

Something thick and cold seized his shoulders, inexorably drew him back from the burning abyss. The heat on his face diminished.

"No . . ." The voice spoke again, this time more closely, with greater familiarity. Almost a whisper, but soothing, so soothing. So gentle—

Darkness settled wings across his face, blotted out the horrible images of fire and death. His stomach righted itself. He lowered his hands, hugged his arms around his chest, listened to the pounding of his heart.

Opened his eyes.

Stone stood next to him. Luke could remember the sensation of coolness, the irresistible comfort of his touch. Glanced down, imagined he could see the fading imprint of Stone's fingers on his flesh.

"Sire."

Luke faced him. He lowered his head slightly, without realizing the significance of the act. For the first time in his existence, the Emperor, in his own Empire, bowed to another.

"Thank you," he said softly, his voice raw and rough from the terrible roaring of his fear. "Thank you, Stone."

Stone shrugged. "My job, Sire. Only my job."

Luke shook his head and considered the wonder of it. What was stranger? The cancerous horror of the blaze that was eating his own entrails? Or the mirror of himself who seemed to know the salvation from it?

He turned away from both, back to the twisting tunnels of golden light. The answer was not here.

Not the answer to either question.

This war would be won elsewhere. He wondered how he'd misunderstood. This was only a battle.

The war was beyond the Empire, perhaps beyond the Web itself. But there wasn't anything beyond the Web. Was there?

He shivered.

"Take us home, Stone," he whispered finally.

Stone nodded, and wrapped him up, and took them home.

For a time . . .

## THE HEGEMONY: CITY ON WORLD

Charlie felt strangely buoyant as he approached his own front door. The light in the corridor was without shadow. No one waited for him. He'd been half-afraid that Eileen would be camped out in the hallway, full of threats and vengeance for his disobedience. He checked his nailtale. Almost noon. What had he told her? Ten o'clock, he thought. He hadn't listed the appointment, couldn't call it to the tiny screen embedded in his fingernail. But it was okay. She wasn't around. Perhaps, he thought with sudden hope, she'd forgotten. Maybe it was all some paranoid game she was playing with him, some hideous joke, and now something had caught her attention elsewhere.

He blinked at the doorway, which checked his retinal pattern, agreed he was the legitimate occupant, and opened itself wide. He stepped through, turned—

"You're a little late, don't you think?"

Her words whipped at him as effectively as a physical attack. Each slow syllable dripped venom. He whirled.

"Eileen!"

"Who were you expecting? The cops? Maybe that's a good guess, Charlie. Maybe you *should* expect the police. Or somebody from the Hegemony. If I was in your position, *I* would certainly watch my back."

She was seated on one of the form pillows, her hair twisted into bumpy, ugly shapes, her eyes glittering. The expression on her face was no more a smile than the grimace of a headsman as he crashed the axe to his victim's neck.

Her lips were bright red.

"What are you doing here?"

She stretched, making him think of a great cat ready to feed. "We had an appointment. Remember?"

"I'm sorry." He stepped all the way into the room, and heard the front door click shut behind him. He'd never noticed before how final that sound was. Now they were alone. Or were they? Panic belched into his throat with a sour, bitter taste. What if she *had* turned him in? Given the incriminating chip to his superiors or, worse, agents of the Hegemony? Perhaps they waited in his bedroom, ears wide for something to seal his final inculpation.

He began again, haltingly, trying to remain noncommittal. "I didn't realize you thought it was that important. I left a message, something came up . . ."

She shook her head. "Oh, Charlie. You still don't get it, do you?"

"What are you talking about?" He felt miserably stupid, playing the ignorant fool in his own quarters, but he still hadn't checked the bedroom. And what would that prove? Cops didn't need to be present to know his every word. Eileen might be wired somehow, or his own comm system.

"Give me a second," he blurted, and rushed for the open doorway to the bedroom. He caught his shoulder painfully on the doorjamb as he blundered inside and halted, rubbing at the sore spot as he wildly peered around.

He checked the closet. He even peered into the shower in the john.

Nothing. But how would he know, he asked himself again. Monitors could be *anywhere*.

Something thick and sludge-like bubbled in his gut. He felt hot, light-headed. I'm overreacting, he told himself. This is crazy.

He forced himself to take deep breaths. After a while the rapid thrumming of his heartbeat slowed. He wiped at his forehead, felt cool moisture. He could smell his own odor, sharp and musky.

He walked back to the living room. She hadn't moved. She smiled at him. "What's the matter, Charlie? You look upset. Don't you want to talk to me?" A horrid little chuckle underlined her words. "Cat got your tongue, you miserable, treacherous little motherfucker?"

"Treacherous! You call *me* treacherous? Go on, Gods damn it! It was a prank, a harmless prank." The memory of Naomia's tired face flickered behind his eyelids. He tried to ignore it, but somehow, her features still exerted a nameless, powerful attraction. "Go ahead. Turn me in. Nothing happened. Nothing with the . . . template. I didn't hurt anything."

He watched her carefully. She'd quit smiling. And was that the tiniest ripple of uncertainty that had quivered across her eyelids?

"Charlie," she said finally. "Oh, Charlie. You think I wouldn't?" She reached into a pocket on her flower-printed, billowing blouse and took out the chip. "Here it is—remember, there are copies. But this one would do it. But maybe you don't understand. Not me, but those who are my associates. Here. Let me show you what you're asking for."

She stood with a single movement—my Gods, her legs are *strong*, Charlie thought—and moved to his comm center. She slotted the chip, brushed her fingers lightly across the touchpad, and stepped away as the big screen on the far wall burst into light.

Charlie listened to the sound of his own voice fill the room. The screen showed his handwritten notes, the indolent doodles that had led to the beginnings of the prank.

As he listened to his words, he began finally to grin. She had it all, true, but to any observer not consumed by panic, there wasn't much in this to fear. Oh, yes, he had "plotted" to hire a hooker to perform fellatio on a template. But he hadn't done it. If this was all there was—and he could recall nothing else—the worst he might expect was a reprimand, perhaps a small demotion. But there was nothing criminal here.

What had he been thinking of, to let this madwoman frighten him so? His gaze slid in her direction. She watched the monitor raptly, her lips parted slightly, a faint sheen glistening on her forehead.

She looks excited, he thought. Almost sexual. Maybe that's it—little Eileen wants a piece.

A warm, gloating feeling filled his belly. Maybe, he thought, after I tell her to stuff this shit, I'll give her what she wants.

Spies. Burning Gods, what a fool I am!

His last notes appeared on the screen, held for a moment, disappeared. He inhaled and began to turn toward her. Saw her nod once.

The monitor flared once again, and a new sound—harsh, alien—filled the room.

Charlie froze. His eyes widened.

The figures on the screen were sharp, clear. Faces easy to recognize. And the words. The words were a horror.

"Oh . . . oh." Nothing else would come out. He sat down, hard.

Dimly, in the background of his destruction he heard Eileen.

She was laughing.

His knees buckled and he sat down hard. The shock of the floor hitting his spine sent a lance of pain into his skull, and he blinked away tears. The nightmare on the screen swam in his blurred vision.

"That's not—I didn't—*that's not me!*" The protest ripped involuntarily from his throat. He tasted blood and realized he'd bitten the soft flesh of his tongue.

Her face was full of malevolent merriment. "Oh, yes it is, Charlie. It's exactly you. And no tech—Hegemony or otherwise—will believe it isn't."

He couldn't tear himself away, even to babble another mindless protest. For it *was him on the monitor.* With the same fascination he supposed a helpless rabbit watched an approaching snake, he watched what Eileen Michelson had done to him.

The backgrounds were familiar—his apartment, this very room—a small park near the Hall of the Web, a favorite cafeteria, even the area near the Street of

Whores in the Scarlet Sector. Yes, he had been in all those places, but—

Not like that! Not speaking to a short, dark, ugly little man whose voice was full of gravel, who sat comfortably on a form cushion and explained how Charlie's proposed act would paralyze the Web at a critical time for the Hegemony, and not standing next to the Grog, the Papa Bear, watching the needle-teeth in that huge face move as Grog told him Naomia's location on the Street of Whores, explaining that the Twisten had selected her as best suited to accomplish their aims. And not as he lifted a mug of wine with another woman who vaguely reminded him of Naomia, but who chuckled evilly as they toasted the destruction of the Hegemon himself!

Treason!

And he'd done none of it. Yet these pictures said he had.

He sucked in a ragged lungful of air as the monitor faded suddenly to black, as the silence in the room became palpable.

"A . . . trick," he said. "A simple trick. Anybody could—"

Eileen shook her head. "That is your chip, Charlie, sealed with your embedded codes. Supposedly unbreakable, certainly impossible to fake. Why, Charlie, in order to alter that chip, somebody would have to be able to duplicate your retinal codes! We all know"—her voice thickened in an ugly imitation of sweet reasonableness—"that's impossible, don't we?" And once again, she laughed. Then her voice went cold and dark as the spaces between the stars. "You want me to, Charlie? Give it to the Hegemony? This chip?"

She paused, and when the only sound was his husky, broken breathing, and the only thing she saw was a quick, stunned shake of his head, she nodded. "Then, Charlie, what you want to do is *quit fucking around with me*! You understand? Just *stop fucking around*!"

"Yes."

"Yes, what?"

"Yes. I'll do . . . whatever you want."

Eileen had half risen from her seat on the cushion, her eyes flashing as she spoke. Now she sank back and smiled a final time. Charlie closed his eyes. He wanted to sleep. Or puke. Or cry.

He didn't want to watch that smile.

"Good, Charlie," she said at last. "I think we finally understand each other." She patted the cushion next to her. "So come to mama, Charlie boy. You come on over here to mama, and she'll tell you just exactly what you're going to do next."

He couldn't move.

Her face changed then, and she smashed her fist into the cushion once, hard.

"I said *come*!"

Charlie went. Not the way he had with Naomia, but he went just the same.


## THE HEGEMONY: CITY ON WORLD/SCARLET SECTOR

She sat in her silent room and considered her Name. Naomia. Names were important to her. She was very old, and she understood the great power in Names. Names were both a shield and a banner, something to hide behind, or use as a weapon.

Names *defined*. She understood this, as well. As for the rest, it was in the hands of whatever True Gods still existed. She had her Name, and her secret Names, as well. The old words, those coined in the dim and

distant ages of the First and Lost Men, held no secrets
for her.

There are no secrets left, she thought suddenly, and
was amazed at how tired this understanding left her.
She felt the weight of eons press her down but, as
always, she straightened. and lifted the weight. As she
always had. As she always would

In the meantime, the wheel turned.

Charlie. For a moment she smiled. Poor little man.
She could imagine what he was going through. He'd
tasted but the tiniest portion of her powers. For one
instant she'd spread the wings of her strength and
shown him Night. But only for an instant, and not the
full, howling truth of Night. He'd been able to shake
it off as a hallucination, and she'd sent him away
unbroken.

But he was hers. He would be no problem.

The rest of it, though . . .

She fingered the necklace of tiny skulls, which
rested across her breasts. It made small clicking noises
against her pointed nails. The rest of it wouldn't be
so easy. Already one sleeper stirred, and the other
would awaken soon enough without any help from
her.

That other one, she feared.

She named another Name softly. Her red lips caressed the word. Kali. She wondered how many in
this new world knew the true meaning of it. Kali destroyed the old, cleansed away decadence with fire,
and when the time came, ushered in the new Yuga,
the new Age in the turning of the Wheel.

Kali, too, wore skulls. Just as she did.

And Kali must slay her consort.

Oh, yes, she did fear the awakening of the second
sleeper.

Poor Charlie. Poor universe.

Poor fallen angel.

# 5

## THE WEB: EMPIRE

The ever-present gray mist was thick as ever. Luke stared out a window of his temporary rooms at the dense, colorless veils moving silently across the huge parade ground. For a moment he considered banishing the fog, replacing it with bright sunlight—but then realized the weather only mirrored his mood, as did all things in the Empire unless he consciously dictated otherwise.

Gray day, gray mood. He was still shaken by what he'd seen in the heart of the Web. In retrospect, details of the conflagration became more clear: he had seen the *bones* of the tree burning there, utterly consumed. A vast section of his own Empire had been destroyed. Here, in the world of the Empire, the effects were becoming noticeable; more and more of his resources—Icons—sacrificed in the increasingly futile attempt to halt the spread of barbarism across his once-predictable land.

*Where were they coming from?*

He forced his fevered thoughts to slow. Panic

wouldn't help here. He seated himself and turned his mind inward, seeking the cool, peaceful heart of his power.

The Empire. What was it, precisely?

It was, at its deepest core, a source. The Icons appeared almost magically, in numbers nearly inconceivable. He took these raw Icons and channeled them where they were needed for imprinting in the daily tasks of the Empire itself. And he had seen a terrifying thing in the Web—the fires that consumed him were fed from the same source. It was as he had most feared. Somehow, he was fashioning raw Iconic power into a tool of his own destruction. At the base of the tree, where the trunk grew and flowered into the intricacy of leaf and branch, the source still functioned, pumping millions of unpatterned Icons up and out. Some were still at his conscious disposal. His new armies had been created from such. But somehow, without his knowing volition, other Icons—incredible numbers of them—were being turned into . . . other. Into the mindless savages that assaulted everything he'd built. Yet search as he might, he couldn't find the source of this suicide within himself. As far as he could tell, he *wasn't doing it*.

Yet it was happening, and his vision of the tree did not lie. He *was* killing himself.

He shook his head. No answers. The trip into the Web had been necessary, but it had given him no answers. Only more questions, problems for which he could divine no solutions, even though he ransacked every Library he had, even though he plumbed the most arcane depths of his own power.

Very well. A sort of fatalistic calm took him. Perhaps the tree, the Empire, perhaps he himself was fated to pass into oblivion. But even that didn't seem right, somehow. The barbarian invaders showed frightening vitality. They killed and burned and died with manic gusto, and more of them appeared with appalling rapidity. Perhaps a final death was not in the offing, but a change. The tree would become wholly savage and, in the end, he also.

But what function would he have then? The commerce, the life of the Empire was dedicated to something beyond it. He dimly sensed the greater reality, what he thought of as the True Reality, from whence came problems for which he supplied solutions. The equation had existed as long as he had. Would that now change as well?

There were other powers, forces beyond his absolute control. True Reality represented one such. But other Empires existed, too. And the more he considered, the more it seemed likely that answers might be found in *those* Empires. Some were far older than his own. Perhaps there had been similar situations, and solutions found for them.

Perhaps. But everybody he contacted admitted no such knowledge. Everybody but one. Only Ice refused entirely.

Ice was one of the first, one of the oldest Empires. For time out of memory, it had defended the rest of them, but now, in his own extremity, it refused even the courtesy of reply.

Very strange.

He had hoped to avoid the trip to Ice. But in its silence, Ice had made that impossible.

Could three—himself, Stone, Durward—crack the secrecy of the Empire whose very function was secrecy?

He shivered. Ice would be cold. Perhaps deadly. But he had no choice. Again, for a few moments, he watched the dancing fog. Somewhere beyond the fog, beyond the mountains, a deadly fire burned.

No choice. No choice at all.

"Stone," he said. "Durward. Come to me."
They did. They had no choice either.

## HEGEMONY: CITY ON WORLD

For the first time, a faint worm of doubt began to
gnaw at Eileen Michelson's certainty. Charlie sat next
to her on the form cushion, as she'd demanded, but
there was no sense of camaraderie. Her logical mind
found nothing odd about that—after all, their relationship was based on fear and blackmail—but she knew
enough about herself to recognize that, however irra-
tional it might be, a part of her hoped for some other
relationship with the young man. Yet, at the moment,
Charlie looked incapable of having even a relationship
with himself. He twitched. He chewed on his lower
lip so furiously that she saw a faint smear of blood at
the corner of his mouth. And whenever she spoke, he
would sigh and look away. Once, by accident, her
hand had brushed his knee, and he'd gone absolutely
white. For a moment she'd feared he would simply
pass out or, worse, vomit.

He was obviously in shock. That could be a problem. Her mentors—she preferred to think of them in
that manner, rather than as superiors or, worse,
bosses—had given her a strict timetable. But now,
judging from Charlie's condition, he'd be lucky to
function at all. It puzzled her. After all, he couldn't
truly know what was at stake. She thought she did,
though she was wise enough to realize that her teachers might have withheld something—perhaps from
lack of trust, or simply as a way of covering their
bets—but she knew enough. What she proposed to
do was change the world, perhaps even change the
Hegemony itself. The dumb show her teachers had
inscribed upon Charlie's supposedly unbreakable chip

had nothing to do with the real problems at hand. She was certain enough of that. It had been designed to instill fear, even panic, and obviously it had done its job well. Maybe too well. If Charlie succumbed to the hysteria that seemed, as she examined him more closely, only a few breaths away, he would be no use to her. To any of them. And he was essential.

Something would have to be done. Something to lower his anxiety level. But what? The answer came in a flash of inspiration. It was so obvious, she wondered how she'd overlooked it.

She broke off her litany of instruction. He wasn't listening anyway, or if he was, nothing was being absorbed. After half a minute of silence, he realized she had stopped. He licked his lips and turned slightly. She nodded at him, reached over, and carefully wrapped the fingers of her right hand around his penis and began to move her fist slowly up and down.

He bucked once, like a frightened animal, at her touch. But she had read him well. Beneath his terrified exterior, a part of Charles Seagrave was still wired, with supreme confidence, into his gonads. Her guess was that Charlie was still totally egocentric, locked into an adolescent fantasy of ultimate male desirability. He was young, good-looking, healthy, intelligent, and always horny. Even though she was his enemy, she was a woman. Why, his unconscious would ask quietly, *wouldn't* a gawky, social maladroit like Eileen Michelson be attracted to him? Even, perhaps, *lust* for him? It was no more than the hidden, teenage version of himself would expect.

And so, though he fought the rhythmic motion of her fingers for a few instants, ultimately he slumped back and closed his eyes. She could almost read his mind. It was the break he'd been waiting for, the sudden revealing of Eileen Michelson's hidden passion for him. Now he had something to bargain with. The upper hand, so to speak.

She smiled as she brought him closer to orgasm. He was such a fool. But that was precisely what she wanted. Wasn't it?

"Why?" Charlie asked. He was sprawled bonelessly on the form cushion, his pants around his knees. His flaccid penis rested, small and pink, at the top of his thigh. Once again, Eileen was struck at the essential helplessness of the male, ruled by hormones he not only couldn't control, but couldn't even understand. She thanked whatever Gods there were that she, a woman, was free of that particular danger, that ever-present masculine threat of destruction from within, and marveled instead at the change that had overtaken Charlie Seagrave. Amazing how friction, a few grunts, and a sudden small spurting could create such a transformation. Where before she'd worried that he might pass out, or worse, now he rested calm, relaxed, his breathing slow and steady, a new flush in his cheeks, a confident sparkle in his eyes.

Just the way she wanted him, in fact.

"I wanted to," she told him, and repressed outright laughter at the way his chest puffed out and a knowing expression smoothed his features.

"I thought you might. How was it for you?"

This time she couldn't help it, but managed to turn what threatened to be rib-shaking guffaws into a small, womanly chuckle of understanding. The arrogance! How was it for her? She'd masturbated him. He hadn't even touched her. This was supposed to be some kind of experience for her? How was it, indeed!

"Enjoyable . . ." she said.

He nodded. "Thanks."

This time, when she moved closer to him, he didn't

move away. In fact, after hitching up his pants—how courteous, she thought—he placed his right arm carelessly around her neck and shoulders, half cradling her against the cushion.

"Eileen, what's going on here? Why are you doing this to me?"

Now comes the tricky part, she thought, and chuckled silently, pleased with herself at stringing so many double entendres together in such a short sentence. She looked down at him, placed what she hoped was an appropriately simpering expression on her face— would he believe it? Yes. His macho arrogance would believe *anything*—and said, "I selected you myself, Charlie. My . . . compatriots asked me for a way to accomplish our goals, and I selected you."

He nodded, as if he understood. Somebody had regarded him as capable, as perhaps even heroic. She watched the thoughts chase themselves behind his slightly narrowed eyes, and thought once again that men were such fools. "Why . . . me?"

He wanted confirmation. Needed it, even. She happily supplied it. "Why, Charlie. Isn't it obvious? Who else could do what needed to be done? I watched you for a long time, wondering. Trying to decide if you were my . . . man." Carefully she laid the slight emphasis on the last word, giving it an extra meaning he couldn't help but hear. He stirred slightly as she continued. "And when I discovered you were already planning something that could be adapted to our needs—had already shown me you were the *man* I needed—why, then, the decision was easy."

She leaned back a bit, the better to observe the effects of this bit of bald-faced lying, and was gratified to see all her hopes verified. Charlie's eyes literally glowed. She wondered just what adolescent daydreams were at last being fulfilled in the barely post-pubescent turmoils of his mind.

"So, your . . . compatriots"—he paused slightly before the word, just as she had, unconsciously gilding those mysterious conspirators with a spurious but acceptable legitimacy—"agreed with you?"

They will *ruin* you, she thought, but only said, "Yes. In fact, they were even more enthusiastic than I was. I was uncertain whether you could take the pressure." She waited a beat, in case he wanted to protest, but he said nothing. She continued; "Of course I see now that my fears were mistaken. Although I wondered, when you didn't show for our meeting this morning."

It was almost laughable, how he seemed to preen, to expand, as his masculinity—I gave the horny little girl what she wanted!—filled him with visions of his own invincibility.

Go on, she urged him silently. Finish it. Trip over your own cock.

"Eileen." His voice deepened. She could read the script from here on out. "You know this is wrong. I could get into a lot of trouble. But that's not what I'm worried about. You could have the same problems—lose your job. Your career. Even difficulty with . . . the Hegemony itself."

Worried about me? Bullshit.

"Charlie," she whispered. "Just let me explain. Once you understand, I'm sure you'll be able to show me how to avoid all that. After all, you're not the man I selected if you can't."

And you *certainly* want to be the man I selected. Or any kind of man, you poor dupe.

He paused. Finally he nodded, as if he'd made a decision. "Okay," he said. "Go ahead. I guess it can't hurt to listen."

Not much, she thought. And only for a little while.

## THE WEB: EMPIRE

"Check it out," Durward said. "Am I cool, or what?" He jingled the arrangements of thin steel chains that made an overvest above the thickly padded shirt that covered his sinewy upper body.

Luke thought he looked something like a strange sausage wrapped tightly for market, but he grinned and said, "Cool. You do look cool."

Durward nodded happily, then slid his eyes sideways toward the corner where Stone silently inserted yet another small black, probably deadly thing into his own jacket—a quasi-military thing that seemed mostly held together by zippers and snaps.

"Hey, Soldier boy," Durward said, his lips flickering into and out of a smile. "Is that what you call camouflage? You look like a human version of one of those tanks the General likes so much."

Stone turned his serious gaze on the Messenger. "It never hurts to be prepared."

Durward shrugged. "All that shit, people'll hear you coming miles away."

Stone shook his head. "No, they won't."

Somehow, the way he said it, Luke knew it was true. And Durward's nervous jabbering was beginning to irritate him.

"What about me?" he said. "Am I . . . cool?"

"You be cool, Sire. Very cool."

Luke saw his reflection in one of the darkened screens still unrolled across the far wall of his living area. He wore a long black leather coat over a suit of soft material the General guaranteed would protect him from anything short of a point-blank ripper blast.

The General had not—was still not—happy about any of this. Even his ironclad confidence in Stone was not enough to make him sanguine about the Emperor—the *Emperor!*—leaving the safety of the Empire. And that the Emperor chose to travel incognito, with only the companionship of one half-crazed and totally useless Messenger and one—however competent—Soldier, that, the General no doubt felt, was madness.

The General knew the truth. The Empire and the Emperor were one. If something happened to the Emperor, what then for the Empire?

An interesting question, Luke decided. No one knew. Not even himself. Once again, he felt a shiver of apprehension about the upcoming foray. He had no idea whether it was the right thing to do. But he couldn't think of any other option, certainly no option offering a greater degree of safety. To plumb the fiery, boiling roots of the cancer itself—he'd seen the tree burning. He still couldn't entirely accept that horror as his own doing. Perhaps some insidious invader, of a kind he'd never heard of, was mimicking the process of creation somehow. It was certainly easier to accept than the evidence he'd already seen.

Ice would know, if anybody did. Perhaps, somehow, Ice was even involved. The expertise was no doubt there. Of course, if Ice was behind the invasion, this little jaunt was doubly dangerous. On the other hand, it would be doubly necessary. Ice could protect itself. Perhaps only another Emperor would have any chance to breach its defenses.

So many questions. So many dangers. Yet it all came down to one thing: he *had no choice.*

"So why worry about it. Just go *do* it," he mumbled softly.

"Beg pardon, Sire?" Durward said.

Luke smiled. "Nothing, Durward. Just a thought. Are we about ready?"

Now Stone spoke. "Sire, let me check you."

"Go ahead."

Stone moved over to him and began to gently pat him down, scrutinizing him to make sure the survival suit beneath his coat was fitted properly. He made no sound as he worked. Luke watched Stone's face, trying once again to get some kind of line on this strange creation. Stone's eyes were slightly narrowed. Once again the color was hard to make out. Other than this mildly intent expression. Stone's face was blank.

"Stone?"

"Yes, Sire?"

"What are you?"

"I'm your protector, Sire."

"That isn't what I meant," Luke said softly. "Not what you do. What you are."

Stone paused. Luke noticed how neatly his hands stopped moving. Just stopped in mid-motion, while Stone thought about it.

"He's an asshole Soldier boy," Durward laughed.

Stone paid no attention. "I think I understand," he said finally. "I'm dangerous. Is that what you mean?"

Luke realized he'd been holding his breath, waiting for the reply. Now he exhaled. "Yes," he said. "That's what I meant."

Stone nodded and finished his check. "You're fine, Sire. Can we go over the ground rules now?"

Luke blinked. "What ground rules?"

"There have to be rules, Sire," Stone said patiently. "You are the leader, of course, but I can't do what I'm supposed to without some understanding. For instance, no wandering off. We let Durward do any talking necessary, unless I decide otherwise. For the rest, you stay quiet and as much in the background as you can. Let Durward be the point. He's the Messenger, after all. You and I, we're fakes. He knows, and it will show. If they buy him, they'll probably buy everything else. And if not—"

"Yes?" Luke prodded.

"One other rule, Sire. If I move, it will be very quick. Just try to stay out of my way. Don't help. If I need help, it will most likely be too late anyway."

Durward chuckled. "Big, bad man." But his heart wasn't in it. As usual, Stone ignored him.

Luke sighed. "That's fine. You heard him, Durward."

"But, Sire—"

"Those are the rules," Luke said flatly.

Durward subsided, his thin features sullen. "At least I get to do the talking," he said.

"Yes," Stone said. "You're good at that."

"Is that supposed to be an insult?"

Stone shrugged. "It's not supposed to be anything."

For a moment Luke wondered if this was such a good idea—Durward seemed likely to become a problem, his dislike of Stone already evident. But why did he dislike the man? Stone hadn't done anything to him.

He pushed the problem away. Too many problems, not enough answers, and way too much at stake. It still boiled down to no choice.

"When do we leave?" Luke said.

"Right now," Durward told him. "Unless you have a reason to wait?"

"No. No reason."

Stone nodded. "I agree. The sooner the better. Durward will lead once I get us past the border."

"*You* get us across? Hah."

"Yes, me. I don't want to cross at the usual Messenger points."

Durward paused, his face suddenly thoughtful. "Oh, uh. Well, yeah, I guess, then . . ."

Luke glanced from one to the other, not understanding. "What am I missing?"

Durward said, "Sire, you're not a Messenger. Or

even a Soldier. In that getup, you might pass a casual inspection, but at the Messenger transfer points, they check things real good. We don't want that." His voice sounded unhappy. "Unless you'd rather, of course . . ."

Luke shook his head. He would never have thought of it. My ignorance will get me yet, he thought abruptly, then pushed *that* thought away, as well. It would haunt him later, but that was ignorance, too. "No, do it your way. In fact, the two of you, don't bother asking. If I have a question, I'll ask, but for now, we assume that you both know what you're doing. Okay?"

Stone nodded. "Fine, Sire," Durward said.

"Then shall we go?"

Stone motioned toward the door. "The General has arranged transport."

"Oh, Burning Gods. Not another tank," Durward groaned.

Stone smiled faintly. "I don't think so," he said.

Stone led the way down the long hall to a pair of doors that swung wide onto the parade ground, Durward behind, Luke following last. A part of him bridled—*the Emperor does not follow!*—but he discovered he was interested in this new, unfamiliar role. There was a feeling of relief, even exhilaration in laying down his perpetual role and taking up another, lesser masquerade. He was surprised to find it so, but the surprise was pleasant. One never realizes the load one carries, he mused, until one lays it down.

Stone pushed the doors aside and led them out into the open air. Today the fog was gone, and a sky built of light and blue steel arched over the shabby barracks and the burnt brown hills beyond, throwing everything into painful clarity.

They stood, a thin, hard breeze slicing at their

cheeks. "The General," Stone said, "will meet us when we board," and that was when Luke realized they were alone.

Odd, lonely feeling. For an instant he considered summoning a crowd, a mass of faceless Icons to cheer him good-bye. Hero off on the journey. But he didn't feel like a hero. The wind whispered to him, messages of desolation.

Why do I feel so tired? he wondered.

"Up, above," Stone said to Durward, and after a beat, Durward breathed softly. "Fire God, look at that . . ."

Overhead, a star was falling. Luke squinted against the light, his gaze caught on the ever-growing flare. At first a point, then a hard-edged oblong structure, and then, finally, with ponderous slowness, the shape of the vessel became clear; a capital ship, layer upon layer of armor, plexsteel, shielded glass. It seemed impossible that something so huge—the shadow of it covered the vast parade ground entirely, and even blotted out ranks of barracks on either side—that something that gigantic could ever become airborne. And slowly it fell, a city of death, toppling . . .

Something bright red flashed beneath the ship. Letters. The vessel proclaimed itself, showed its name in configurations of flame: *Lucifer Imperator*.

As a boarding tube extruded toward them from the underside of the gargantuan battleship, Luke thought of the awful dichotomy. So much power, and yet so helpless.

There was something basic, intrinsic, wrong with the Empire. Something flawed within his very structure.

Would he live? Would he die?

The wind blew. They watched the beast settle, and a moment later, to the sound of drums and horns, climbed into its belly.

The General bustled forward, exuding confidence, hiding his fear well.

Live? Die?

A nagging thought finally surfaced: Are these even the right *questions*?

## THE HEGEMONY: CITY ON WORLD

"Charlie, have you ever thought about the Hegemony? Or the Hegemon himself, for that matter?"

They lay sprawled on the form cushions. They'd made love—made sex—once again. This time she'd taken command of the act, led him into the ritual movements but kinked them against his desires so that she took, and took, and in the end finally gave a grudging release in return. Even so, as she stared at his satisfied face—it took so *little* to satisfy him—she marveled again at the inherent weakness of men. Charlie was not stupid, nor was he ignorant. He was, in fact, a highly representative example of a certain class of man in a particular time and place. In his own milieu of education and employment, he would be competent, at times even brilliant. But so narrow was his field of knowledge that once outside its constricted walls, he was essentially helpless. Which, in fact, he was yet again in the process of confirming.

After they'd finished, Charlie lit a bowl of Suma oil and placed it on the floor in the middle of the room. Now, as he considered a reply, he watched the flames chase themselves in hypnotic patterns across the surface of the oil, colors of blue and rose, picking up the ancient lily patterns of the Suryma bowl itself. "The Hegemony?" he said. "It just . . . is. Always has been, I guess. And the Hegemon. Who knows *anything* about him? I'm not even sure he exists. Has anybody ever seen him?"

She stroked his forehead lightly, and he closed his eyes. Like a child, she thought, a baby. So trusting . . .

She smiled. "Nobody's ever seen him, Charlie. And that's part of the problem."

"What problem?"

"The one we're going to solve."

His voice slowed, overlaid with a patina of drowsiness. The room felt hot. smoky, full of the dusky incense of the Suma oil, although the air seemed clear as old crystal, gravid with flickering light.

"What are we going to solve?"

"The Hegemon is dead, Charlie. Has been for a very long time." She inhaled, exhaled softly. "So, long live the new Hegemon."

"Crazy talk," he mumbled.

"Charlie, the Hegemon is dead. I'm serious. Who do you think runs the Hegemony?"

He licked his lips. The fluttering light caught the glossy reflection, the faint hint of white from the perfect teeth beneath the vulnerable flesh. "Never thought about it. It runs, that's enough."

She sucked air, a muted sound of irritation. "The Web, Charlie. The Web. and the Council of Ten. The Hegemon is a fiction, kept in place to maintain the illusion that all is well. But it isn't. And some of us have decided to do something about it."

He opened his eyes. In the light, his pupils were dark, clean-edged, like beads. "You're nuts, Eileen."

Her fingers, which had been playing with his earlobe, clenched suddenly. nails digging into the flaccid skin.

"Ouch!"

*"Don't ever call me that, Charlie Seagrave. Don't ever call me crazy."* Her voice was a hiss that echoed in the room.

He stared at her. "Hey. I'm sorry."

"You'd better be." But she released his ear. "I hurt you. I didn't mean to."

He settled back. "Eileen, who put you up to this? Who are these people? Something in that chip you trumped up . . . Twisten? What are the Twisten?"

Ah. Now that it was too late, he'd finally begun to think. Typical. She kept her tone light, unconcerned. "The Twisten? It's just a name. For a group."

"Of concerned people, right?" He was sardonic. "Maybe they meet on Tuesdays, discuss revolution— that is what we're talking about, isn't it?—after tea?"

"Not exactly."

"Damned right not exactly! Eileen, don't you understand? It took real tech to get into my chip like that, change it. They told you it couldn't be detected? If that's true—and it would have to be, for the thing to have any blackmail value—whoever did it has to have some mega connections. You can't buy tech like that off the shelf. Heavy people, Eileen. You're mixed up with them. And now you've got *me* mixed up, too."

Poor thing, she thought. You don't even know the half of it. "Charlie, these are good people. There's no danger . . ."

"How can you be sure? Eileen, admit it. You're in over your head. You need help."

Oh, yes, little man. I do indeed. So come on, make your offer. You can't believe how ready I am to accept. "Charlie, I can handle myself."

"You can't. Look. You set out to blackmail me, and you end up in bed with me. You can't even control your own drives."

She didn't laugh. She wasn't sure how she kept from it, but she didn't laugh. "Charlie, there's something about you."

"Well, maybe." He paused. "Listen, Eileen. I like

you. At first, the blackmail and all, but now—things have changed. This half-baked scheme—overthrow the Hegemony, for all God's sake—you can't go on with it."

She let a bit of steel creep into her voice. "But Charlie, I *am* going on with it."

He heard the faint flick of metal. He paused, then plunged ahead. "You have to bring me all the way in."

"I don't know . . ."

"No, really. I still don't understand how a practical joke will help your crazy conspirators, but you have to admit, I'll do a better job if I'm a willing participant. How could you trust me otherwise?"

How could I trust you period, she thought, if what intelligence you had wasn't wired directly to your balls? "Maybe," she said. She let him wait. "Maybe you're right . . ." It was the second time she'd said it, and its effect was all she'd hoped.

"Of course I am. So tell me, what is this supposed to accomplish with the template? Go ahead, you can trust me."

She reached over and gently ran her fingers down the cord of his scrotum. *"Of course I can."*

## EMPIRE: THE BORDER

Luke's booted feet crunched on the ragged stretch of gravel that bordered the small, icy stream. Behind him, Durward made harsh, panting noises as he wrestled a backpack from the door of the small flyer. The fog had closed in again, making the outlines of the sharp series of ridges that led down to the creek a gray, hazy blur. Noises were eerily muffled.

"Gods *damn* it!" Durward muttered, as the final pack slipped and landed on his foot.

"Here," Stone said softly. "Let me."

"I got it, thanks," Durward grumbled as he lifted the pack. "Sire?"

"Yes?"

"Here. The smallest one is yours."

Luke hefted the proffered pack. "It doesn't seem heavy. Are you sure you two can carry the rest?"

Durward looked shocked. "Sure, we should carry *everything*. But I don't know—"

"The Emperor can carry a pack," Stone said.

"Of course I can," Luke said. "I want to do my part."

Durward glared at Stone, who had already festooned himself with the two heaviest packs, seemingly without effort, and now stood off to one side, watching them.

"Stone," he said, "you don't seem to understand. This man is the Emperor. The Emperor shouldn't *carry* things."

Stone shook his head. "Durward, where we are going, Luke is no longer an Emperor. He will have to do his part, just as we will."

No longer the Emperor? The strange idea picked at him like a bad tooth. How can I not be the Emperor? The Emperor is what—is *all* that I am.

An errant burst of damp, cold air billowed down the narrow canyon and brought tears to his eyes. He brushed them away, conscious of how chilled he'd gotten.

I've never been this cold before in my life, he thought. I should just—

Suddenly the temperature began to rise. The wind died instantly. A glimmer began to show through the fog.

"Sire, *don't*," Stone said.

"What?" Luke said, astounded.

Stone's voice was urgent. "Sire, this close to the border, don't display your powers. Remember, we are talking about *Ice*! Who knows how closely, or how deeply, they watch? Why give them an engraved announcement of our impending arrival?"

Stupid, Luke thought. I am so stupid. I have to learn to *think* before I do things. "Yes," he said. "You're right." Even as he spoke, the frigid breeze returned, and the fog closed its leaden roof again.

"Better," Stone said. Then, "Sire?"

"Yes, Stone?"

"Perhaps it might be a good idea if you asked me, from now on, before you attempt to use any of your . . . abilities."

"Now wait a minute!" Durward said. "You can't order him—"

"Sire?" Stone interjected.

"It's okay, Durward," Luke said. "He's right, as usual."

Muttering to himself, the Messenger subsided. Luke was surprised to note how fiercely ready the flamboyantly garbed Icon was to leap to his defense. Somehow it had to be more than simply a programmed reaction.

The pack straps were relatively simple. Stone showed Luke how to adjust his belly strap, and how to position the weight of the pack itself for the least amount of strain. When he was finished, he stepped back and said, "You look fine, Sire. You must take to this sort of thing."

Luke was oddly warmed by the compliment, even as he realized it was probably the first time in his whole existence he'd ever *carried* something.

Durward, muffled by his heavy coat and strangely clumsy in a pair of bulky hiking boots, muttered something indistinguishable, then said, "Well, we're not getting anyplace standing around, are we? Everybody ready?"

"I'm ready," Luke told him.

"Okay. Follow me." He paused. "If that's acceptable to you, *Mister* Stone?"

Stone grinned. "Lay on, MacDuff."

Luke chuckled, but Durward didn't get the joke. He snorted and turned abruptly, beginning to make his way up the bank of the stream, leading them against the current, higher into the canyon.

Stone said, "You go in the middle, Sire. I'll keep an eye on our rear."

Luke nodded. Suddenly he smiled widely. The mad spirit of the thing had taken him, and now, without warning, he felt as happy as he'd ever been. It's crazy, he thought. But I love it.

The idea of using bicycles had been discarded almost immediately. Stone pointed out they had no idea of the kind of terrain they might encounter. Now Durward set a brisk pace, his legs moving deceptively slowly, but eating up the ground. He never seemed to stumble. Always he set his boot down on solid earth, easily missing treacherous spots of sliding rock and slippery gravel. The stream made a soft, bubbling roar to their left, but Durward's low-spoken instructions easily carried to Luke at his back.

"Just step where I step, Sire, and you'll be safe."

Luke tried to do so, but found himself much more clumsy than his Chief Messenger and, within several hundred yards, he stumbled twice. Each time, without any appearance of effort, Stone caught and righted him smoothly. After a time Luke began to feel the pattern, the rhythm of the trek, and took fewer missteps. The frigid air pouring down from the canyon was bracing. For a time, in the bliss of the hike, he was able to forget all his troubles, his fears, and concentrate only on the beautiful simplicity of physical exertion.

What have I been missing? he wondered. I never do anything like this, and it's *wonderful*.

The path beside the stream began to rise sharply, even as the trail itself narrowed and became strewn with ragged, cracked boulders. Beside them, the sound of the water became a dull roar; white froth danced over broken piles of granite, caught by the wind and whipped into a fine silver mist.

". . . Up ahead, Sire."

The tail end of Durward's warning interrupted his reverie. "Uh? I'm sorry, Durward, I didn't hear—"

The Messenger raised his right hand and came to a full stop. He waited until Luke and Stone caught up, then said, low-voiced, "We're approaching the border now. At the head of this canyon, maybe half a mile on up."

Curious, Luke asked. "Have you come this way before?"

"No, Sire."

"Then how do you know what's ahead?"

Durward's cheeks took on a bit of color. He shrugged, awkwardly. "I don't know how I know, but I *do* know, Sire. I'm a Messenger—your Chief Messenger. My true function is to carry things from one Empire to another. In this case, it just happens that instead of a more normal load, I'm carrying an Emperor. But I *always* know where I'm going. Just like Stone always knows how to do whatever it is he does." He stopped, glanced at the stream that now made thunderous, grinding sounds as it dropped a series of rocky steps, almost waterfalls, and said unhappily, "You'll just have to trust me, Sire. Can you do that?"

"Of course I can." The words sounded lame in his ears and, without thinking, Luke blurted, "I always have, haven't I? Why should I stop now?"

Durward grinned. With his face suddenly alight, he

resembled some small, fairylike being, dancing in the mist and the rumble of rock and water. "Well, then," he said. "Shall we go, oh fearless leader?"

Now Luke grinned in return. He couldn't help it. "Not so fearless," he said, "and maybe not very much of a leader right now. But yes, let's go. Lay on, MacDuff!"

"Sire, what does that mean? That 'lay on' shit?"

Luke glanced at Stone, who eyed him without expression. It figured, that Stone would somehow be familiar with one of the greatest of the war poets, but it would take too long to explain the history of ancient English to Durward.

"It's an old joke," he said. "I'll tell you sometime."

Durward's smile remained, but Luke thought it looked a bit strained. I shouldn't take these two for granted, he thought. Either one of them.

The next thought stunned him to the roots of his being. *Because they have feelings, too.*

He hid this epiphany from them, however, and merely nodded thoughtfully as Durward turned and led them upward once again. After a time, Durward paused and said, "Soon, Sire. Just over that ridge."

A moment later, still in the Empire, they crossed the final ridge, and the Emperor Lucifer saw the Land of Ice for the first time.

Later historians have chronicled the moment—usually in prose so purple it begs for a broiler and some cooking, or artistically, in paint and other media so garish it has become a staple of the cheaper souvenir shops.

This junk always remarks on the configuration of three: the Emperor, the Killer, and the Messenger. Much symbolic nonsense has been said of this, and always there is light on the scene, as if to illuminate some basic human principle—or, as some of the more thoughtful would have it, some basic human joke.

But that was all later, when history had become history. The reality was a bit more plain.

"Gods . . ." Luke muttered.

"Pretty, isn't it?" Durward said.

Stone said nothing, but Luke heard him click his tongue against his teeth, once. A rare display of emotion. The path reached the peak of the ridge and stopped at a small overhang before beginning a short, winding trail to the border proper. Luke's eyes followed the dim trace to where it finally vanished into a wall of ice nearly half a mile high. A blazing sun sparked over the vast plain, turning the tortured surface into a field of diamonds, sapphires, topazes. Here and there ice mountains bulged like monstrous tumors above the lower reaches, their tops tinted crimson in the pitiless light. Even from this distance the buzzsaw whine of the gales that swept those fearsome steppes tugged and cut at his ears.

"We're going there?" he whispered.

"Yes, Sire," Durward replied. He sounded not at all awed by the grotesque vista before them. In fact, his voice was filled with exhilaration. Luke stared at the back of his head, at the dark, curly hair, half-shaved, whipping in the wind on the other side, and imagined Durward's eyes alight and glittering at the fields of ice.

"You . . . don't seem afraid."

Durward turned, his smile fading. "But I'm not," he said seriously. "It's only another place. That's what a Messenger does, Sire. Goes from one place to another. I don't know what I'd do . . . if I had to stay in only one place."

Luke stared at him. "I've never been out of the Empire," he said at last.

Durward's eyes narrowed as he considered the statement. Its import burst upon him all at once.

"Oh, Sire! I'm sorry. I didn't understand." He half turned away, toward the endless plains of ice, then turned back. "It's wonderful, Sire. You'll love it. I promise."

"Don't make promises you can't keep, Messenger," Stone said.

Luke shifted his weight onto one foot and turned to face the warrior head on. "Stone. What about you?"

"How do you mean, Sire?"

"What promises do you make?"

Stone shook his head. "I never make promises, Sire."

"Even to your Emperor?"

Stone grinned faintly. "Especially to my Emperor."

They stood and listened to the howl of the wind, distant and rising. The sun flared in their faces, half blinding them.

"There, Sire. Can you see it?"

Luke shaded his eyes and stared in the direction of Durward's upraised hand. "I don't see anything."

"Follow the path with your eyes to where it ends."

After a moment's search, Luke was able to pick up the faint markings of the trail. Down and turn and down again, moving away from the stream that branched nearly at their feet, its source rising somewhere above them on the top of the ridge. Disappearing into the wall of ice at—

"That dark spot?" Luke said.

"Yes, Sire. Ice comes right to our border here."

"What is the spot?"

"A hole, Sire. I hope, a hole in Ice's defenses."

"You mean you don't know?"

Durward moved his shoulders up, down. "Sire, I'm only a Messenger. I know the points of entry and exit, but as for forcing my way through—"again, the shrugging motion—"well, I assumed you'd know the answer to that."

"Sire?" Stone interjected.

"What?"

"Do you understand what is necessary?"

Luke shook his head. Perhaps this was a complete mistake, better aborted at the beginning then continued into a further, possibly more complete, failure.

"Very well," Stone said. "Then I'll have to teach you."

For once, Durward voiced no objection to Stone's usurpation of leadership. He moved closer to them, his body shielding Luke from the cutting winds. "Sire, this would be a good place to stop, build a camp. There's a lee just beyond the spike of rock there. We can wait while Stone tells you what you have to know. And you can rest." He stopped, then slid a worried, knowing glance in the Soldier's direction. "You'll need your rest. You'll need to be strong."

"Strong?" Luke asked. "What for?"

"To fight our way into Ice," Stone replied. "And do it without destroying us all."

Luke felt his jaw drop. "Fight? Me?"

Stone stared at him. "You have to, Sire. You're an Emperor—and here, nothing less will do."

## THE HEGEMONY: CITY ON WORLD

"How are you going to smuggle this . . . woman into the Hall of the Web?" Eileen asked.

They sat in a small restaurant perched halfway up the side of a slablike business structure whose roots were buried far beneath the ground, but whose pyramid-like tower thrust a full three thousand feet above the surface of World. They sat near the edge of the over-hang, where they could look down on a few wisps of low-lying cloud scudding below, protected by force baffles that admitted the muted roar, but not the force, of the wind.

Charlie lifted his mug of coffee and sipped. The restaurant was nearly deserted in the early afternoon, a place of slow movement and low, tinkling sounds of glassware and silver. In the background, human wait-ers glided deliberately by, intent upon their tasks. Charlie was unaware of any oddity in the scene, but Eileen, whose historical grounding was much more ex-tensive than his, understood that the scene could have taken place in nearly any period of modern human history. Knives, forks, waiters, coffee, white table-cloths: humanity had been dining in much the same way for most of its recent existence.

There had been no change. And why was that?

"I thought I'd just dress her up as a tech or something, walk her right through. It wouldn't be for long, and nobody pays much attention to us anyway."

She lowered her own cup of coffee and stared at him. "You're kidding, right?"

"Why?"

"Charlie, do you have any idea of the security protecting the Hall of the Web?"

He blinked. "I've never thought much about it, no."

"Your chip," she said flatly.

"What?"

"The one that controls your socket. You know."

Involuntarily, he reached up and touched the hard knot of the socket beneath his right ear. "This?"

She nodded, impatient. "For starters, you are scanned every time you enter the Hall. If the chip isn't there, you can't get in. Alarms sound, and guards come."

"I never knew that."

She sighed. "And then, to enter the actual template areas, you have to plug in, right? What you're doing is downloading entry and access codes. Have you ever tried to go somewhere you weren't supposed to go? Like the programming areas, where the big hard systems are?"

He shook his head. It had never occurred to him to explore beyond his designated work space.

"If you try, doors won't open. If you keep trying, you get alarms and guards again."

He finished his coffee, relief suddenly filling his thoughts. "Oh. Well, then, it doesn't matter, does it?"

"*What* doesn't matter?"

"All these games you want to play. I wanted to pull off a joke, but obviously we can't." He stopped, then laughed shortly. "Picture it, this hooker trying to get through all of that. We'd be stopped in a second. Hell, we wouldn't even get inside."

Now Eileen smiled. "Oh, yes she will. If she's properly equipped. And that, my friend, is where you come in."

"What are you talking about?" He raised his head, alarmed.

"Chips and sockets can be had, Charlie. All you have to do is talk this woman into going along."

Charlie thought of Naomia, of her tired face, of her barren life. "She'll never go for it!"

Eileen shook her head slowly. "Charlie, you have to make her go for it. You can do that, can't you?"

He remembered other things now, the hunger, the fire. "I don't know," he said, doubtful.

"Well, at least you can try."

He thought about it. "Yeah, I can try."

Eileen smiled. "Good. That's settled. You get her to agree. I'll arrange for the implants."

He regarded her with mild awe. "You can do that? Fake Hegemony security chips?"

"Not me, personally, but—you saw your own chip. You told me what it meant."

He recalled his own words: *"You can't buy tech like that off the shelf. Heavy people, Eileen."* But heavy enough to counterfeit truly sensitive stuff like security chips?

Yes, he supposed. It was possible. And if he went along, then he was snared forever. He'd never get free of these lunatics.

There had to be another way. All he had to do was think of it. As he stared at her, the answer came with surprising ease.

"Sure, Eileen," he said finally. "I'll talk to her. All she can do is say no."

Eileen glanced down at her nailtale. "Can you do it today? We don't have a lot of time."

Again, the cryptic reference to some agenda hidden from him. Eileen might be rolling in the cushions with him, but she was a long way from trusting him fully. Or trusting him at all, he warned himself.

Yet, if he could handle this the way he planned, none of it would make any difference. "Yeah. I can go today."

"Good. Oh, and Charlie?"

"Yes?"

"Make sure you do talk her into it. I'm sure you can. Just use your masculine . . . wiles."

He nodded, watched her fold her napkin carefully, rise, and turn away. She walked with a smooth undulation, much more attractive than he remembered. Was it the sex? Or had he simply not noticed before?

He didn't even think of the third possibility. Granting Eileen with powers of real deception was completely beyond him. After all, he knew her as well as a man *could* know a woman.

Didn't he?

## THE WEB: BORDER

They followed the second branch of the stream downward toward the point where it vanished into the opening in the ice. As they descended, the air grew even colder, and now Luke's nose twitched at a whiff of ozone which tainted the crystalline air. This close to the mighty rampart they walked in shadow, yet light, the color of dilute blood, filtered down through the ice along ancient fissures, cast a dull crimson glow upon the rushing water. Fire and ice, Luke thought. He shivered.

"It's cold," he remarked, his words sending two frosty puffs before him like tiny, guiding clouds. Durward, who had slowed and now tramped along beside him—Stone still watchfully bringing up the rear—nodded.

"It will be warmer when we get across," he said.

"Is that true?"

"Yes, Sire. Despite what it looks like, Ice is a hot place. It's not really ice, you know."

Luke glanced up at the frozen overhang. "It looks like it. What is it, then?"

Durward shrugged. "I don't know. I told you things are different in other Empires. I don't even know if Ice considers itself an Empire. The Icons here are very strange."

"Oh?" Luke still struggled with the idea of other Empires and their mystifying differences, bound as he was by his own experience, and his knowledge of only one Empire. Rationally he could accept that there might be other ways of doing things, but he'd not yet hurdled the emotional barrier of actually accepting such things as real, or relevant to him personally.

Personally—what a laugh. What could get more personal than leaving my own, and going into someone else's Empire? And for that matter, someone else? What if more than one Empire is involved? What if—

His uneasy musing was broken by the sound of Stone's footsteps approaching quickly. "Sire, stop," he said abruptly.

Luke and Durward halted. Durward turned. "What is it?"

"There's something wrong here," Stone said.

Durward turned back and faced the opening, which now yawned, dark and threatening, less than a hundred yards away. Waves of frigid air rolled off the ice facings, brushing their noses with red, silting their brows and lashes with frozen rime.

Durward peered intently ahead. "I don't see anything . . ."

As far as Luke could tell, nothing had changed at their approach. There was no movement near the tunnel mouth, no alteration in the rhythm of water sounds and wintry gusts that had so far shepherded their steps.

It was a lonely place, but nothing threatening revealed itself to his eyes.

Stone said, "Can't you feel it? A tension, something *waiting*?" He turned to Luke. "Sire, we are still within the Empire. You have your powers yet. If you can search on levels beyond this, now is the time."

Luke studied the scene again, still unable to find anything out of the ordinary. What did Stone want him to do? Sink into the Web itself, examine the reality beneath the reality?

"There are hidden guardians here," Stone said, his words harsh and urgent. "Can't you feel them?"

Trust Stone, his instincts told him, but he was still unsure what he could do. "You remember when I took you to see . . . the burning?" he asked slowly.

Stone nodded agreement. "Yes, Sire. But that wasn't what I meant. We are very close to Ice here, but the guardians will be on the far side of the border. Is there any way you can see the truth of the situation? See into Ice without leaving the Empire?"

Luke thought about it. All Empires floated, like sprawling continents, upon the darker sea of the Web—and viewed from that sea, their true shapes became visible. He'd never entered the Web in close proximity to another Empire. But there was another possibility as well—this close, he might see across the hidden borders, but so might the watchers on the other side.

And if one could see, could one *reach* across?

He had no idea.

"Can you go with me?" he asked Stone.

"If you wish, Sire."

"Very well. I'll do it."

"I want to go, too, Sire," Durward said.

Luke shook his head. "If I take Stone, we won't be aware of what happens here, Durward. Someone must remain behind, to give warning if it's needed."

A look of worry moved Durward's pixie features. "But Sire, if something *should* happen, I wouldn't know what to do."

"Oh." Luke considered. He'd never bothered to check on what his Iconic form did when he entered the realm of the Web. It hadn't seemed important. Now it did.

"Let me try something," he said. He closed his eyes, let his inner eye slide open for the tiniest instant upon the brawling vistas of the underworld—not long enough to actually see anything—and then snapped himself back.

"What happened?" he asked.

"You became very still, Sire. As if you'd turned into a statue."

Hmm. So a representation of his body *did* remain behind. He searched his memory for a reason, and after a moment, found one. "There is a connection," he told Durward. "If anything unforeseen occurs, just shake me, pinch me, anything to create some kind of physical sensation. That should be enough to bring me back."

"What about Stone?"

"I don't know," Luke admitted. "Since he will travel with me under the influence of my own power, he may not even exist here after we go. But it doesn't matter. My return will automatically bring him along, too."

Durward nodded dubiously. "If you say so, Sire."

"Fine, then. Let's get out of this wind, though, if we can."

Stone said, "Over there. That formation of rocks offers both shelter and some concealment. Will that make a difference?"

Luke shook his head. "Not at the level of the Web, but perhaps it would be helpful here, where the Icons of Ice—if there are any—function."

"They're here, Sire. You'll see."

Durward led them to the granitic outcropping, several dark, jagged spears that leaned away from the walls of Ice as if tilted by some ancient blasting gale, and opened his pack. He withdrew a large blanket and spread it on the ground. "It will help to keep you warm. I think you two should lie down. If you're going to turn into statues, I don't want you toppling over."

Luke nodded. Wordlessly he sat, then leaned back until he rested in a nearly horizontal position. His face unmoving, Stone joined him. Luke felt the heat of his protector's body as Stone snugged in as close to him as he could get. The warmth was welcome, reassuring. "That's good," he told Stone. "As close as you can get. I'll try to keep it that way as we enter the Web."

Stone nodded. "I'm always close to you, Sire."

Durward snorted softly. "I don't understand what you two are planning, but it's starting to feel like snow."

Luke glanced up. He was facing away from Ice, looking back into his own realm. In the distance, where wind had rent the curtains of fog, dark clouds rolled. Once again he resisted the temptation to banish all this. Stone had called for secrecy. It wasn't as if Luke had an army to protect him.

Why am I doing this? The question drummed at him, in counterpoint to the equally insistent answer—no choice, no choice.

And I want to, he realized. I *like* doing this.

Does it take the threat of impending death to illustrate the boredom always there, always unrecognized? Yet as he closed his eyes and began to slow his breathing, a final thought intruded; I'm learning. I'm learning new things.

I'm even learning how ignorant I really am.

"Sire . . ." Stone said.

"Come with me, Stone. Come with me."

The Web opened, and they fell in.


## THE HEGEMONY: CITY ON WORLD

Charlie trammed directly from the building that had housed the restaurant to the Scarlet Sector. He hadn't paid much attention to time-zone shift, so when he stepped out of the terminal into a corridor beyond, he staggered sharply, buffeted by the surging crowd that choked the passageway.

"Gods," he muttered. "Rush hour."

The faces that surrounded him, topping every kind of garb he could imagine and some that were beyond even his numerous fantasies—frills, chains, leathers, furs, neon, makeup, bells, even a rack of antlers apparently grafted to one more or less masculine forehead—those faces were closed, intent, filled with unrelieved lusts.

Horny.

The place reeked of sweat, sickish sweet pheromones, musk. The mob was in every kind of heat imaginable, and, against his will, he felt himself responding to the overwhelming stimuli that battered against his none-too-solid resolve.

Naomia. He couldn't remember—that way, he thought, turning against the flow of the crowd and attempting to shove through by brute force.

He quickly discovered that brute force wasn't an effective stratagem when one only weighed a hundred fifty or so. His left hand pushed against flesh, soft and yielding, and somebody squealed, a high-pitched, frantic sound. Fingers clutched at his clothing, brushed his face, tugged at his hair. Somebody grabbed his crotch and squeezed, hard, and he let out a sharp yip of pain.

"Hey!"

No reply, but the hand released him, leaving a lingering memory of strength and hunger unsated. After a few more minutes futilely shoving and wedging himself into the tide of aroused humanity, he found himself being swept backward, farther and farther from his goal.

The lights had been adjusted to a flaring red again, so that this corridor seemed an adjunct of some ancient hell, complete with doomed revelers.

His body was thick with sweat. He turned himself around and let the crowd carry him along until, finally, as bits of the swarm broke off and were swallowed by branching corridors that led to areas specializing in every form of release, he washed up in a small cranny that, after he caught his breath and straightened his rumpled clothing, he decided would do for a short rest.

It was darker here. Overhead an unseen ventilation outlet sighed darkly, emitting a long whoosh of cool air. Other sounds, a bit louder and more intense, issued from the shadows across from him. Two, maybe three shapes, indistinct and blurred, and moving in unmistakable rutting harmony.

He brought his nailtale close to his face and subvocalized a request. Obligingly the tale, with magnified holographics, supplied him with a map and his position. The address Naomia had given him blinked invitingly, a tiny crimson dot. He saw that he'd been forced even farther away than he'd guessed, and wondered if any alternate routes existed from his location to the right place on the Street of Whores.

The tale obligingly threw up three different paths, marking the way in blinking green lines. He moved to the opening of the cul-de-sac and glanced out; the crowds seemed as thick as ever. Behind him, in a crescendo of moans and gasps, the human pile on the floor approached some sort of climax—the sharp odor of ammonia smote his nostrils. He wondered what weirdness they were engaged upon, but his curiosity wasn't strong enough to lead him to investigate.

He sighed heavily. With a final glance over his shoulder, he reentered the swelling crowds in the main corridor. All of City on World appeared to have but one goal—fucking its collective brains out.

Charlie, a youth of his time, found nothing remarkable about it. Decadence was not a part of his working vocabulary, nor would he have recognized any of his daily life as symptomatic of it. Like the rest of his culture, he was trapped—and Eileen could have told him the best traps are those of which the victim is completely ignorant. She would not have added, however, that ignorance itself was a trap. She couldn't— for that was her own particular cage.

The passages he chose did seem to be less crowded. Within ten minutes, he began to recognize the seedy familiarity of the Street of Whores. Here the glass boxes, each fronting on a small crowd of sweating men, women, and indeterminates, displayed their contents like exotic aquariums. Charlie barely glanced at the brightly lit wares as he pushed through the panting knots of worshipers—Naomia! As he came closer and closer to the place he remembered, he began to recall other things.

A low heat thrummed his brain and, despite himself, his penis began to throb into deliciously painful hardness. Conflicting images overlay themselves on his mind's eye: Naomia tired, cynical, a burned-out whore; but dancing like a flame over the drab reality, the indelible recollection of her lips on his flesh, of darkness, of irresistible lust, of a vast, loose *letting go* that no other experience could induce. His tension-filled dalliance with Eileen faded away, and with it, his fears for himself, for her crazy schemes. He could *feel* Naomia's tenebrous lure, summoning him to her.

A final turning, another crowd, and then he stood, sweat running off him, his breath as hard as his dick, at the rear of the group gathered before her window. Two men watched with shiny eyes, openly masturbating, oblivious to anything else. Nor did Charlie notice them in anything but passing—his own eyes, now red and itchy, were focused completely on the spectacle of the woman who danced with skulls.

*Naomia!*

Tonight her small cubicle was lit by a cool blue glow. The sagging glow strips he'd noticed before were nowhere in evidence. Resting across her shoulders and dangling down across her small, perfect breasts, the necklace of skulls shimmered as a line of discrete lights, each tiny skull a glittering star. The aureoles of her nipples glowed similarly, drawing attention down to the perfectly defined muscles of her belly, and to the large snake that coiled sinuously over her hips, its flat, triangular head an arrow pointed at her pubic hair. Yet compared to the lascivious movement of Naomia's dance, the motion of the snake seemed crude, disjointed.

Charlie's eyes goggled, and his lips went dry as bone. No music sounded from the cubicle—Naomia danced to her own rhapsody, just as every watcher swayed or jerked to the dusky melodies that filled their own skulls.

Pipes, he thought, distant pipes. His education had not encompassed the ancient mythologies, but had someone told him of the reedy flute of Pan, the Goat God, he would have nodded knowingly. A thick, turgid warmth suffused his balls, flowed slowly into his penis, rose up and up—

No!

He turned away, forced himself to close his eyes. Not this time! The woman held him in thrall too easily. Dimly he sensed that her incredible sexual wiles destroyed his ability to think, to act rationally. More was at stake now—his job, his future, perhaps even his freedom. Strangely enough, he didn't even think of Eileen. Perhaps, he would decide later, no other woman could stand comparison with Naomia, her skulls, her snake, her infernal dance.

After a few moments he regained control of himself, and was relieved to find there had been no embarrassing accidents. Then another thought struck him. Carefully avoiding direct observation of the spectacle in the small cubicle, he scanned the rest of the crowd warily. Already some of the onlookers were waving small chips, and beginning to move toward the barely outlined door next to the window.

What if somebody got there first? He had to see her tonight!

Panicked, he shoved his way forward. Voices from the shadows muttered surly threats—"Watch it, asshole," or the all-purpose, "Fuck you!"

Close by the door, the small mob grew more thick, and more envenomed in their harsh protests. Somebody punched him in the chest, and air whooshed from his lungs. Somebody else yanked painfully on his hair, and a third form, huge and menacing, reared up to block his path.

He balled his hands into fists and struck out blindly against this final obstacle, tears starting from the corners of his slitted eyes. But the shape was soft, yielding, though he felt a hint of hard muscle beneath the initial filmy barrier.

Breath rasping, he lurched forward again, but this time a set of fingers like steel cables clamped onto his shoulder and lifted him neatly forward.

"Hey!"

"Hey, yourself," a familiar voice rumbled in his ear.

He opened his eyes wide, saw a flash of white needles in a broad, furry visage.

"Grog!"

A cloud of pheromones enveloped him, and once again he felt the persistent, itchy fingers of sexual arousal in his groin.

"Come back to see me, Charlie?" Grog said. Then he laughed. "Of course you didn't." His voice turned playful. "How come I can't compete with the holy bitch, there, Charlie? Don't you think I'm cute? Just a little bit?" He shook Charlie's shoulder for emphasis.

"I have to see her, Grog!"

"That's what they all say, Charlie boy."

At his back, Charlie could sense the crowd reaching some kind of exultant group climax. She must be ending her dance. Any minute all thought would turn to the door.

"I have money!" he babbled desperately.

"Of course you do, Charlie," Grog said. His voice was low, soothing. "But this time, she actually wants to see *you*. No payment is necessary. That's why I'm out here—to make sure you get right in."

Charlie listened to the sound of his pounding heart subside in his ears. He stepped back a bit, against the pressure of bodies building up behind him, and searched Grog's face. "Is that true?"

Grog flashed his disconcerting mouthful of teeth once again, swept out one massive arm, and magically a rectangle of darkness appeared behind him.

"Go right on in, Charlie." And laughed one more time, as a guttural moan of disappointment rose from the inflamed onlookers.

"Just wait," he roared at them. "You'll all get your chance." And in a lower tone he hissed at Charlie, "Get your ass inside, kid. And don't take all night."

Charlie started to move forward, then felt Grog's grip on his shoulder tighten suddenly. One more beat—the sound of the door slamming behind him—and he stood in darkness.

In the distance, the sound of pipes.

Calling him.


## THE WEB: EMPIRE AND ICE

He'd never entered the Web this close to a border with another Empire. He didn't know what to expect; certainly not what he found this time.

All around him swirled the familiar signs of his own domain; endless swathes of glowing snakes, the hyper-texted Iconic tentacles of his day-to-day operations smoothly entwined in a throbbing, moving sea of light. But now there was a boundary. His previous paradigm of the Empire—a great tree made up of trillions of branches and leaves—had been learned from a partic-ular viewpoint. He'd been able to see the tree as if viewed from *beyond*, hanging pristine in darkness. No other Empires visible. Now the others were evident. His domain stretched out before him, but above were other stars, other skies, and the dome of them was crushing. Seamlessly the architecture of otherness arced over his head, so crowded it seemed pieces of it must fall. He faced out and swayed slightly. Vertigo. The crazy quilt map of other space continued endlessly, tilting slightly down at his border, then stretched into misty distance where the universe itself seemed to arch up to become the sky patterns that loomed overhead.

It was like being inside a sphere, centered perfectly on the base of it.

It was very quiet.

No words sprang into his mind to describe this vision of the Web so different from what he'd expected. The Web should be all dark and points of light, not this jeweled tapestry that encompassed all. Why so different?

A flicker of movement caught his attention. He was drifting above the Empire, a tiny mote of awareness, oblivious to the curling fire below, but now he turned. Something . . .

There.

The Empire came to an end, a perfectly sharp line of demarcation. On one side, the familiar, writhing lines of his stacked Icons, and on the other—Ice.

But Ice didn't resemble the awesome wall he'd seen before. Here, in the more poignant reality of the Web itself, Ice lay revealed in all its perfect geometry.

For that was what Ice was—a rank of crystal lines, geodesics in infinite construction, the ordered path of them summoning the eye inward, ever inward . . .

Flick.

Flicker flack.

He moved closer to the edge, to the demarcation where the two Empires butted against each other like vast tectonic plates. Now, again, all was still, silent, but he had the sense of great pressure, of strain building, of the potential for some vast cataclysm.

Flick.

He still couldn't see what made those bright, knife-sharp movements. Something right at the border, though. Something hidden. The motion always occurred just beyond the limit of his immediate vision, so that he could make out nothing more than the fact of the occurrence, as if sunlight glinted only for an instant on choppy water.

Beyond, the crystal Empire lay still, drawing his attention, beckoning . . .

"No, Sire."

Stone spoke softly. As before, Luke couldn't quite make him out. The Soldier was there, somewhere, but always just behind him, much like the hidden snake-tongue flickings that made the border itself so intriguing.

"I just want to see."

"So does it, Sire. Don't go too close. Can you make out anything?"

Luke paused. Stone was right, of course. Hadn't he worried about much the same thing just a few moments earlier? He halted himself and let every sense he possessed extend gingerly toward the line of demarcation between Empire and Ice.

Flick.

Again! A strange excitement seized him. There was great danger here, he understood abruptly. Ice itself, not only those who inhabited it, was full of peril. But still he probed, trying to plumb the secret of this particular, border-side menace. Unconsciously he reached out, took Stone's hand, felt a wave of confidence, of support, wash into his awareness, strengthening him, strengthening his power, until—

Flick. Flicker flicker flack!

Like disturbing a covey of birds. He gained a fragmentary impression of teeth, of glassy, razored claws, and drew back.

"Sire!"

"It's all right, Stone," he whispered. "I know what it is now."

"Yes." He stopped and considered what he'd learned. "And I can handle it. I think."

Relief. "Good. Can we go, then?"

Luke shook his head. "I have to do it here. Ice is more . . . vulnerable at this level."

Stone didn't say anything, but Luke had the impression that he'd drawn closer to him. It was as if a familiar coat had just been snugged down and buttoned more tightly. A warm, comforting sensation. It heartened him.

"Stone, I have to get very close. And you mustn't interfere. Not for my protection, not for anything. Do you understand?"

"Sire . . ."

"If you get in the way, it could be disastrous. And I *have* to do this, if we are to get through on the other levels."

Waves of unhappiness surrounded him, but within them, an underlying sense of resignation, as if Stone had expected something like this all along. "Is there anything I can do to help?"

He considered. "If things go wrong, you can try to pull me back."

"Don't worry, Sire. I will."

Given a definite task, Stone seemed much more at ease. Luke waited a moment, then put the other from his mind. What he had to do was delicate. It would require all his concentration.

Slowly, he moved forward again.

Flick. Flicker flack.

## THE HEGEMONY: SCARLET SECTOR

He had expected the sudden disorientation. He was becoming used to the tricks Naomia played. He hadn't yet figured out how she did it, but at least this time he didn't lose his head.

"Naomia," he called sharply. His voice seemed flat, devoid of the usual echoes his brain subconsciously recognized. It was like shouting in a very small, well-padded room.

Which, he discovered as he extended his arms, was precisely where he was. He felt quickly around, discovered the enclosure to be less than two meters square.

What had happened to the hallway that had been here before? Surely Naomia didn't have spare money to remodel her squalid quarters so often?

"Where are you?"

No reply. Stupid, the voice in his mind told him. She hasn't finished entertaining the mobs yet. Just wait. She'll be along. He concentrated on his breathing, trying to iron the ragged wheezing into some semblance of calm. He was amazed to find that the exercises he'd learned in some long-ago biofeedback course actually worked. After inhaling deeply and slowly, holding it for a count of six, and then exhaling for the same count, a measure of serenity came over him. His heart rate slowed, and his penis finally went limp. After that he stood unmoving, his hands at his sides, and waited.

His nailtale informed him eight minutes went by before a door opened almost in his face. Light spilled forth, framing Naomia's lithe, naked form.

Naked except for the dark shape that still coiled menacingly around her shoulders and down to her waist, that flat, evil head aimed at him like a weapon.

Flick, flick. The movement was too fast, but he imagined he could see the fork in the tongue of the snake. She stepped back and said, "Come in, Charlie." He followed her into a larger room. It was nothing like what he'd seen on his previous visit. This was filled with white light, harsh and penetrating, suitable for fine microelectronics work. The comparison was brought even closer by the spotless white tiles that covered the walls, floor and ceiling. The light itself burned from recessed strips outlining all right angles, leaving no shadows.

"What's this?"

She carefully removed the snake—a large python, gaudy in splotches of gem-like color, and placed it on the floor, where it began to coil languidly at her feet.

"A room," she said.

"I don't remember it," he told her.

She shrugged. She seemed entirely unaffected by her nakedness. In the light, the chain of tiny skulls around her neck no longer glowed; the beads seemed to him small and nasty, almost obscene in their intricate detailing, as if actual human skulls had been shrunk to make the dirty little beads.

"Things . . . change," she said, and waved her left hand vaguely. Her dark eyes were distant, shadowed even in the pitiless glare. He suddenly longed to take her in his arms and hold her gently. She seemed exhausted. Could the dancing take this much out of her? But as he stepped forward, she spoke again, briskly. "Charlie, what do you want? Is everything ready?"

He stopped. "No. Not quite."

She stared at him. "What do you mean?"

He sighed heavily. "Naomia, it isn't going to be as simple as I'd planned. Things have come up. I'm going to need your help."

She looked down at the snake. "Is this going to take a while?"

The tone of her voice made him feel a stab of guilt. She was just a hooker, true, but that made her no less a human than he. And now he was going to drag her into the morass that had already claimed him. "It could," he replied.

"All right," she said. "Let's go somewhere else and get comfortable." She grinned faintly, but he couldn't see the humor. Besides, she looked comfortable enough already.

"Okay."

She turned. A hidden panel against the far wall slid aside, and she motioned him through. "Go on in, grab a seat. Drinks and drugs in the wall dispenser. I'll be along in a second."

Then she was gone. He stood in the middle of a large living area, of a kind he'd never seen before. Slowly he turned, his eyes narrowed slightly, clicking his tongue softly against his teeth at each new wonder.

Just a hooker? But how did a whore afford such luxury?

Could he have made another mistake?

He found the dispenser, an ornate thing paneled with what appeared to be genuine tortoiseshell, and dialed for a frothy concoction of Arrean *bollo*, the potent liquor that was Arrea's principal export, and whipped cream—the current drink of fashion among those few he considered his crowd. The machine responded quickly and quietly, disgorging a stainless-steel mug so cold it almost stuck to the pads of his fingertips. Gingerly he carried the cocktail to a long, low sofa that, at the first hint of his weight, molded itself to his body. A moment later, invisible fingers began to knead the tension from the muscles around his spine.

He sipped the cocktail. It was perfect. No more than he'd expected, he decided, as he slowly cataloged the other details of the room.

Smoked-glass dividers, which played caged holographs that seemed to be keyed to his breath patterns—although he noticed they also mirrored his physical movements as well. A carpet so soft and thick that, when he glanced down, he saw his shoes buried in amble fluff almost to the ankles. Not an ordinary carpet, either; as he watched, it hunched up and began to squeeze his feet with firm, relaxing pressure, while wisps of it rubbed against his calves like some sort of disembodied cat.

Soft music, strings and mellow, distant horns. The smell of sandalwood and violet. Dark woods polished to such a sheen they picked up glints from the crystal and glittering, shapeless *objects* that populated the area in random groupings.

Unutterable luxury. Cost a fortune, he ruminated, his eyes musing. A lot more than a hooker could afford—or if she could, she wouldn't live in a place as sleazy as the Street of Whores.

Then he shook his head. Why wouldn't she? He couldn't claim to be an expert on the life-style of prostitutes. In fact, he decided, he couldn't claim to be much of an expert on anything. Certainly not Naomia. And not Eileen, and her crazy schemes, either. Or the Twisten, whatever they might be. Even, he realized suddenly, the template, that near-thirteen-year-old enigma that had inspired this whole mess in the first place.

"I don't know fuck, to be perfectly honest," he mumbled to himself.

"I wouldn't go that far," Naomia said.


## THE WEB: BORDER

"Wait," Luke said.

He felt the infinitesimal pressure against his back

that was Stone's presence lessen. He brought them to a halt just at the border. Directly in front of him, across the barely visible separation, the glittering shapes of Ice waited silently. He was aware of the chaos of the Web flaring around him, but only dimly so; his entire concentration was forward, into the realm of the defenders of the Web itself.

He held himself steady, waiting for any sign of the lightning movements he'd sensed before, but all his hyper-activated senses brought him was a feeling of watchfulness. Did Ice even know he was here, or were those flashing shards of motion only some automatic process, mindless, without volition?

Briefly he considered what he knew of his own Empire. Everything within it was either his own creation—the physical reality serving as a matrix for his Icons—or the Icons themselves in their endless stacks. Could Ice be so very different?

He doubted it. Everything he knew of the Web told him that Empires, despite their differences, functioned in much the same way. Just as he had his tree with its roots deep in the process of Iconic creation, so must Ice have a similar heart, no matter what bizarre forms the final results of that creation took. And bizarre they were; as he examined the structures more closely, he noticed tiny details.

The basic structure of Ice at this, for lack of a better concept, "Webular" level, was a six-sided hexagon. The shapes varied from very large to very small, and the connections followed patterns beyond his understanding, but the basic form of Ice was that shape. As he peered further, he saw that each shape contained within its boundaries a shimmering point of light. The lights were of various colors—he saw red, blue, green, yellow, purple—and they moved constantly, traveling the outline of the hexes themselves. The hexes seemed to be constructed of tubes, and the lights moved within the tubes, circling and circling. Occasionally, where a pair of hexes joined along one section, two lights might intersect, and then a tiny spark of brilliant white would occur. The overall effect, he decided, was somewhat cheerful, in an antiseptic sort of way. But the movement of the lights bore no relation to the other movements he'd barely perceived. Those snicker-snacker flicks had been larger, quicker, hinting of threat. He was convinced that danger was near, even at the level of the Web itself. What that danger might mean at the more complicated level of Empire and Icon, he could only guess.

Not that it mattered. In the universe of the Empires, control extended from the bottom up, not otherwise. He controlled his own Empire at its most basic level in the Web. Ice was, for all its strangeness, its intrinsic age, only another Empire. The true level of control was here. If he could somehow disengage the hidden watchers, then—

"Closer," he whispered. Obligingly, the pressure against his rear increased. The space between him and Ice narrowed until bare inches separated him from the ultimate boundary.

"Stop, and hold me steady. Do nothing else," he ordered softly. When Stone had done so, Luke relaxed. He wasn't sure he could do this. In theory, of course . . . And the fact remained that he was Emperor, and though only bare inches from another Empire, he was still in his own, and master there.

He stared at the closest hex, its traveling bit of green light growing almost hypnotic as he absorbed as much of its shape and structure as he could without actually crossing the border. Finally he was ready.

"You will see a change," he told Stone. "Don't be alarmed. Do nothing unless I tell you."

"Yes, Sire" came the disembodied answer.

"All right." Then, still watching the hex, Luke gathered his powers.

And changed.

Stone's first reaction was panic. He couldn't quite understand why Luke couldn't see him, but seemed aware of his presence just the same. But Luke was the Emperor, and though Stone had a better idea of an Emperor's capabilities than perhaps Durward might have given him credit for, what happened after Luke's final words was utterly shocking.

Where before, Stone had carefully held on to Luke's shoulders, somehow being pulled by him and at the same time guiding him, he now grasped something entirely different.

The Emperor was gone!

In his place, Stone found himself clinging to a giant white hex, within whose depths glowed a shimmering blob of sapphire light. His first instinct was to release himself, to immediately search for his missing leader. But Luke had told him, warned him.

*Do nothing!*

Discipline was rigidly ingrained in the Soldier. He might, in order to protect Luke, be able to disobey him. But now Luke was nowhere to be seen. Stone's prime directive was protection, and there was no longer anybody to protect. Faced with this conundrum, he relapsed to his second instinct, and obeyed the orders of the one being whose orders were absolute.

He gave another start as, still clinging to the great, pulsing shape, he felt himself being drawn forward. Slowly, slowly, this new hex approached the border until, almost imperceptibly, some invisible line was crossed.

Stone felt the shock of it travel through his fingers, the palms of his hand, up his arms, leaving a tingling numbness in its wake.

Flick!

The movement was preternaturally quick, but so was Stone, and he saw the sudden gathering of a host of hex shapes as almost in slow motion. The shapes . . . *congealed* at the point where Stone's hex had entered their territory. There seemed to be further movement, a great straining, and the royal blue light of his own hex throbbed brighter.

Now many hexes gathered there, and more appeared out of nowhere. The blue hex flared suddenly, and then its light seemed to *stretch* as it flowed outward, entering the other hexes, overwhelming and finally extinguishing their own multicolored glows.

As each hex was overwhelmed, another shock rolled up Stone's arms and jolted back down his spine. He held on grimly, wondering whether he was doing the right thing, wondering what else there was he *could* do.

Finally, the rate of jarring impacts lessened, and a few moments later, ceased entirely. What remained was his own hex, the blob of sapphire light undimmed, and beyond, a forest of similar blue hexes whose lights all moved in identical rhythm. Far beyond this tangle, the colors gradually returned to normality, but at this point everything had become twin to his own hex.

What did it mean? He couldn't imagine.

"Pull me back," a familiar voice urged.

Without thinking, he tugged on the giant blue hex form. Soundlessly, but with a sucking feel, it came loose, and Stone discovered the Emperor, grinning faintly, within his encircling arms.

The great hex was gone, but the others still remained blue.

"Back now," Luke said. "We don't have much time." He paused, glanced at the glittering sapphire forest. "But enough, I think. If we hurry, we have enough."

Luke opened his eyes. The first thing he heard was Durward.

"Would you fucking look at *that*," Durward said.

# 7

## THE HEGEMONY: SCARLET SECTOR

Charlie started at the sound of her voice, nearly spilling his drink.

"I'm sorry," she cooed. "Did I scare you?"

*You scare the shit out of me*, he wanted to say, but instead, after wiping a stray fleck of the *bollo* and cream mixture from the cuff of his shirt, he grinned weakly. "I didn't see you," he said.

She spread her arms and pirouetted slowly. The movement sent the gauzy veils of her crimson gown swirling out like the petals of a great flower. The fabric of the dress was so sheer, it enhanced, rather than concealed, the slender shape of her body. He could still make out the dark, circular shadows of the aureoles at the tips of her breasts, and once again felt the onslaught of desire, murky and barely controlled.

"Naomia, sit down."

"What's the matter? Don't you like to look at me?" She giggled, a sound he found incongruous with his image of her.

He shook his head. "Of course I like to look at you. But—things have come up."

She glanced down. "I bet they have."

Something about her cutesy little girl routine felt rancid, spurious. It made him even more uneasy. She was so unpredictable. She could have any man she wanted, it seemed, and yet preferred him. Or was that just his ego talking? The idea was uncomfortable—probably even stupid, he decided. Only him? What about all the others—the ones who made up the crowds outside her window? Surely she didn't remain chaste when he wasn't around. She was, after all, a prostitute. Sex was her business.

Which brought him full circle to his own problems. "Naomia, we have to talk about the . . . plan."

Her eyes crinkled faintly at the corners. She moved over to the sofa and sat beside him. He noticed she wasn't wearing any perfume, nor did he detect the more subtle scent of pheromones. She smelled fresh, clean, a faint, woodsy odor that reminded him of forests he'd visited as a child.

"I thought everything was all set," she said.

Careful, he told himself. Got to do this just right. His problem was basic; somehow, while trying to sound convincing, he had to force *her* to reject Eileen's plan to install a socket and chip that would allow Naomia free passage into the Hall of the Web. His paranoia, running now at full tide, made him question everything. What if unseen listeners—the Twisten?—monitored him even now? If he simply told her not to go along with Eileen's plans, or made them sound too dangerous, what might happen then?

He took a gulp of his drink, grateful for the relaxing coolness of the smooth liquid. "Naomia," he said, then paused and took a deep breath, "how would you feel about an operation?"

He'd gauged the opening carefully. It sounded a

properly plaintive note, but he guessed that the prostitute, who made her living with her body, might find the idea of slicing into that body and installing implants a bit unsettling.

"An operation?" He felt her body stiffen slightly.

Good. He turned to face her, and arranged his features into what he hoped would be a properly somber expression. "Yes, an implant. Don't worry, it would be done quickly, easily. And there would be more money for you."

"I don't understand, Charlie. I thought this was a joke . . . a game. Why an operation?"

Keeping his tone as neutral as possible, he explained to her the intricacies of the Hall of the Web's security systems. As he did so, he was careful to mention the dangers involved in detection, without stressing them unduly for any hidden listeners. When he had finished, he reminded her again of the extra money. That would sound good if his conversation was being monitored, although he guessed—if she was able to afford a place like this—that money might not be a primary consideration with her.

She leaned back, away from him, and pursed her lips. Her eyes narrowed. "Charlie, this doesn't sound anything like the original deal."

A wash of relief swept over him. She was going to turn it down! He could go back and tell Eileen her stupid scheme—at least as it involved him—was finished. And, perhaps, if he was lucky, he could keep on with both women.

She nodded once, as if she'd come to a decision. "No, not at all like what you told me before." She paused. "It sounds *better*."

Something indigestible tumbled from his throat into his gut. She patted his knee happily. "Now, let's talk about that money."

## THE WEB: ICE

Luke awoke on the blanket, his face turned toward his own Empire. The storm clouds had rumbled closer, and a sharp, biting wind numbed his face. Durward's words echoed in his ears, barely heard above the low, continuous roar of the wind. He hitched himself up on one elbow, noted that Stone was already sitting up, and turned toward his Messenger.

"Over there," Durward said, and pointed.

The wall of Ice, and the forbidding tunnel into it, had changed. Now a narrow canyon extended back into the glacier, a deep gash in the ice as if a giant ax had shattered the wall in two. The path at the bottom of the canyon was narrow, but easily passable, and the way well lit by the harsh light overhead. The stream that had disappeared into the dark hole before, bubbled merrily alongside the path.

"What did you do?" Durward wondered.

Luke shrugged. "I convinced Ice to change a bit at this point. I . . . fooled it." He hadn't forgotten Durward's admonishment that other Empires changed visitors to suit their own matrices. The only question he'd had was whether he could change himself sufficiently to convince the secret guardians that he, and his small troupe, were compatible with the standards of the new Empire. He knew that now, when they crossed the border, they would appear at the level of the Web itself as hexagons containing spinning lights. The only difference between such happenings in other crossings was that he'd imposed the change himself, rather than allowing an alien power to do so.

He hoped it would be enough. Any Empire's primary defenses were at perimeters, set up to deny entrance. Detection systems—even his own—were much more loose in the Empire proper.

Slowly, he levered himself to his feet. His legs felt numb. Physical discomfort was entirely new to him, but he resigned himself to the idea. Once in Ice, he wouldn't be able to draw on the powers of his own well of creation, and would probably have to put up with whatever came. He wasn't certain of it, though; actually, he had no idea what he might be able to do in this new place.

He hoped—in fact, this whole journey was based on the idea—that something extra would remain, some ability that might allow him to pierce whatever secrets regarding the invasion of his own Empire that Ice might hold.

He didn't want to consider the alternative. "We should be getting on," he told Durward. Already Stone was repacking the knapsacks, getting ready for the next step of the journey. "I don't know how long my arrangements here will hold."

Durward stared at the beckoning canyon. "The watchers are gone," he said finally.

"Yes," Stone agreed. "But the Emperor is right. We have to move quickly."

"When we get across," Luke said, "we have to pretend to be just another group of Messengers, right?"

Durward nodded. "Yes, Sire."

"Then no more of this 'Emperor' and 'Sire' stuff, okay? Just call me Luke."

Durward grinned. "Yes, Sire—Luke, I mean."

"Better," Luke replied. "See that you remember it."

Stone tramped up and placed a pack on Luke's back. "Here, Luke. Hold still. I want to tighten these straps."

As the weight settled across his shoulders, Luke felt again that wave of exhilaration. He had no idea what might happen now, but at least he was doing *some-*

*thing*. Something *new*. And he had good friends and stout allies to do it with.

Durward, fully loaded, his face wreathed in clouds of frozen breath, joined them. He looked like a small, woolly bear in his thick fur coat. Luke imagined that he looked much the same. Stone wore no fur. His coat of many straps and zippers made small, tingling sounds in the chill air. Unbidden, Luke suddenly reached out and placed one arm across each of the other's shoulders and pulled them close.

"One for all, and all for one, eh?"

Durward hooted. "The Three Musketeers!"

Luke grinned, and wondered how Durward knew about *them*.

"Let's go," he said.

A moment later, they crossed the barrier and started up the canyon. At their rear, just as they left the Empire, the sun broke through the clouds, and the storm began to dissipate. Luke didn't notice, but Stone did, and a worried expression crossed his face. He dropped back a bit, and began to pay even more attention to their surroundings. He'd seen the flicker flacks, as he thought of them, in the naked reality of the Web. They were still around, although Luke's magic seemed to have neutralized them.

He'd felt their essence, and it was powerful and evil. He grunted softly to himself as he marched. If they came, they were in for a surprise. He didn't think of himself as evil.

But he was powerful, too.

## THE HEGEMONY: SCARLET SECTOR

After Charlie had gone, Naomia wandered out of the chamber in which she'd entertained him, and entered another. This was the squalid little room that she'd showed him before. The incongruity of it had no affect on her. She was a woman of many personalities, and designed her quarters to suit. There was no way a simple apartment could ever confine, or ever reflect, her infinite moods, and she didn't even try. Charlie had no idea, but the warren of rooms, halls, passages, and galleries that occupied the space behind her tiny windowed cubicle numbered more than a hundred enclosures, each designed to mirror some facet of her personality. Of course, she reflected as she strode out of the second room and into a long, vaulted passageway that always gave her the feeling of Alice down the rabbit hole, Charlie didn't need to know any of this.

He was simply a means to an end. The look on his face! He'd been as easy to read as the newspapers that she'd once perused, with much eagerness, in long-gone times. She'd enjoyed picking out the emotions that rose, as plain as headlines, to his smooth, baby-like cheeks.

Or was she being uncharitable? He was young, true, but not an infant. It was just that, compared to her, *everybody* was young. She stopped and stared at her reflection. The skulls were a nice touch, she thought. Just the right hint of ominous threat, subdued, yet impossible to ignore.

Charlie had come, with all his unsubtle wiles, to talk her out of going through with the little "joke" he'd planned. But how could he know it would take far greater powers than his own puny persuasiveness to prevent her entrance to the Hall of the Web?

Such a power slumbered now, awash in its own peculiar madness, and she would have once been perfectly content to let it sleep. But time had trapped her. Humanity decayed slowly, but it decayed, and she was one of the few who remembered the first bright promise. Now the dissolution had become critical. The sleeper must awake. But first another must be roused, and Charlie was her bell ringer.

The Hall of the Web was guarded by demons far fiercer than Charlie could ever imagine. She knew. She had designed some of them herself, in another, better time. Those demons she could defend against. It was the simple things that prevented her entrance now, stupid things like chips and implants. But Charlie would see to it, he and Eileen.

They were fools, but willing, and Naomia had learned one thing in her long career; the workman used those tools that came to hand.

It was the best she could do. Time grew short.

It would have to be enough.

## THE WEB: ICE

"Where are we going?" Luke said. The canyon had widened somewhat, and at a point perhaps an hour to their rear, the little stream had twisted sharply, then dived beneath the ground amid a welter of huge boulders. Now only the sound of their breathing and the crunch of their boots on the scaly rock underfoot broke the silence. Even the wind had died, and Luke noted the temperature seemed to be rising. At least, he could no longer see smoky clouds in front of his face.

They halted for a rest, sprawled against a few scattered boulders. Above them, the ice had gradually given away to naked black rock, and Luke wondered uneasily where the boulders had come from. Probably tumbled down from the heights, some weathering process.

They had seen no one. Even Stone, his professionally paranoid feelers fully extended, admitted that as far as he could tell, they were alone.

Durward chewed slowly. He had brought a huge package of chewing gum in his pack. After offering it around and finding no takers, he'd popped a couple of pieces in his mouth and begun chewing. "Raspberry," he'd said. "Good stuff."

He shifted the wad from one cheek to the other and said, "I don't know this part of Ice. But as we get further in, I ought to come across something I recognize. All of Ice isn't like this." He gestured vaguely with his right hand. "This is fucking weird, in fact."

"Oh?" Luke said. "What's the rest of it like?"

Durward rotated his head, listened to soft popping sounds in his neck. "Different . . . flatter. And a lot of bizarre shit. The things that live here—like machines, but different. Big crystals, sort of, but they move. Soldiers, I guess. But you can talk to them."

Luke thought about it. "Then we'll stick out like sore thumbs. We don't look like crystals."

"Doesn't matter. Not everybody changes when they come here. I don't, sometimes."

That was interesting. "What do you mean, sometimes? You mean sometimes you change, and sometimes you don't?"

"I dunno. To tell the truth, I can't tell the difference. But every once in a while, I feel like I'm not myself. That's when those crystals seem more familiar, almost friendly. But I've never come here with anybody else, and I never talk to anybody except a crystal, and we don't discuss what I look like. It's all business, you see. I just speak my piece, or hand over whatever I've brought, and turn around and go home. Sometimes I see others. In the paths, I mean."

"What are the paths?"

"The regular places, where Messengers go. We

don't just wander around, you know. In, out, gone, that's us." He considered what he'd said, and chuckled.

Of course it would be that way. Why hadn't he considered it? In his own Empire Messengers only traveled on designated paths. Aliens were not allowed to wander about freely. But what mechanism did he use to assure the arrangement? He squinted, dredging up the information as best he could. Strange. What he'd once been able to locate with only a thought, now came hard. He had to think, to labor after a bit of information. Could it have something to do with being cut off from his own Empire? And if so, what other faculties might have been dulled, even lost?

He sighed. So much to worry about. But even as he thought this, the answer came. Messengers—they were controlled by his own Icons. There was nothing intrinsic in the construction of the Empire that demanded aliens keep to certain areas. His own Icons made sure they stayed where they belonged. So, most likely, there were Icons in Ice that performed similar functions. Like police.

But they'd seen nobody. He knew they were far beyond the guardians he'd kinked at the border, yet no alarm had been sounded. Could Ice be this deserted? Or was some other factor at work, something he hadn't considered? He didn't know how the Emperor of Ice operated his domain. Were there police? Given the nature of Ice—that is, defender and protector of the Web as a whole—it seemed to follow that the defender would defend itself. He had no lasting confidence in the shape-changing trick he'd pulled off at the border. He knew his own powers, and assumed another Emperor would be no less powerful, particularly in his own realm.

Could their disguises stand up to scrutiny? Real

scrutiny? He doubted it. But, so far, they had proceeded undisturbed.

"Uh, Luke?"

Durward halted slightly as he spoke the name. He still wasn't used to addressing his Emperor in so familiar a way. Luke nodded encouragingly. "What?"

"Your hand. Your left one."

Luke glanced down. "Oh," he said.

"Doesn't it hurt? You must have scraped it somewhere. Here, let me put a—"

"No!" Luke drew back from Durward's sudden movement. He shook his head again. "No . . ." he said more calmly. "It doesn't hurt."

And it didn't. He looked down at the ugly red blotch that marred the otherwise smooth skin on the back of his hand. It didn't hurt. But it itched—and the more he stared at it, the more persistent the itching grew.

What could it be? He knew he hadn't scraped or otherwise wounded himself. Gazing at the unsightly sore brought no recollection of anything that might have caused it. Nor could he remember seeing it before Durward's sudden show of concern. How long had it been there?

What was it?

The question was halfhearted, though. He stared broodingly at the livid disfigurement. He knew the answer. It was cancer. The cancer of barbarian fire had followed him, even into Ice.

He looked up. "Let's go," he said.

"But Si—Luke. We need to rest."

He bared his teeth in what he'd intended as a reassuring smile, but from the look on Durward's face, he knew he'd failed. It didn't matter.

"We have to hurry," he said.

Stone was already hoisting Luke's pack. His glance

flicked across Durward like a razor. "Luke's right," he said. "We have to go."

"But *where* are we going?" Durward asked. It was almost a wail. "*He* doesn't know. Do you?"

Stone nodded at Luke. "Luke?"

"The Emperor," Luke said grimly. "The Emperor of Ice."

# THE HEGEMONY: CITY ON WORLD

Eileen Michelson was puzzled. She glanced at the digital readout above her workstation. Eleven o'clock in the morning, nearing lunchtime. Charlie had called in sick earlier in the day. She hadn't talked to him, but their supervisor, an elderly, overweight woman named Joanna Dieterling, had grumbled about Charlie's excessive absentee rate over the last few days.

"If he's sick, he ought to get it fixed. It's not like we're one of those primitive outback Worlds with no decent medical facilities. This is City, after all."

Eileen had listened patiently, waiting for the inevitable request. Joanna ran fingers through her ragged mop of gray hair, sighed and said, "You wouldn't mind, would you, dear? Doubling up for today? I know it's a load, but you can skip everything but the basic observations."

Eileen nodded. Usually her shift didn't overlap with Charlie's, but today happened to be one of the exceptions where she came on only four hours after he did. She knew what had happened—Joanna enjoyed her position. It had been a long time since the older woman actually worked the floor. In theory, she knew the ins and outs of the various templates under her charge as well as any of the line techs, but the truth was, she'd let herself go. And so she'd done nothing about Charlie's templates, except to wait for Eileen to show up, then dump the whole thing on her.

"Double time?"

Joanna nodded, relieved that the younger woman wouldn't put up any argument. Normal pay for extra duty was time and a half, but the extra money was easier to explain than a complaint from Eileen of overwork.

Neither woman liked the other very much. The arrangement was fine with both of them. It kept things . . . honest, Eileen thought.

"Of course, dear. And if you see that young man before I do—"

Eileen blinked. "Why would I do that?"

"Well, I thought perhaps you saw him . . . away from work."

Eileen wrinkled her nose and made a small, disgusted sound. "Charlie? Are you kidding, Joanna? Charlie is a . . . he's a worm. Hadn't you noticed?"

The supervisor waved one hand in airy dismissal. "He doesn't seem any different than most young men, dear." She paused, then smiled bitterly. "Actually, they're *all* worms, aren't they?"

Both women laughed at their shared judgment. A moment later Joanna waddled off, most likely to return to her perusal of travel folders, Eileen guessed. The older woman had planned of nothing else for years but her escape to one of the new planets, after a body refit and brain scrub to make her attractive to the horny-handed sons of the soil that she was certain she would discover in some faraway place like K'Mill or Savaboa or King's World.

Eileen suspected Joanna would most likely croak of an irreparable stroke, probably in her small, stuffy office, and not be discovered until she began to stink like a dead fish. Which was of no concern to her.

Charlie was, however. Why had he called out today? Trouble? She was coming to believe that anything involving Charlie Seagrave included trouble as an integral part of the package. What a joke. Her lips curled at the memory of the bullshit she'd handed him, all about her so-called "selection" of him as the best man for the job. Actually, she'd fought long and hard against using him at all, but Harrison had been adamant that Charlie Seagrave was necessary for the success of the plan.

Her memory of those arguments now made her uneasy. Harrison had never actually convinced her of Charlie's indispensability, merely finally overridden her protests with two solid hours of sexual persuasion.

Now, *there* was a man. She never thought much about it anymore, but when Harrison Lever had accidentally brushed her arm that day, knocking the load of shopping bags she carried out onto the slide walk, it had been the beginning of the best time of her life. There were moments when she thought the accident had not been as accidental as Harrison told her it was, but that only made things better. If he'd done it on purpose, then it meant he'd *wanted* to meet her, that he'd found her attractive from the very beginning.

Charlie and his puerile, constant sexual drives, as persistent and unimportant as the buzzing of a gnat, wasn't even close to Harrison's league. All Charlie knew was the satisfaction of his adolescent needs, while Harrison, a *real* man, did everything he could to make sure she was totally taken care of before giving any thought to himself. Harrison was a strong man. It took strength to be a giver. And he had given her a new life. She wasn't sure she cared much about Harrison's plans, about this weird plot of his, but she nodded attentively each time he explained, because now, after six months with him, she fully believed she would, if necessary, die for him. She'd even told him so, once, and he had laughed.

"I don't think that will be necessary, Leenie," he'd told her, but there had been a look in his gray eyes. She would never forget that look. And whenever a third-rate twit like Charlie Seagrave exasperated her too much, she would take out that slow, fond glance from the pages of her memory and examine it again, like a still-living flower from some forgotten date.

Not that she had so many dates to forget. Her early life had not been pleasant. She'd been part of a triplet out of an office crèche—Gods only knew who had been her sources—and raised in the sterile conformity of a corporate arcology, trained and refined just as any other corporate machine might be. But she'd wanted something better. Her two sisters still remained with GilNex, but she'd negotiated a government loan to buy out her contract. Now, working in the Hall of the Web, she was repaying the loan. Eventually, she would be free.

Or would she? Harrison, for all his fanatic intensity, had opened her eyes to things she might never have seen for herself. He understood the tides of history, the inevitability of rise and decay, the cycles through which mankind passed without ever seeming to learn anything new. But he claimed it was conspiracy, and she wasn't at all certain he was wrong.

There had to be a reason. She had, by way of following his obsession, educated herself as well as she could in the history of humanity. And eons before, experts of one stripe or another had predicted an "end to history." They had been laughed at, even as they cited telltale signs; the collapse of ancient enmities in the face of the corporate state, the triumph of the market economy, the geometric rise in the rate of knowledge and technology. It seemed to her that humanity had trembled on the brink of some vast change, but, for reasons she couldn't discern, had drawn back. Oh, there was the Hegemony, true, and humanity would never again be bound to a single planet, all its gametes in a single womb. But as for the rest, man lived much as he always had—only the trim on the toys changed.

She glanced up at the monitor in front of her. It was down, a blank, light green screen, showing her reflection clearly. She looked at herself, amazed once again that a man like Harrison and a woman like her could—

No. Don't take that thought further. Just pretend it's you he wants, that this isn't merely another step in his long climb to the pinnacle of whatever it is he seeks.

Believe that he *loves* you. That everything will be all right. That dreams can come true.

Sure, she thought wearily. Meanwhile, I've got a job to do. She sighed, pushed her form chair backward, and clambered to her feet. She smoothed the tight skirt she'd selected this morning on the off chance that she might see Harrison after work, and noted that her thighs—always one of her better features—were still firmly muscled and trim.

Harrison always told her he liked her legs. Charlie Seagrave hadn't even noticed.

Maybe Charlie likes boys, she thought suddenly. Maybe that's why he's so concerned with that miserable template. Lucky thing. We are, too.

Which reminded her that part of Charlie's job was to do an eyes-on monitor of the template every two hours. She glanced a final time at the readout. Time to go.

Worm!

## THE WEB: ICE

They came down from the mountains slowly, picking their way through blasted shards of rock that baked beneath the unremitting sun. The temperature had risen greatly; Luke and Durward had rolled up their heavy coats and strapped them to their packs, and now moved more easily, clad only in thin shirts. The sound of Durward's many chains played a continuous metallic counterpoint to their march. Stone still wore his be-zippered coat. "It's temperature sensitive," he'd told them, but explained no further. Luke guessed that much of Stone's armory resided in the many pockets of the garment, and that the coat itself might be a weapon, at least a defense, of some kind.

The ancient rock over which they strode gave off a bitter, sulfuric odor that stung their nostrils. Luke swiped at his brow and felt his fingers go slick with sweat.

"Is any of this familiar yet?" he asked Durward.

"I dunno. Can we hold it a minute?" The Messenger was breathing heavily, although both Luke and Stone, though running with perspiration, had no trouble with the strenuous pace.

"Sure."

Gratefully, Durward collapsed to the ground in a cross-legged position, then shrugged out of his pack and leaned against it. He shaded his eyes against the furnace of the sun and scanned the vast bowl of earth ahead.

Much of the land was blackened. Luke remembered the condition of the battlegrounds in his own Empire. Absent the smoke and fire, this looked much the same, a vista of desolation and silence. Nothing moved out there. He saw no evidence of civilization as he knew it, no roads, towns, or moving vehicles.

From this vantage point, Ice seemed to be a deserted Empire. Yet the feeling of watchfulness had
returned as they descended from the heights. Stone
had noticed it first and cautioned them, and then Luke
had begun to feel it. A pressure, a constriction that
made the air feel heavy, stifling. Yet he'd seen nothing
that recalled the flicker flack of the border guardians,
nothing overtly threatening beyond the pervasive threat
of Ice itself.

I don't like this place, he thought.

"Well," he said, "anything?"

Durward pointed. "See that?"

Luke squinted, trying to focus in the direction of
Durward's gesture. He couldn't make out anything
specific. "What am I looking for?"

"Those dots of light, like something reflecting."

Now he could see them, far out in the huge depres-
sion they were beginning to enter. Here and there, a
random pattern, things glinted, much the way shiny
stones in a gravel path will catch the sun in sudden
sparks. But these sparks were far away; they must be
*huge*, he decided.

"Are they as big as I think they are?" he asked.

Durward nodded. "Yeah. Crystals," he said.

"You mean cities made of crystal?"

"No. Individual crystals. They don't really have
cities, except for one place."

Luke tried to imagine a single crystal large enough
to show the flare he was now observing. Ice was, indeed, a very strange place. A single crystal the size of
a mountain? What was it, then? An Icon? Or some
representation of the deeper Web reality, an equivalent to the institutions of his own Empire? Crystal
universities, or manufacturing complexes? Libraries,
perhaps?

He couldn't guess. Ice would follow its own logic,

the logic of its Emperor. And that Emperor, he was beginning to realize, operated on principles far outside his own understanding. Yet that same Emperor must, by his very nature, have the same powers of memory and recall that Luke did. Moreover, it was that Emperor who had refused even a reply to Luke's original request.

"Can we reach the Emperor through one of those crystals?" he asked.

Durward shrugged. "Luke, I honestly don't know. I have never seen the Emperor of Ice. All I know is what I've picked up in my travels. There is one city here, and rumor is that's where the Emperor stays. But I've never visited the city. I'm not even sure how to find it."

Another problem. "Stone?" Luke said.

The soldier stared thoughtfully at the distant crystals. "If those things out there are connected in some way, then most likely the connections eventually lead to this city Durward's talking about."

Durward brightened. "Oh, they're connected, all right. Those paths I told you about, the ones we Messengers use."

"Durward," Luke said, "go slow. Tell me exactly what happens when you bring messages to Ice. Think about it. Don't leave anything out."

A hot, dusty breeze bellied up from the valley below, bringing a faint sulfuric stench, ruffling Durward's hair. He thought for several moments before replying. The wind lessened, and he said, "I always come in through one of the regular gateways across the border. There are crystals there. Sometimes I go no further. I just give my messages to the crystal. Other times the border crystals tell me I have to go to another place. Then they show me which channel to get on. I get on, and the channel takes me where

I'm supposed to go. Then I pass on whatever I'm supposed to, turn around, and go back home."

"That's it? That's all?"

Durward gazed out over the burnt umber and onyx plain. "I don't know what you want, what else to tell you."

"The channels. What are they? How do they work? Like roads? Do you walk? Or ride something—you said the channels *took* you where you were supposed to go."

"Yeah. They take me." Durward turned back to face him. Already the fair skin on his nose and cheeks was turning red from the sun, and faint patterns of freckles were beginning to show. "I don't exactly ride anything. At least I don't think so. It's more like a tunnel. But slick. You go in, there's this feeling of movement, although you can't see anything, and then a door opens, and you get out when you arrive. That's all."

A tunnel. "You mean a tunnel like the one at the border? What was there before I changed things?"

"No. Different. The channel starts at a crystal, always, and ends at one, too."

Luke tried to picture it. "You mean next to a crystal?"

"Uh-huh. Inside a crystal. I told you, some of those crystals are real big."

Luke glanced at Stone, who raised his eyebrows slightly. "Some kind of transmission? Instant, perhaps?"

"How long does it take, Durward?"

"I dunno. I mean, I don't keep track." His voice was faintly resentful. He stared at Stone. "Not instant, though. It takes *some* time."

"How do you know?" Stone replied, keeping his own tone low and reasonable.

"I said I did. You doubt my word?"

"No, of course not. But how do you know time passes? Can you see things? Something else, outside these channels? Some marker or way station?"

Durward's tongue darted across his dry lips. "Can't see nothing. It's dark. But it takes some time."

Luke said, "I don't think it's important."

"Then why are you making such a big deal of it? I mean, Stone, you make a thing about it."

"It's good to know how your enemy operates," Stone replied.

"Is Ice my enemy?" Luke asked.

"Maybe . . ."

The sun did not seem to be moving. It hung in the sky like a hole into a furnace, perfectly overhead. Maybe it's always high noon in Ice, Luke thought. He glanced down at his left hand. The itchy, prickly feeling was constant. The malignancy there was spreading. Now it covered most of the back of his hand and part of his wrist. One crusty, flaking tendril had extended perhaps an inch up his forearm.

It looked like it should be painful, but it wasn't. Yet it would continue to grow. It would take his hand and then his arm and, eventually, devour him whole. Just as it was devouring his Empire. Unless he could find a way to destroy it before it destroyed him.

Was Ice the answer? He didn't know. But he didn't know what else to try, and he had to do something. Very well. Turn away, ignore the putrescence of his flesh. Concentrate on the problem he could do something about. Concentrate on Ice.

"If we could get to one of these channels . . ." he mused aloud.

"Luke?"

"What?"

"I'm a Messenger. The channel will accept me. I don't know about you."

Luke stood up. His knees ached. The air was completely still. When he moved, a small cloud of gray dust rose, then slowly fell. He breathed in deeply. His chest seemed filled with heat. When he exhaled, he fancied he could see a faint quivering, a refraction in the air. "What makes you a Messenger?" he said.

"I am a Messenger."

"Yes, I know that. But is it something intrinsic, or something functional?"

Durward looked confused. "I don't understand."

"I think it's a bit of both, but mostly it's functional. You are a Messenger because you carry messages."

"Well, of course."

"What's the most important message you could carry?"

Surprisingly, Durward's answer was immediate. "One from you—er, from the Emperor, Luke."

Luke nodded. "And so you shall. And so shall we all."

They rested a few minutes more. They drank some water, and Stone checked their packs. Then they got up and began to walk down into the great, burning bowl of Ice.

It took them two days to reach the crystal. Luke could keep time well enough—two Empire days and the sun never moved. He wondered if time moved differently in Ice, more slowly. Perhaps their two-day trip had only taken two seconds. It didn't matter.

They would trudge onward until they got too tired to go farther. Then Stone would lead them to the shelter of some barren ridge of rock, where the omnipresent sun didn't glare directly into their eyes, and spread blankets in whatever shadow he'd found. They slept on blankets spread over the rocks. They needed no other covering. The heat never wavered, and they woke coated with sweat and dust that had turned to a rime of dark gray, hardened mud where their sweat didn't wash it away.

They drank from water carried in bottles in their packs, and ate dried food they soaked in the same water. Luke was astonished to find he needed to eat. He had never needed such nourishment before, but when he'd tried to go without food, he'd become weak and dizzy. Again, he marveled at the consequences of his separation from the Empire. Had he become entirely helpless? Were all his powers gone?

Now he understood how much he'd always taken for granted. He didn't blame himself. How could he? He understood that he'd only known what he'd always known. Now he had to learn new things.

It was frightening, but it was also invigorating. He had already resolved to devote, when he returned to the Empire, a great deal of his capacity to determining what he didn't know. Of course, he thought as he glanced up at the great, crystalline pile less than a mile away, first I have to get home.

"What do you think?" Luke said.

"It's a big one," Durward replied. The trek had drained him greatly. His face was pale beneath a peeling sunburn, and lines had begun to show at the corners of his eyes. He looked much older than before. Stone, however, was unchanged. He never showed any effects from his exertions.

And I smell like a goat, Luke thought.

"Do you think this one has entrances to the channels?"

They were about a mile away from the gigantic, intricately faceted jewel. It hulked above them, even from this distance. Half a mile high, Luke estimated, and twice that wide, flanks catching prismatic reflections in the light, red, blue, green. The black rock around the crystal was splotched with wide sprays of color, and the whole thing shivered silently in the heat distortions of the atmosphere around it.

Durward picked at a stray bit of peeling skin on his nose. "I don't know. Probably." His voice was dull, flat, leached of any emotional content. Luke hoped this crystal would prove to be a way into the mysterious city of Ice. He didn't think Durward would be able to march much farther.

"We'll just have to try, I guess," Luke decided. He went over to Durward. "Come on, my friend. Put your arm over my shoulder. We'll go together."

"I can carry him, Luke," Stone broke in.

Durward glared at the Soldier, then gently pushed Luke away. Neither he nor Luke took any notice of this lèse-majesté. "I can walk . . . Luke. Don't worry about me."

Luke stepped in front of him, stared into his eyes. The usual emerald color had washed out of his gaze. Now a thin, grayish film seemed to cover his corneas. "Old friend," he said. "I do worry about you."

For a moment, moisture glittered in Durward's eyes. He nodded slowly. "It's okay. I'm okay. I won't let you down."

He hoisted his pack without another word and set off. Face troubled, Luke followed. Stone brought up the rear, silent as usual.

*What if we die here?* Luke thought.

It was the first time he'd ever thought anything like that. He brushed the thought away. Emperors didn't die.

Did they?

There was no barrier, no demarcation point or wall. There was only seared rock, and then, rising from the ruined stone, a wall of shimmering glass.

The crystal was faceless. It took no notice of their

presence that Luke could detect, although he had to remind himself that his powers were limited here. This was Ice. The rules were different. Perhaps the gigantic thing had observed them all the way from the distant mountains.

The three of them stood before one towering facet. Luke stared into the crystal, watching the light refract across hidden lines and angles, drawing the eyes deeper into its center.

"You see anything that looks like an opening?" Luke asked.

Durward shook his head. Luke stretched out his hand to touch the slick surface of the thing.

"No!" Stone tugged at his shoulder, pulling him back.

"Stone, don't do that," Luke said calmly. He noted the serenity of his reaction. Only a short time before, his reflexes would have fried Stone to a cinder.

"I'm sorry . . . Luke. But it could be dangerous. We don't know—"

Luke faced him. "We don't know a lot of things, Stone. That's the problem. I think we have to start finding some things out."

Stone stepped back, craned his head back, and eyed the wall of crystal before him. "I can't feel anything specific. But that thing is dangerous."

Luke shrugged. "I think everything here can be dangerous. But—there are other dangers, too. We have to take some chances."

Looking unhappy, Stone nodded. Luke pressed forward, and placed his palm on the unyielding surface. For a moment, nothing. Then a deep, thrumming tone sounded inside his skull. He glanced around. None of the others seemed to have heard anything. The tone repeated itself, a long, slow tolling. He removed his hand. The sound stopped.

Silence. The other two stared at him. "Well?" Stone said.

"I don't know," Luke replied. He waited a moment, but nothing else happened. There had been no information in the tone, nothing he could decipher. Merely the sound itself.

A warning? A guidepost? He couldn't begin to guess.

He tugged at the straps of his pack, adjusting the weight to a more comfortable position. "Let's walk around it," he said.

"It must know we're here," Durward said.

Luke considered, then turned right and began walking. "Probably," he replied. "But that's only fair. We are here."

Half an hour later, they found the channel.

They stared up at the huge opening, at least three times their height, and twice that wide. They could see some distance in, before the passage became lost in the refractions of the jewel itself.

"Is this a channel?" Luke asked.

Durward wiped sweat from his forehead. A cooling breeze drifted from the mouth of the tunnel, and he turned his face gratefully toward it. "Looks like one," he said.

"Fine," Luke said. He started forward.

Somehow, without seeming to move very quickly, Stone was in front of him. "I'll go first, Luke." His coat was fully zipped. Both his hands were in pockets.

Luke nodded. This was, after all, what Stone was for.

"Go ahead, then."

Cautiously, Stone stepped up slightly and placed his foot on the lip of the tunnel entrance. He paused, his head cocked alertly. The crystal did nothing they could detect.

After ten seconds or so, he stepped all the way in. Again, he waited. Finally he walked forward about ten feet or so, until he was completely enclosed by the huge gem.

"I guess," he said at last, "you can come on." He didn't sound entirely cheerful about the idea.

Luke turned to Durward. "You follow me," he said.

Then he took a deep breath and stepped forward into the tunnel. A moment later, Durward followed.

They gathered in a small group at Stone's position. Durward sighed at the sudden drop in temperature. The glimmering throat of the tunnel beckoned them on.

Luke turned slowly for a final glance of the barrens outside. The other two were staring down the tunnel itself. They didn't see the teeth begin to form.

Thus, as was perhaps only fitting, one Emperor was the first to taste the defenses of another—and Luke recalled, wondering how he'd ever forgotten, why Ice was the most feared Empire of all.

# 8

"You see the problem?" Naomia said to Harrison Lever. The heavyset, dirty blond man seated across from her raised his glass of bubbling *grill* in silent toast.

This room of Naomia's hidden castle was light; flashing mirrors, glittering chrome, and a glowing form carpet for their feet. The room was all hard edges and shimmering refractions, yet the overall effect was not overwhelming. It was much like being inside a snowflake. The cinnamon smell of Lever's drink floated in the air.

Naomia wore a long, simple white gown, which set off her wide, red mouth, her scintillant emerald eyes, and the chopped raven charcoal of her hair. Lever thought she resembled a sort of dark candle given unnatural life.

"Of course I see the problem," he told her, grinning crookedly. "You've talked of little else for the past several months. Haven't I managed to reassure you yet?"

She stood and flicked a switchblade glance in his direction. "Zero, don't fuck around with me. You know what we're opposing. You know the risks, probably as well as I do. Everything depends on getting him out of there after I wake him up."

He raised one big, broke-knuckled hand and waved it reassuringly. "If the schematics you provided are correct," he said, "everything will go like cake." He paused. "And it looks like your plans are okay. Little Miss Michelson has confirmed everything I checked with her. That is one hell of a security system, but they don't call me Commander Zero for nothing."

Her black eyebrows arched. "Spare me your macho posturing. And by the way, what do you think of this woman?"

"Eileen?" he replied. "She's in love with my dick. She thinks it's me, or maybe even this bullshit *cause* we dreamed up, but it's only that I'm the first man to ever treat her like the woman she wants to be."

Naomia stared at him with obvious disgust. "Zero, you are a chauvinist swine. You do understand that?"

He grinned again. "Such charmingly archaic insults. Would you have me be any different?"

She turned away. "Just don't pull that shit with me. I'm not in love with your dick, unless"—she paused thoughtfully, her eyes narrowed slightly—"well, it might make an interesting wall ornament."

He shuddered faintly. He knew her well enough to understand that she was not intending humor. A chill of fear jangled through his scrotum, but he thrust the nasty image away.

"Forget I mentioned it. She'll be all right. Even without the sexual attraction, she's too stupid to figure out what we're really after."

Naomia seated herself on something that resembled a floating snowball. "Let's go over it one more time," she said. "I get him awake, and then . . . ?"

He shrugged. "My team will penetrate the outer perimeter approximately three minutes before the event. We will secure the escape route and arrive in the template chamber no more than thirty seconds after you have him up. Are you absolutely certain he'll be able to move under his own power? Or will we have to carry him?"

She closed her eyes. "Yes, that would make a difference, wouldn't it?" She considered the question. "I think you'd better prepare for any eventuality."

He nodded. "I'll need a somewhat larger team, in that case."

She moved her shoulders slightly, signifying no consequence. "Whatever," she replied. "Just make sure you get it done."

He drained his glass and tossed it over his right shoulder. It disappeared in midair. He took no notice. "The tough part is going to be getting off this miserable fucking planet. Everybody thinks it's a harmless bureaucratic quagmire, but I've never seen protections built into a World Traffic Control System like they have here. I can handle the assault on the Hall of the Web with no problems—but it's going to take more than I can bring to the party to get us out of this system."

She nodded. "*He* designed the security, and you know what *that* means."

Zero said, "There isn't anyone better. God help us if he gets involved too soon."

"Don't worry about *him*," she said. "When the time comes, I'll deal with that problem personally."

Zero's gray eyes widened. "Are you sure you can handle him?"

"More sure than anybody else could be," she replied.

He shrugged a final time. "It's your neck," he said.

Her face was grim. "Both of our necks. I suggest you don't forget that." She lapsed into silence as the blond-haired man stood suddenly.

"I'm thirsty," he said. "Where's the bar around here?"

Wordlessly she pointed in a direction to his rear. He turned, found the proper equipment, and began to make himself another drink. "Did you ever notice," he said, "what a strange mixture of archaic and modern technology our lives are today?"

She made an unintelligible sound. "It's *his* doing. *He* shaped things to his own satisfaction, and we let him do it."

Zero brought his drink back and sat. "Well, it wasn't entirely our doing. He had his own vision, and we trusted it."

*"Then we were fools!"* she replied. "We call it the Original Sin now, but the real sin was ours."

He laughed. "Don't you find this discussion ludicrous? I mean—sin, and all? You'd think this was some sort of religious crusade instead of the most complicated assassination plot in history."

There was a stillness about her that was frightening. Finally she said, "It was my mistake, actually. I knew him best of all. I should have seen the Godhood complex before it occurred. And known how it would go bad."

Zero sipped his drink. "You can't blame yourself for everything."

"Why not? I tried to *do* everything."

They both remained silent for a time. Zero finished his cocktail, but this time set the glass on the floor, where it remained. "I'll get the kid out," he said. "The rest is up to you."

She grinned, and he recalled once again just how dangerous she was. "It always is, isn't it?"

"Yes," he replied. "There is that . . ."

## THE WEB: ICE

Out from the walls of the crystalline tunnel new shapes were forming with preternatural speed. These crystals resembled arms, or even worms, but the strands of multifaceted gemstone accreted to each other with such speed, the overall effect was like great reaching tentacles made of multicolored glass. Two of the tentacles completed themselves almost instantly, and Luke saw the gnashing, whirring teeth that revolved like buzz saws at the ends of them. The tentacles waved blindly for a moment, then, visionless but seeking, turned toward him.

"Sire!" barked Stone.

Luke felt something cold and icy wrap itself around his ankle. A moment later, another gem-like rope enveloped his chest, its vacant, grinding mouth seeking his face. The overall attack was so swift, Luke had no chance to do anything but gasp once before the crushing weight tightened on his lungs. He struck out frantically, then screamed as he saw the soft flesh of his palms shredded on the razored edges of the deadly worms. The stench of his own blood was harsh and coppery on the cold, still air.

A heavy weight slammed into his upper body, knocking him forward. Even as he felt this new attack, more tentacles dropped from the ceiling, sprouted from the sides of the tunnel, and grew like diabolical shrubbery from the floor. Somewhere in the dim distance, he heard Durward shouting unintelligibly. He stomped at the tentacle that held his right leg imprisoned, desperately trying to evade the crushing, heaving mass of new tentacles that choked the tunnel second by second, each sucker-like tip seeming to seek him and him alone.

Luke heard a thin, high-pitched shrieking noise, and

somewhere in the dim recesses he understood it was his own voice. Panic struck at his bowels. His vision clouded. He had never been physically attacked in his entire existence. The shock of it temporarily short-circuited his conscious thought patterns. Involuntarily he closed his eyes. He thrashed and heaved against his bindings, giving into the sheer terror that threatened to overwhelm him and sink him into darkness. As if from the bottom of a black well, he heard Stone calling to him.

"Sire!" Stone yelled. "Hang on. I'm coming!"

Luke forced himself to open his eyes. In front of him, his body moving back and forth through the forest of tentacles, Stone flashed like a God. His hands moved more quickly than Luke could follow. Each time Stone struck one of the tentacles, a sharp flash of light illumined the darkened chamber. The tentacles cracked as if made of rotten glass, where Stone's deadly hands did their superhuman work. For a moment the pressure on Luke relaxed, as Stone severed tentacle after tentacle, but even as he did so, Luke realized it wouldn't be enough.

Stone was truly a machine of destruction, but even his awesome power was doomed to fail against the swarm of new tentacles that rose around him. Luke saw that within a few more instants, Stone himself would be enveloped and brought down.

Now Durward joined the fray, his small face pinched and intent, his hands beating against the encroaching ropes of glass that sought to overwhelm them.

"Stay back!" Luke shouted. "Durward, get out of here!"

Durward barely glanced at him. He continued his futile attack. Luke watched in horror as, within a few heartbeats, the small Messenger began to fall into what appeared to be a cocoon of icicles. His fear threatened to paralyze him. Was it all to end like this, and worse, not even in his own Empire? The concept of death was entirely alien to him, yet now that it threatened, it seemed almost familiar, as if he had died before, in some far distant time or place.

The idea seemed almost welcome. His vision began to blur around the edges. A red fog filled his eyes. He felt himself begin to fall, but as he began the final downward spiral, something bright flickered deep within his fading consciousness.

*"No!"* he screamed. *"Not this way!"*

The icicles made a dry, rustling noise at the sound of his voice. Even Stone paused momentarily in his inhuman battle against the crystals. A part of Luke seemed to raise a questioning signal, as if to ask what was he doing?

Why don't you do what you *know* you can do?

This part, this *other*, would not let him sink into oblivion. Rather, it pulled him within himself, leading him further and further from the scene of carnage toward a dark, cool spot hidden even from his own conscious awareness. His last sight was of a heaving curtain of crystal and blood and light, falling across his face. Then the cool dark claimed him.

It was a release. Freed of the moment-by-moment distraction of the attack, he was finally able to think again. Dimly, he sensed the battle continuing beyond his current awareness. He knew he didn't have much time, but somehow, here, in this nameless place, time itself was plastic and changeable. He considered. He was not on his own ground here in Ice, yet Ice was an Empire, not unlike his own. It could be no other way. The very weave of the Web dictated what could survive within it, and the Web itself could be manipulated by those who had the keys to its secrets. He knew that he possessed such keys, but he couldn't think for the moment how to use them.

The darkness soothed him. A moment later an idea began to form. It was the darkness that triggered the beginning of the revelation, a darkness similar to the interstices of the Web itself. Surely the Emperor of Ice was bending the power of the Web into his own defenses, into the deadly trap that had caught him. Once he realized this possibility, it took him only instants, a flex of power to view the Web, which underlay all.

Immediately the dark and light of the underworld sprang up around him. He focused on the reality beneath the reality of the attack. Once again, he saw the sharp, hexagonal forms that made up the Empire of Ice.

Yes! Here was the true scene of battle. Immediately he saw what had gone wrong. The shapes of the three blue hexagons were literally encrusted with thousands of tiny white hexes, an analog to the battle going on at another level of perception. He could see nothing different in the protective forms he'd created, yet the white hexagons no longer ignored them; instead, they attacked in ever-growing numbers. Something had changed. Something had riven his deceptive wall of protection. The white hexagons themselves looked no more unusual than before—but he could sense a difference in their intensity and awareness.

Something new. But what? He racked his brain, even as he extended every particle of his awareness as far as he could, seeking the source of the new onslaught. He felt himself stretch. The giant blue hexagon that represented his reality on this level of the Web appeared to stretch in response. His awareness followed the long blue line of his seeking. Finally, deep beneath the most basic fabric of the Web, he found what he had sought.

For a moment he didn't recognize it. Accustomed

as he was to the ordered stacks of hypertextual existence, this nugget of alien shape and form awakened
no response or recognition. Faintly, he knew he'd left
behind all the conflict and terror of the assault on
his person and his party. Here, buried in electronic
darkness, he stared at the strange apparition that had
drawn him to itself. The familiar hexagonal shape was
nowhere to be seen. Instead, pulsing on the stygian
background, a single, hard-edged, rectangular shape
that reminded him of a coffin—something he was
aware of only as a hypothetical structure.

In his world, there were no funerals. There were no
burials. Only existence or nonexistence. Yet something was trapped in this shining silver shape.

Carefully he moved toward it. Finally he came close
to one sheer, mirrorlike face. He saw his own reflection. Once again, he wore the clothing of his usual
body. It seemed odd to watch his own approach in
the glittering mirrors of this bizarre shape—but he
knew the key to his survival lay here.

What was it?

He didn't know, but as he approached, he sensed a
new feeling of watchfulness, of danger. His own eyes
gleamed greenly back at him. He felt the chill that
emanated from the hidden structure. Along with the
frigid wave of awareness that juddered out from it
came also a questioning as strong as his own.

*Who are you?* What *are you*? It drummed out at
him in long, sonorous tones.

Luke held his position. *I am Lucifer. Emperor!* he
replied.

A slow, greasy chuckle echoed within his mind.
*Emperor?*

A wave of anger seized Luke. Whatever this thing
was, whatever demoniac trap that Ice had set for him,
he was, indeed, Emperor. Even out of his Empire, he
still held True Power.

*Yes*, he snarled. *Emperor!* And hurled the full weight of his rage and fear against the silver box.

Immediately the sensation of cold amusement ceased, to be replaced with an equally maddened reply.

*You dare!*

Luke said nothing. He focused the ultimate forces that had slaughtered millions of Icons unthinkingly, this time directed with full knowledge and power against his enigmatic adversary.

Stasis held for a moment. Then Luke saw a change. Two tiny red dots flared in the side of the structure. Swiftly their shape became apparent. Two eyes, pinpoints of fire rimmed in dull gold. They grew, jousting with his own green gaze until he feared the very structure of the Web must crack beneath the forces unleashed.

Once again, Luke felt a scream begin to jerk its way up from his tortured lungs. He stifled the sound, gritted his teeth, and concentrated on the one thing of his true desire—the destruction of this grotesque creature.

The struggle continued. Wave after wave of power battered against Luke's own defenses, while his attack slowly began to fail. Fear seized him in a vice. He knew the true battle was here, and if he lost it, there was no recourse. He would die in darkness, and his Empire with him.

A cold wave of triumph rolled out from the silvery box. The reddened, fiery eyes grew larger, full of venomous mirth.

*"No!"* Luke screamed.

*Yes*, the deep, lust-filled voice replied.

Luke felt his identity begin to disintegrate. Lances of personality darted outward, seeking escape, yet each feverish attempt ended in futility, battered and ruined on the awesome powers that flowed endlessly from the red-eyed destroyer.

A bell rang. A tinkling sound, distant, a growing rhythm. A silvery chant.

At this level of the Web, the individual Empires were remote stars floating in darkness. Here he faced Ice alone, but now something new slowly filled the void. A star grew closer, and the sound of bells rang more loudly in his ears. Evidently Ice was aware of the intrusion as well, for Luke sensed a lessening in the strength of the other's assault.

For one long moment, the battle went in abeyance as both combatants awaited the new arrival. Then Luke saw her. Faint and tiny, but growing sharper, more clear as she approached. A woman. Naked. Around her neck, a chain of tiny skulls flashed brightly. She danced across the abyss, a faint smile upon her face. Her eyes were as green as Luke's own. His breath caught in his throat as she approached. Something about her slow, languid dance snagged his attention on spikes of awe. She danced between them at last, interposing her lithe, muscular form betwixt Luke and Ice.

Still she said nothing. The sound of bells was loud in the darkness. Her frame obscured the fiery eyes within the coffin. Luke realized that somehow the power of this new intruder was nullifying the terrible force of Ice. Quickly he gathered his defenses in as tightly as possible. She faced him, her back to the coffin, and smiled. Her teeth came to sharp white points.

He stared at her face. She nodded in reply. Her lips did not move, but two words formed, as clear and simple as the chiming of bells that accompanied her every movement.

"Go now," she told him.

Abruptly he noticed that the bonds that had tied him to the coffin in deadly embrace, no longer existed.

He felt the awful rage that had energized his enemy lessen. It was almost as if that creature was equally mesmerized by the dance.

Luke questioned no longer. Clasping his hands over his chest, he bowed his head and reentered the world of hexagon and Web. Once again, he extended his power to the three giant blue hexagons that represented himself and the others. It was but the work of a moment to make necessary adjustments. The encrusted white hexes fell away in a shimmering rain. A great weight lifted from him. Then, weak with relief, he allowed himself to sink into the welcome dark.

"Sire, wake up!"

Dizzily, he heard Stone's voice, echoing and tinny, urging him awake. His eyelids felt heavy as lead. He groaned. Every muscle in his body ached. His hands were patterns of fire. He inhaled slowly, and felt his chest fill with dry, burning heat. Something gritty scratched against the back of his neck. Sand. Slowly, he opened his eyes. Stone's face swam into his vision, and, dimly over Stone's shoulder, Durward's equally anxious features floated like a fuzzy balloon.

"What . . . what?" Luke mumbled. His voice was choked with phlegm. He coughed. Something bitter and sour-tasting filled his mouth and he spit.

Gently, Stone propped his head up and placed the mouth of a canteen to his lips. He tilted the canteen. Cool liquid flowed into Luke's parched throat. The water was like an elixir of life. He swallowed greedily, choked once, and swallowed some more.

"Easy, Sire," Stone said softly. "Don't take too much."

After a moment, Luke felt well enough to try to sit up.

"Here . . . let me," Stone said, and pulled him upright while Durward arranged one of the packs behind his back. Luke blinked and stared around, astonished. The horrible vision he had left was gone. They were outside the great crystal. He could see its sheer, multi-colored walls out of the side of his eyes. The sun beat down mercilessly.

"How are you, Sire—Luke?" Stone said.

Luke shook his head. "You can forget about the Sire and Luke thing. I think Ice knows we're here well enough." He paused, taking stock. "I guess I'll live," he said, and realized with a flash of joy that it was true. He hadn't been certain until this moment.

"What happened?" he asked.

Stone squatted on his haunches and faced Luke. He seemed entirely unmarked by his recent battle. Luke found this impossible to believe, but then he recalled the supernal skill with which Stone had opposed the attack of the crystal tentacles. Durward looked okay, too, although his eyes were puffy, as if he'd been crying.

"You remember anything?" Stone asked.

Luke tried to concentrate. What *did* he remember? Strangeness piled on strangeness, and the sound of bells. What was it that had saved him? He was certain it hadn't been entirely his own strength that had brought him back from the prospect of certain destruction. He shook his head. Pain lanced through his skull at the sudden movement. "I don't know," he said. "I remember something . . . but it doesn't make any sense."

"You disappeared," Stone said abruptly. "One moment you were there, and then you were gone."

"What happened then?" Luke asked.

Stone smiled grimly. "The tentacles relaxed, and I was able to break free. I pulled Durward out of the tunnel, and we came here."

"I wanted to go back in," Durward interjected.

"But I wouldn't let him," Stone finished. "I didn't know what had happened to you, but it seemed senseless to sacrifice ourselves. Better to wait and see if you returned. We wouldn't have been any good to you dead." He paused. "Was that right?"

Luke smiled. "Of course it was. What else could you do?"

Stone nodded once in assent. "There *is* something else," he said.

Luke regarded him silently.

Stone seemed uncomfortable. "When you returned, it was—you just sort of staggered around the corner of the crystal and collapsed in front of us."

"Oh? And then?"

"Well . . . *she* was with you."

"She?" Luke felt his pulse begin to throb.

"Yes, me," a new voice interposed. The woman who had danced between him and death walked easily into his field of vision.

She was still naked, but seemed unconcerned by the blazing heat of the sun above. In fact, her natural dignity was so great that it clothed her more effectively than any gown could.

Luke stared at her in wonder. "Who . . . what are you?" he finally sputtered.

"I'm Naomia," she said. "And I think it's time we got the fuck out of here. What do you think?"

Luke felt his mouth fall open. His vocal cords had frozen solid. She nodded. "Me, too," she said. "So let's get your ass in gear, buddy. It's going to be a short trip, but maybe not a nasty one. If we hurry."

## THE HEGEMONY: HALL OF THE WEB

Charlie Seagrave walked slowly up the broad, marble steps toward the massive rank of pillars that made up the facade of the Hall of the Web. The building reeked of antiquity. He paused and stared up at the massive black pile that towered five hundred feet above his head. The main pillars themselves stretched half that height.

How old was this place, anyway? He realized he had no idea. History had never been his strong suit. The Hall of the Web had always been no more than a place to go to work.

The day was clear and bright. The blue sky overhead held no clouds. The sun blazed with brilliance. For a moment his cares fell away. It was a beautiful day, and a great time to be young in the City on World. Then, like black curtains drawn across his hopes, the memory of what had happened, and the fear of what he had yet to do erased his feeling of goodwill.

Suddenly the Hall of the Web became dark and threatening. He shivered, then continued on up the steps to the first checkpoint just beyond the mighty pillars. The first barrier was merely a single attendant approximately his own age, dressed in a familiar black uniform that sported the crossed swords of the Hegemonic Guard on wide shoulder boards.

Charlie paused at the station and extended his chip, which the guard inserted into a reader. A moment later, the guard returned the chip and sketched a half salute.

"Good morning, Mr. Seagrave," the guard said.

Charlie didn't recognize the young man, but that wasn't unusual. The guards changed often. He had never considered the reasons behind this rotation before, but now, his senses heightened by Eileen's warnings, he began to notice things he hadn't noticed before.

This was one of the main entrances to the Hall of

the Web. Beyond loomed a vast, cavernous space called the Great Rotunda, open to the public. Here were displays depicting high points in the history of the Hegemony, where curious citizens and tourists wandered freely.

Charlie usually didn't pause here, regarding the Rotunda as a somewhat confusing barrier in his path toward the smaller entrances that led to the Hall of the Web proper. As he passed the guard, he glanced back and saw a thin, silver line embedded in the marble floor. Decoration? Or something more dangerous? He really didn't know.

He walked on into the Rotunda. This time he paused before a few of the displays. The first to catch his attention was a long diorama depicting a moment in the discovery of a faraway planet called K'Mill. The only thing Charlie knew about K'Mill was that it was the source of an exotic liquor whose name he couldn't remember. Other than that, his knowledge of K'Mill lumped it vaguely in with the vast sprawl of what were called the "frontier planets."

A woman whose clunky brown shoes and shapeless green smock betrayed her off-World origins shepherded two bored, smeary-faced children along the length of the display. As they stopped at certain spots, holographic guides sprang into existence and began to explain the details of the display.

Charlie stood back to let them go by. The younger child, a boy maybe four years old, kicked him viciously in the ankle. He yelped. "Gods damned little brat!" he snarled.

The woman gave him a glare mixed equally of fright and anger, and jerked the child forward, away from the wrath of the big City native. Though his ankle throbbed, he almost chuckled. He didn't find it strange that tourists regarded the citizens of City with awe. City was the heart of the Hegemony, and had been for as long as anyone could remember. There were rumors of an even older World, a place called Dirt, or Earth, or some such similar generic term, but the origins of that planet were lost in antiquity. Charlie thought it was most likely legend.

Once the woman and her two unruly charges had proceeded a safe distance away, he turned back to regard the display. Through a trick of holographic imaging, he seemed to be looking directly into a forest. Gigantic, thick-needled trees jostled against each other, blotting out the light of a sun that had a faint orange tinge to it. The earth beneath these trees was barren and sprinkled with dead brown needles. The light was so dim that no foliage but the trees could survive. As he watched, a small, six-legged animal with bright eyes darted from one tree to another, then scampered up the rough blackish bark. He decided the whole thing was utterly boring. A forest, whether the tame variety carefully tended on World, or the more authentic species of K'Mill all looked pretty much alike to him. The intricacies of their fauna interested him not at all. He shrugged and walked on, little knowing that the diorama represented a reality that no longer existed.

Just before the unobtrusively armored door that opened into the bowels of the Hall of the Web where the real work went on, Charlie paused before a small display. He found this one of more interest. It was a relatively accurate rendering of a template chamber. He saw that it had been simplified and cleaned up a bit—the template on display was fully clothed—but otherwise it was a good example for the general public. As he approached the display, the holo image of a white-coated guide appeared. The guide was male and had a fatherly, professional air about him. He smiled blankly at nothing and gestured at the template.

"Hello, Citizen," the guide said. "You are in the outer reaches of the Hall of the Web right now. Inside, away from the public eye, one of the most important institutions of the entire Hegemony functions in its daily routines. As you can imagine, any political structure as large as the Hegemony"—here, the guide paused, smiled, and added as an aside—"over fifteen thousand worlds and counting—needs a great deal of supervision to keep everything rolling along on an even keel."

Charlie smothered a grin at this string of clichés.

"The enormity of the task makes it beyond the grasp of any one man, or even computers made of metal and crystal. Luckily, there is another answer— the Web of the Hegemon, housed within this very building."

Now the guide assumed a serious mien and pointed at the template, which lay on its slab of steel, as if on display in preparation for sacrifice. "This is a template," the guide said. "Please note the enclosure that surrounds the head of the template."

Obediently, Charlie glanced at the familiar silvery shape. "Templates are designed from conception to serve the Hegemony," the guide said. "Selected gametes are specifically nurtured until mating, growth, and full brain development is achieved. Each template is carefully protected from outside stimuli, so that the brain remains essentially a blank slate. Then, through many complicated processes"—Charlie grinned at this— "the eventual neural pattern of the template is duplicated electronically thousands of times a second. Each one of these patterns has all the potential capability of a single human brain.

"These neural patterns are stored within a microelectronics environment that allows them to function to the limits of their design. The template copies, sometimes called Icons, are stored in long stacks, or hypertextual strings. Each Icon is connected to every other in a stack, and each stack is also connected to all other stacks. The result, called virtual hypertextual reality, is far more efficient a computing device than anything ever before created."

The guide turned away from the template and smiled reassuringly. "Inside the Hall of the Web, hundreds of these templates labor ceaselessly to oversee the Hegemony, solve its problems, predict its future, and make safe and happy the daily lives of all its citizens."

Charlie snorted and turned away before the guide could launch into another slavishly fawning discourse on the wonders of modern technology. The truth was not quite so wonderful, but the guide had essentially outlined the function and operation of the Web correctly. The guide didn't mention the Web was under the complete and total control of the Hegemon himself, and had no more volition than a pile of rock.

He suspected most people would want it that way anyhow, but the Hegemon, and his Hegemony, on the surface at least, hewed to a form of self-representation that claimed to express the wishes of all citizens equally. In fact, the governance of the Hegemony, through the Web, represented only the Hegemon. Charlie knew this, but didn't care. His life had been good enough, and despite the horrible invasion of Eileen and her invisible friends, he had some hope that it might once again become so. The larger implications of absolute control escaped him entirely.

At the first of the inner doors, Charlie placed his

palm and finger pads on a black, glassy plate, while at the same time he opened his eyes wide and stared into a goggle-like retinal scanner. The door opened immediately, sliding aside with what he noticed for the first time was a weighty, ponderous thud. This time, as he entered the room beyond, he glanced at the edge of the door and saw with some surprise that it was at least eight inches thick. Armor of some kind, no doubt.

The chamber he walked into was about thirty feet long and twenty feet wide. The ceiling was relatively low. Here, two guards stationed behind massive transparent slabs of plex identified him visually. Once again, he presented his chip and was passed on. He thought he remembered one of the guards, but the other was, as usual, a stranger.

The chamber was otherwise barren. The floor looked like ferroconcrete, although it gave back no sound as he walked across it. In fact, the atmosphere of the room was oppressive. He felt as if he were in some thickly walled box. As he approached the door at the far end of the chamber, he looked up and saw wide-mouthed nozzles spaced evenly along the length of the room. Gas? Or something worse?

One of the attendants keyed the final door open before him. Charlie wondered at what point the chip inside his skull had been scanned. He'd seen no sign of such an operation, but given Eileen's warnings, presumed that it had. He shook his head and stepped through into the familiar, comforting brightness of the interior of the Hall. Seen with new eyes, it was obvious that the interior of the Hall was much better protected than he'd ever guessed. It was, in fact, a fortress.

None of it was reassuring. Somehow he had to smuggle Naomia past all this. The task looked impossible, but there had to be a way. He could only hope that Eileen was right, and that her fellow conspirators were as technologically proficient as she claimed. Otherwise, his options were quite limited. He didn't want to think about the results of failure. Then a terrible thought struck him. The results of success could be no less dangerous.

*Gods damn it!* he thought despairingly. It was only a practical joke! He remembered what had first given him the idea. For a moment he wished he'd never seen an erection, neither his nor the template's. Both seemed to be leading him further and further into ultimate catastrophe.

## THE WEB: ICE

They marched down a low, sandy rise into a bowl of blasted rock, beyond which reared the great black ramparts of the border mountains. This time Stone led the way, and Durward brought up the rear.

Luke walked with Naomia. His left arm throbbed in tune with his stride. The cancerous growth now covered most of the flesh there, and had extended tendrils up across his shoulder and back. He tried to ignore the pain, but it was impossible. Naomia was still naked and unconcerned. Luke could feel Durward's disapproval of their new compatriot as a palpable wave against his back. Stone, as usual, remained noncommittal, neither seeming to approve or disapprove. But that, Luke thought, was the way of a Soldier. As long as Naomia did not present a threat, Stone would show no concern.

The fact that Stone ignored the woman reassured Luke. If she were dangerous, he trusted that Stone would know it and take action.

"Let's stop awhile," Luke said.

Stone paused and glanced over his shoulder. "Sire, I don't think that's a good idea. We know that Ice is aware of us, and I think we also know it isn't friendly. It seems to me the best thing we can do is get out of here as quickly as possible."

Luke turned to the woman. There was something about her . . . She had said little after the march began, merely smiling at his occasional sally, sometimes replying in sentences of one or two words that said nothing.

Luke was fully aware of the mystery of her presence. She was obviously not of Ice, unless Ice had created an even more devious trap than he'd imagined. He was certain she'd saved his life in the battle against the silvery coffin that housed the red-eyed demon. Yet if she weren't an enemy, then what was she? How did she come to be in Ice? And why had she taken on reality at this level and joined their march? Most important of all, where had she come from?

A hundred questions bubbled in his mind, but for some reason he had not brought himself to ask them. Her natural dignity created a wall of reserve he was loath to break. He thrust his confusion aside and answered Stone instead. That was, at least, a problem he could deal with.

"I think we'll be okay for a short rest," he told the Soldier. "I've been checking our protective structures on another level as we march, and I've seen nothing that indicates further attack. Do you sense anything?"

Stone lifted his head. The impression he gave was of a dog listening alertly for sounds beyond human ken. After a moment he shook his head. "Well, perhaps for five minutes," he said. "But no more. Agreed?"

Luke nodded. "Five minutes it is," he said. Gratefully, he sank to the ground, shrugged out of his pack, and leaned against it. Durward came around and did likewise, settling in a position facing him. Stone remained on his feet, though he moved in closer to the group and took up a protective stance.

Naomia squatted on her haunches, showing little signs of wear beyond dark smudges staining the thick calluses on the bottom of her feet. She placed her long-fingered hands carefully on her thighs and regarded him calmly.

He stared back at her. He had an empirical knowledge of women in his Libraries, but had never seen one in the flesh. Her ribs were outlined in a ladder of shadow, and her small breasts, with their nipples surrounded by dusky aureoles, fascinated him in a way he couldn't comprehend. He found the effect of her both tranquilizing and exciting, as if she were a wellspring of contradiction. Or was it simply himself? Everything he knew about her was confusing. Why shouldn't her elementary presence also be a confusion? Yet he was equally certain that she was very important, even vital, not only to him personally, but to the survival of the Empire itself.

He took a canteen from his pack, opened it, and offered it to her. She smiled and shook her head. He shrugged and drank, then replaced the canteen in the pack.

"I don't understand," he told her. "And if I can't understand you, I don't see how I can trust you."

"You can trust me," she said flatly.

"I'm sorry," he replied. "That's not good enough. In a day or so we'll reach the borders of Ice. I can't let you into my Empire without the answers to some questions."

She smiled at him and said, "You can't stop me."

He shut his mouth. Couldn't stop her? It was a new and disconcerting thought. In Ice, it was true his powers had been somewhat limited, but once returned to the Empire, he would be at full strength again. Nothing, not even Ice, could challenge him there. Yet she had challenged, and defeated, the Emperor of Ice, if that's what the silvery coffin had been, on *his* own ground. Could she do the same with him?

He realized he had no idea. In fact, he really knew nothing about her. And, as he had already learned, ignorance could be his most dangerous enemy. He nodded thoughtfully. "That may be so," he said, "but I am Emperor. I will have to oppose you at the border, if you don't tell me what I need to know."

She stood up and stretched. Once again, the strange feelings welled through his body as he watched her languid movement. She looked down at him. "Poor little boy," she said.

Her words were such a non sequitur that Luke could only gape. What did she mean?

"Sire, don't let her talk to you that way!" Durward interjected fiercely. The little Messenger rose to his feet and glared at Naomia. "I say we dump her now. You don't know anything about her. She could be a trick."

His face, distorted with anger, went dark and ugly. He took a step toward her. "I'll get rid of her, Sire!"

She paid him absolutely no attention. Her gaze fastened on Luke's face. "Is that right?" she said.

"No. Sit down, Durward," Luke said. "She's not an enemy." Then he returned her searching look. "Are you?"

"I am Naomia," she replied simply.

"That's not an answer," Luke said.

"It's all the answer I can give you," she replied.

Luke seized on the incongruity of her statement.

"All you *can* give me? What does that mean? Does someone control you?"

"No one controls me." There was no pride or arrogance in her tone. It was a simple statement of fact.

Frustration boiled over in him. "This is crazy. You *have* to tell me more. I don't want to fight you, but I can't let you into the Empire if you are a danger to it. My nature is to oppose danger to my Empire. I can't help myself."

She nodded. "I understand." She turned away from him then and walked a few feet out from the group. Luke couldn't tear his eyes from the ropy muscles working in her buttocks.

She stood a moment, arms akimbo, her shadow a long scrawl on the heated ground. Finally she turned and said, "I am not your enemy, Lucifer. You have enemies, but I am not one of them."

He waited to see if she would say anything else, but she didn't. She simply stood, back to him—something he would have once considered an insult—and waited.

Luke sighed. "Is there anything else?"

She didn't reply.

"Sire . . ." Stone began. "Five minutes."

"All right, Stone. All right." He heaved himself to his feet and reached down for his pack. Durward bustled over to help.

"Let's go."

Naomia turned and looked at him. "You, too," he told her. "We can settle this later."

She moved her head slightly. "It's already settled," she told him.

He didn't know what that meant, either, but at least he had a day to think about it. He adjusted his pack, and she reclaimed her position by his side. The small group walked on, and a moment later were swallowed in the dark rock and burning sun of Ice.

## THE HEGEMONY: K'MILL

The great ships swung in their ghostly orbits above the blasted surface of K'Mill like an immense flock of vultures. Beneath them the ruined surface of the planet seethed and bubbled. The atmosphere was gone, boiled off in the first attack, and the single ocean not long after.

Vast craters, magma-filled wounds, marked the footprints of antimatter bombs. There were new mountain ranges spewing deadly fumes into the vacuum, where subduction had occurred, so great was the force of the attack.

Yet, deep beneath the scabbed and broken skin, Karl Hayden monitored what few instruments were left to him in disbelief. The temperature within the small, guarded chamber miles beneath the surface where he lay hiding was still creeping up. Over a hundred degrees now, but the rate of increase had slowed. For the first time in three hours, Hayden began to hope he might survive.

As far as he could tell, the planetary computers, armored against the incredible heat and pressure of this depth had come through in good shape. He wasn't surprised. The marvelous machines of K'Mill were a great secret. Their protections were far greater than usual. But he didn't allow himself to muse on that, except to wonder if those hidden processors had something to do with the attack. Evidently not, for they still survived.

There were even a few of the deep space sensors remaining, so that he could keep track of the activities of the invading armada—although there were gaps in coverage.

He was stunned. He knew he was in shock. He wouldn't let himself think about his wife, Maria, or their two boys. His family had been on the surface. The surface was gone—ergo, they were dead. He accepted it as a fact among the others. Later, perhaps, he would go mad. Now his overloaded emotions were deadened, and the pain couldn't seep through to do any damage. He was, in a curious way, grateful for that.

The suddenness and ferocity of the attack was almost hallucinatory. He felt light-headed, dizzy. Now, on the surface, everything was quiet, with the peace of the grave. The great forests of K'Mill were no more. It seemed the marauders had overlooked his hiding place. He had no idea how he might escape. The attack had no doubt sealed every entrance and exit from this complex.

He noted, however, that a few relay transmitters still remained, scattered here and there about the system. If the invaders didn't complete their work by busting the planet entirely or tipping K'Mill's sun nova, he still might be able to get off messages to Oranda, the nearest Hegemonic capital. He had plenty of food and other supplies. He guessed he could survive as long as it took for somebody to come dig him out.

Hayden turned back to his screens and gasped. One of the gigantic ships had begun to disgorge a cloud of tiny golden fliers. The midges descended, protected by force fields, toward the surface of the planet. His projections showed the focus of their arrival would be directly above his location.

*Did they know he was here?*

Suddenly he felt suffocated by the miles of rock above his head. He watched in panic as the landing craft reached dirt side. He was barely able to increase magnification enough to make out the tiny figures that disembarked beneath the protection of a transparent force dome. Machines followed. They were building something.

Sweating and limp as a wet rag, he stared with resignation while the emissaries completed their odd construction. The entire process took no more than an hour. The electromagnetic spectrum of K'Mill had been badly disrupted by the assault, yet his own machines monitored the high-pitched chirps and wheeps of electronic communication. Despite appearances, the things on the surface were all machines. Evidently, there was no need to risk living beings in the hell that K'Mill had become.

When they had finished, the landing party boarded their ships again and rose like a cloud of butterflies toward their mother vessel. Shortly after, one by one, the great crafts began to pull away from the husk of K'Mill. Finally, one remained, poised above the enigmatic construction they had left behind.

*"Go, you bastards! Get the fuck out of here!"* he breathed, torn between despair and hope. Then, with no warning, every alarm in his chamber went off. Klaxons hooted. Screens flashed red. The sensory input through his induction ring burst into a blazing white cloud of overload. Screaming, he ripped the ring from his skull. After a moment, his vision returned and the static in his ears lessened.

A flat voice filled the room. "Task Force to computer base. Task Force to computer base . . ."

Slowly, hands shaking, he flipped the manual override keys, which allowed him to transmit directly to the few remaining relay stations.

"Ye . . . yes . . ." He gulped. "This is computer base. What do you want?"

"Task Force to computer—" The machinelike message stopped. Another voice, more high-pitched and rhythmical, replaced it.

"Hiya, Jack. You okay in there?" A horrible, liquid humor suffused the words. "Well, it doesn't matter, as long as enough of you survives to skull-scan. Or I suppose *he* can get it out of the machines." The voice paused. "Whaddya think, buddy? Did we make an impression or what? Listen, tell the fucker we're coming. Booga booga, y'know? Tell the fucker we're coming. We left him a thank-you note. The thing on the surface. He wants to be real careful how he opens it, right?"

And all throughout, the voice displayed a geniality made even more awful by the spurious air of camaraderie it tried to express.

Hayden thought of Maria and the kids, of all his friends, even of his few enemies. Nobody deserved death like that!

Choked with rage, he interrupted the invisible speaker. "*Who is* he? *Who are you?*"

"What? Didn't I mention? So sorry, cholly. Ha, ha, y'know? That old lump of shit, the Hegemon. That's what he calls himself these days, right? Yeah, old Heggy. Tell him we're coming. The Twisten are coming. You got that?"

A pause.

"That's right. The Twisten are coming. He'll be real happy. I promise you. Really."

# 9

## THE WEB: ICE

"There it is, Sire, up ahead," Stone said. For the first time, Luke thought he detected an undercurrent of emotion in the normally phlegmatic Soldier's voice.

They had traversed the long, narrow canyon that Luke had created upon first entering Ice's guarded ramparts. He thought the canyon seemed more constricted. The needle-sharp peaks that surmounted the canyon's rim loomed like fangs in a mouth slowly closing on the small party.

Behind him, Durward muttered, "Thank Gods."

Stone was correct. Five minutes of hiking brought them to the border itself, where the glacial barrier ended abruptly. The temperature had been dropping rapidly for the past several hours as they drew farther and farther from the superheated heart of Ice. Luke and Durward had donned their heavy fur coats. Stone had zipped up his own strange garment. Naomia, however, had refused their offer of clothing and still walked at Luke's side completely naked, the sound of her necklace of skulls making a dry, raspy whisper, like the rubbing of insect wings in the crystalline air.

The stream that had bubbled alongside the path when they first entered made a dull roar off to the right. It reminded Luke of the warning, guttural tones a threatened beast might emit.

"Stop," Luke said. He came to a halt and glanced around.

"What is it, Sire?" Stone said. "Do you sense something?"

"No, nothing like that," Luke replied. "Ice may know we're here, but it no longer seems interested. There's something else."

"What, Sire?"

Luke didn't reply directly. "Stone," he said, "I saw what you did against the crystal snakes. Do you have other weapons of power?"

Stone's face went blank. "Yes, Sire, I do."

"Activate all of them"

Stone glanced at Naomia. "They are."

"Good."

"What's going on?" Durward said.

Luke ignored him. "Naomia, I told you before that I wouldn't allow you in my Empire without a few answers."

Naomia darted a sideways peek at Stone, who now faced her, knees slightly bent, fingers curled, hands held neatly at his sides. For one moment, Stone personified menace. She smiled at him.

"You don't need your weapons with me, Stone," she told him.

Stone said nothing. He stood motionless, waiting.

Luke's own powers bubbled in his veins. He had felt his strength returning to him the closer he got to his own borders. Now, with his Empire less than a hundred yards away, he summoned all the destructive potency of which he was capable. He had no idea if it would be enough. Once again, he felt the unfamiliar thrill that was fear.

"Naomia, this goes no further, unless we can resolve our difficulty," he said.

"What difficulty is that?"

"Surely you understand. I don't know anything about you, except that you appear to have saved my life back there in the heart of Ice."

She shrugged. "It was nothing."

"No," Luke said, "it was something. But what? Ice was very strong. It was beating me. I think it was the Emperor himself."

She nodded. "It was, indeed."

"And then you appeared. Dancing across the void, somehow you deflected his power and allowed me to escape. How could you do that?"

"I can't tell you."

"But you must," he said. His voice was urgent. "If you intend to continue along with us."

"Perhaps I don't."

It seemed to him that mighty events were teetering on this moment—that what occurred next would determine whether he succeeded or failed in his ultimate task of saving his Empire and himself. He took a deep breath and let it out in a cloud of silvery steam.

"Fine, then, we're going on. But you can't come." Luke turned away from her, nodded at Stone, and said, "Let's go."

"It's about time," Durward muttered.

As usual, Stone said nothing. He merely took up his point position and began to walk. Luke followed and Durward brought up the rear. He was conscious, as he strode briskly away, of her jade eyes on his back, but he ignored the feeling.

They had gone perhaps twenty yards when her raspy voice shivered through the frigid air. "Wait," she called softly. The day vibrated with menace.

He ignored her plea and continued. There was a

further moment of silence. Then, "*Wait*." The single word cracked like a whip, full of power and command.

He felt the approaching crisis as a long, electric ague through his nerves. Stone had slowed somewhat and without showing any outward sign, appeared tense.

"Sire?" he whispered.

"Keep walking."

Twenty yards, thirty yards, forty yards . . . The mouth of the narrow canyon that led into Ice was only a few yards away. Every one of Luke's extended senses quivered at the storm that brewed at their rear. Whatever Naomia was, she was a being of puissance. Was she some extension of the Emperor of Ice? Some trick? Or was she an anomaly—a creature perhaps of the Web itself? He had no idea, but he had to learn the truth.

A moment later, Stone crossed the invisible border that separated Ice from the Empire, Luke close behind, and Durward last across.

"I said *wait*!" Naomia commanded.

This time Luke stopped, turned, and faced her. She stood perhaps ten yards away, still in Ice, but now Luke felt his own power surging and bellowing within his own skull, dizzying him with its nearly forgotten strength. The pain in his left arm and shoulder was a constant, throbbing distraction, but he pushed it away.

Naomia half ran toward him. When she was within a few feet of the border, Luke said, "Stone." He held up his own hands, palms outward. "You can't cross," he told her.

She snarled her frustration. He noted once again that her teeth came to hard, bitter points. The skulls around her neck glowed in colors, ruby, sapphire, emerald. Every whipcord muscle in her narrow frame stretched like drawn cables beneath her dusky skin.

Her face went black with rage. "I'm coming across," she told him.

"I can't permit that."

"You can't stop me."

He shrugged. "I don't know whether I can or not. But I'll try." He gestured, and a low wall suddenly began to grow out of the rock of the Empire. Swiftly it molded itself into a barrier perhaps four feet high, stretching all the way across the mouth of the canyon.

"What's that?" she said. "You expect a garden hedge to stop me?" But she drew back from it, her eyes narrowed. A flicker of uncertainty crossed her features.

"Naomia? You told me you weren't my enemy. If that's true, then you can answer my questions."

She stood a moment, her hands swinging loosely at her sides, her head cocked slightly to her left.

"You saved my life back there," he went on. "Was that all a trick?"

For a moment he thought she wouldn't reply. It seemed to him that her features softened just a bit, a window to some unknown he could not penetrate. Then, once again, her visage went blank and empty. The tip of her red tongue protruded slightly between her lips.

"It was no trick," she told him.

He waited. She said nothing more.

"Who are you?" he blurted.

No reply.

"*What* are you?"

Again, silence, broken only by the soft jingle of Stone moving up to stand on his right hand. The moment stretched like a great diamond turned to taffy and pulled across the bitter light that emanated from Ice. He reached his decision.

"You may not pass into my Empire," he told her.

Slowly, she brought her arms up, wide palms and long fingers outstretched. She raised her hands over her head. He tensed, expecting some violent, shattering blow of energy. No such thing occurred. Her crimson lips spread in a wide smile, revealing pointed white teeth, and in the dark cavern of her mouth, the lolling red tongue.

Her shoulders began to sway. The movement traveled languidly downward as her small breasts began to quicken, then the navel in her belly, and finally her narrow hips and taut, muscular thighs. She raised her right foot and put it down. She raised her left foot. Then her right, again.

Suddenly the sound of bells filled the air. Silver chains garlanded her ankles, from which depended chimes that sounded the sweet music.

The melody was infectious. It tugged at his ears and filled his brain. He couldn't take his eyes from her gently swaying body. A red-tinged darkness clouded his vision. Everything went hazy, until all he could see in the stygian emptiness was her form, elemental and dancing upon nothing.

Heat grew in his belly. It spread out and down. He felt his own hands and feet twitch. An infernal joy seized his muscles. His bones became fire.

She smiled her hideous smile at him. Her tongue was now so long, it hung almost to her breasts. Spit, the color of diamond, dropped from the tip of it, hypnotizing him. The music grew wilder, more frantic.

"Dance, my Lord. Dance!" Her voice was thunder.

The joy of madness took him then. His feet pounded in rhythm to the supernatural beat of her own frenzy. He laughed. The darkness shivered at the sound of his voice.

"Oh, yes!" she shrieked. A mighty wind arose. "Dance with me, my Lord! It is your destiny to dance!"

He knew it was true. The skulls around her neck laughed hysterically and clashed their dry teeth. A nimbus of ruby light surrounded her, outlining her against the blackness that enfolded them. He saw that now she carried weapons: in one hand a fan, in the other a noose. A third hand held a sword, the fourth, an axe. She clashed the weapons together. A blare of trumpets shattered all else.

His own body was gravid with molten gold. He felt loose and happy, as if for the first time in his life, he had begun to understand the meaning of his existence.

She shook her weapons at him. He howled in release and shook his own in reply. It didn't seem strange that in one hand he brandished a three-tined trident. In another, he grasped a sharpened axe that shone like the sun. He also held a noose made of snakes. Finally, he wielded a discus made of human faces and arms that blazed with supernatural fire.

Across the void she moved to him, her madness a dark cloud before her like a banner. He howled and joined her in the dance. Beneath their feet cracks appeared in the darkness and light shone forth. A part of him understood the very fabric of the Web was being destroyed, yet she didn't seem to care. Her dance became more furious. He found himself responding. Now she came to him and clasped her arms around him.

"You summoned me," she growled, and he knew it was true. He looked down and saw his own erection grow like a spear between them. In their hallucinatory revel, slowly she began to mount him.

Great rents manifested across the darkness. The cracks beneath expanded like volcanoes. Gigantic lights appeared overhead. A long, low vibration filled the region. It was the sound of death. It was the sound of destruction.

That part of him that was always there, silent and observing, said, "No. It must stop. Now."

He knew it was true. The reddened fog that had blinded him began to diminish. "No," he said softly.

She shrieked and urged him on, but he pushed her away. They had in some arcane manner been forever joined by the dance. He knew the dance was a true thing, a part of his power and hers. Yet now was not the time.

Without thinking, he knew he couldn't calm her in any normal manner. She had become elemental. Left to her own devices, with or without his help, she would destroy the Web entirely. Slowly he leaned away from her, then dropped to his knees. He rolled over on his back and lay prone before her.

She accepted this odd movement as her due. She stood upon his belly and danced, but now she was calmer. His erection pointed up at her like a tree. She bent to it, still dancing. Her long tongue touched the tip of his penis. A shuddering excitement racked his body. Even so, he knew again that now was not the time. He made no response. He closed his eyes and arranged his hands across his chest.

After a time he had no way of measuring, he knew the dance had ended. He opened his eyes.

She looked down upon him, only a woman, old and thin and tired. The emerald flame had gone from her gaze.

"Arise, my Lord," she said slowly. "I am calm now. The worlds still live. The dance is over."

He stood then and took her hand. The darkness rolled away. In the bright sunlight that flowed thick as honey over his Empire, he reached across the border and took her hand. "You may enter, Naomia," he said. He pulled her gently across the border.

"Thank you, Lord," she replied, and came to him.

The moment she entered the Empire, a mighty sound shattered the stillness. The walls of the glacial canyon clashed together like monolithic cymbals. When they looked again, nothing—nothing at all—remained to mark the passage into Ice.

"The way is closed," he said.

"The way is always open to you," she replied.

He started to ask, but she shook her head and would say no more. The hinge of his fury opened, but he remembered the dance. He took her hand and squeezed it. They walked on. The sound of bells was soft on the morning.

## THE HEGEMONY: CITY ON WORLD

"What do you think, Zero?" Naomia said. She shoved her long black hair aside to reveal the gleaming circle of the socket that had been implanted beneath her left ear.

Harrison Lever, Zero, sat on a low black leather sofa in yet another of the many rooms in Naomia's house. The atmosphere was gloomy, strange shapes of brassy metal, the hides of dead animals, the tang of rust in the air. The muscles of Zero's shoulders bunched and relaxed as he flexed his big, calm hands experimentally. His gray eyes were serene as he regarded the broken knuckles of his fingers, souvenirs of other, older battles. They made a good match for the sideways bump at the bridge of his nose. "It's pretty, darling," he said. "Real nice. Did everything go okay?"

Naomia wore a jumpsuit of blood-tinged leather. It was so tight, he could see the outlines of her ribs as she strode back and forth, tight as a stalking cat. "It went fine," she said. "That woman and that . . . boy picked me up here and took me to the bootleg tech place you set up. They did the work there, nice and clean. Didn't take more than a couple of hours."

He glanced at her in speculation. "Are you sure they put the right shit inside your skull? I mean, it could be a real problem if you can't get past the defenses into the template chamber."

She nodded. "What's her name? Eileen—she had the right specs. She got all the codes from Charlie, the ones she couldn't put her hands on herself. I know. I checked. Don't worry, Zero. It'll go fine."

She stopped, put her hands on her hips, and glared at him. "And as far as that goes, pal, are you sure you can get in there and bring him out when the time comes?"

Lever spread his hands wide. "Listen, darling. You do what you know best, and leave the rest to me. I've got a diversion set up that will pull most of the regular Guard detachments away from the Hall. We'll blast straight through on the third level and go down. We're not gonna bother with doors. We'll just punch holes in the floors."

Naomia nodded, thoughtful. "Will that pile stand up to that sort of damage? I don't want the motherfucker falling in on my head at the critical moment."

"That thing was built to take direct nukes," Zero told her. "It won't stand up to Twistor projectors, of course, but if we chop a few rat holes in it, it won't make any difference. Don't worry, I keep telling you, it's gonna be all right."

For a moment, both were silent, each considering their own thoughts. Finally Zero sighed, stood, and went to the bar. It seemed every room in Naomia's house had a bar. He wondered if it was for his own convenience, or whether she just pictured herself as a gracious hostess. That bizarre idea made him chuckle.

"What's so funny?" she said.

"Just you," he replied as he finished mixing his drink. "I was seeing you in my mind, handing out little cocktail hors d'oeuvres, making sure guests had a good time."

She wasn't amused by his comment. "You know, Zero, once upon a time I did things like that."

He laughed out loud. "It must have been a long time ago."

"It was. Back when I was a woman."

"You're a woman now."

"I only wish," she replied.

He carried his drink back to the sofa and seated himself. "You know," he said, "there's a lot of shit I don't understand about this whole project."

"You don't have to understand it," she told him. "It's enough that I understand it."

"I'm risking my life on your understanding."

"We all risk something. I'm risking more than your life and mine put together."

He drained off half his drink in a single gulp. The potent liquor—some sort of imported whiskey—warmed his belly. "I don't understand why the kid."

"You mean the template?" she asked.

"Yeah. Him. That, it, whatever. There's hundreds of those things. Why that particular one? You never told me, you just told me what to do, not why."

She paused. Her green eyes narrowed. "And that's fine for you, Zero. You don't need whys. All you need is whats and hows. Is that understood?"

He grunted, uncomfortable at her vehemence. He didn't trust emotion, not on a job. "Look, Naomia. I've been around for a real long time."

She interrupted. "Not quite as long as I have. Don't forget it."

He dropped the subject, aware he was treading on dangerous ground. "Why the kid?" he tried again.

She dropped her head. "The kid is something special," she said slowly.

"How is he special?"

"You don't need to know that. All you need to do is get him out of there, and get him off this fucking planet before that old madman gets his hands on him. It's very dangerous right now. Already that ancient fucker is searching for him. He just doesn't quite know where to look." She paused. "Let's say I threw some sand in his eyes."

Zero snorted. "I'll bet. You could throw sand in anybody's eyes."

"It's a talent," she replied, smiling. "One of my many."

'It seems like we've been planning this thing for a lifetime."

"You've only been involved recently," she told him. "I actually started this project almost fifty years ago."

Even with his own vast age, Zero found it disturbing and difficult to look at this woman, who at times seemed ancient, and at other times seemed but a girl—and realize she was even older than himself. Sometimes he thought she'd been alive as long as humanity itself. He knew the Hegemon of old, but she'd known him before the beginning, before even the Lost and First Men.

The Hegemon. That would be a problem, too. "I can get the kid off planet," he assured her, hoping it was true. "But I still don't understand. What can one kid do against the full power of the Hegemony?"

She didn't answer directly. She looked away from him, over his shoulder, and he had the feeling she was examining paths of unmeasurable distance, of time, space, and pain. "The Hegemon," she said, "at least before he went as crazy as a dope-sticked bedbug, believed that the universe had been changed."

It was a new thought. He'd left the merry little band after the beginning, and had missed much. But how could the universe change? Zero blinked. "Changed? How?"

She shook her head. "I don't know. But he believed it was so."

"And what about you? Is that what you believe?"

She nodded slowly. "I think it was changed. I think the universe has been changed twice in my own lifetime. The first was the Original Sin, and the second . . . something else."

Zero felt confused. "I don't understand. What does that have to do with the kid, with what we're doing?"

"Zero, you worry too much. Let me do the worrying. At least I know all the things there are to worry about."

"I don't like that, Naomia. It smells like you're keeping me in the dark about things. You shouldn't do that. It isn't safe. For anybody." He glanced up at her, his gray eyes hooded.

"That a threat?"

A long interval of silence. Then he said, 'No. A warning, maybe."

She nodded. He sighed and finished his drink. "So it's whatever you say, babe? Whether I like it or not?"

She grinned. "That's just the way it's gonna be. Whatever I say. Come on, Zero. When have I ever let you down?"

He listened to her words, to the velvet underplay of threat and lust, and recalled why he had once loved her, and why he no longer did. When had fear replaced the softer feelings? He didn't know, only that it had happened. It was interesting that the same answer could suffice for two such different questions. Love and fear. The answer was always death. And he knew all about that, too, didn't he? Almost as much as she did herself.

He shivered, and got up to make another drink.

## THE WEB: EMPIRE CENTER

He sat upon his throne and regarded the vast scene spread before his eyes. Nothing seemed changed. At the foot of the steps, his Chamberlain, gorgeous in gaudy crimson robes, deftly fielded the throng of supplicants that sought audience with the Emperor on this day. The air was golden with the smoke of incense. The fragrance of poppies, raspberries, and musk filled his nose. The crowds of courtiers babbled and chattered and laughed. Gongs sounded. Tapers were lit. Light flowed through huge stained-glass windows and the gigantic crystal dome that surmounted the chamber.

His own robes were of heavily embroidered silk. The sleeves had been lengthened to cover the deformity on his left arm. He tapped the fingers of his right hand on the throne and squirmed against the form cushions. Pain was a constant now. A half jacket of agony scrawled down his back, across his chest, and onto his belly with fingers of fire. None of his shape-changing abilities seemed to help. Whatever form he donned, immediately assumed the disfigurement. Each morning brought more of his flesh under its control.

As he mechanically spoke to ambassadors, Messengers, Librarians, and all the other visitors and residents of his Empire, his mind drifted elsewhere. Durward had gone, off on an extended trip through a series of other Empires. He'd left the day after their return. He'd come to Luke privately, saying he wished to take up his old duties. His face had been white and drawn. He'd shivered as he'd spoken to Luke.

"Sire," he'd said, "I can do nothing for you here, and I feel the need to refresh myself with old ways and habits."

Luke thought the journey into Ice had nearly broken the little Messenger. Gently, he'd bid him go, and hoped that Durward, at least, might find some peace.

The destruction of his Empire was spreading in unforeseen ways, even to those closest to him. Stone, ever phlegmatic, had returned to the now gigantic military complex beyond the far edge of the capital. He seemed unchanged by his dangerous journey. Luke found that comforting. Stone was a staunch ally.

Naomia still remained. He'd caused a part of the palace to be transformed into quarters for her. She seemed to have a taste for many rooms, each of different design. She remained an enigma, but a hugely interesting one. Now, faced with the boredom of the day, and even the boredom of his own pain, he suddenly wished to see her.

He raised one hand. The Chamberlain immediately faced him. "Sire?" the Chamberlain said.

"This audience is over," Luke told him.

The Chamberlain nodded. He turned and began to disperse the mob of guests, visitors, and supplicants. Luke rose from the throne, traversed the broad steps, and followed by his usual retinue, strode directly down the length of the chamber to the colossal brass doors at the far end. Once beyond them, he vanished.

"I don't know what to do," he said.

"Of course you don't," Naomia replied. "You're just a baby."

He had created for her a room of crystal and gold. Her bark-brown body moved through the shards of light like a fish. She seemed at home here, he thought. It definitely wasn't to his taste, although the strange, angular chair upon which he reclined was certainly comfortable.

She brought him a bowl of some unfamiliar liquor. He wondered where she'd gotten it. It was slightly warm. It fizzed against his tongue as he swallowed. He felt the bubbling heat grow inside his stomach. For a moment, the ever-present pain lessened.

"I'm going to die," he told her.

It was a relief to have someone from outside close to him. Someone who could hear his deepest fears without endangering the Empire further with panic.

"No, you're not," she said.

"How do you know?"

"I know there's a way out."

It was the first time she'd mentioned such a thing. How could she know? The old questions rumbled around inside his skull. He pushed them back. She'd been here three days, and spoken only in riddles or silence.

"What's the answer, then?" he asked, surprised at how urgent his words sounded.

She shrugged and drifted slowly away. "I don't know what the answer is. I just know there is an answer, and I know you can find it."

Once again it came back to his own ignorance. Before this had started, he'd thought he knew everything. Now, he thought he might perhaps know nothing. Nothing, at least, that mattered. Nothing that could save him.

He could barely make her out. She had moved so far away, the crystals obscured even the faint dark flashes of her narrow body. He stood, set his drink aside, and followed.

"Why do you always wander off when I'm talking to you?" he asked.

She ignored him and kept on walking. He had not realized how huge this room was. It took him a few breathless moments to catch up to her. "Wait! Stop!"

She turned, a faint smile on her wide lips. "You almost didn't wait for me once. Why should I wait for you?"

The automatic answer—*because I am the Emperor*—seemed stupid and hollow. "Naomia." A thought struck him. "The dance. What about the dance?"

"What about it?" But she stopped.

"What happened then? I felt . . . a power. A strength I didn't know I had."

She nodded. "Yes. The strength was real. It was my strength, but yours also."

"There was something else." He closed his eyes and tried to remember the long moments of frenzy when it seemed the Web would fall to ruins beneath their pounding feet. He recalled how maddened she'd become, and how he'd known without understanding why that it was his job to calm her, lest—what? Lest she destroy the worlds? No, that wasn't quite it. There was more. Somehow, he knew, it involved him, his own power.

And how had he calmed her? Strangest of all, he'd laid down on his back and let her dance on him. Dance around his . . . erection. He blinked and inhaled sharply.

Erection!

It was the first erection he'd ever had. There had been a feeling of strength to it, of warmth, of freedom. Joy, almost. The same joy that came from the dance itself.

"Why do you always call me a little boy?" he asked suddenly.

"Because you are. You're not quite thirteen years old."

He shook his head. The concept was so odd. Time was endless and unmarked within the Empire. He'd been here forever. He ransacked his many memories and found the image of "year" easily enough. An order of time involving the travel of a planet around its sun. But he didn't live on a planet, and the sun was of his own creation. This body of knowledge was something that he knew, but considered useless in his own day-to-day life. These were from the facts he used to solve problems brought to him from beyond the Empire. It was the work of the Empire to solve these problems. The Librarians cataloged such esoteric knowledge in order to do so—though it had nothing to do with his own reality.

"That has nothing to do with me," he told her.

"Perhaps. But remember this." Her emerald eyes began to glow. "When you danced, you had no pain. Your penis was hard, and your pain was gone."

He strode alone across the wide floor of Command Central, scattering Colonels and lesser Generals in his wake. No one called to him. Frightened faces watched his passage. He hadn't announced his coming.

He saw his quarry up ahead. General Hendrickson stood atop the raised dais in the center. He leaned against the railing that surrounded it and watched his progress.

He sensed that Hendrickson was as startled as the rest, but his General concealed it well. In fact, long before Luke reached the steps leading up, Hendrickson was there waiting for him.

The General bowed as he came close. "Sire. An unexpected pleasure."

Luke wasn't in the mood for pleasantries. "I want Stone. Where is he?" He rushed by Hendrickson and mounted the dais. He found an empty seat, plopped down, and waited for the General to scurry up after him.

"Stone? Why, he's—I think he's around some-where."

"Bring him. I need to see him now."

The General bowed deep. "Yes, Sire." He signaled. An aide scrabbled away, terror on his features. The tempers of the Emperor were well-known.

"It should only be a few moments, Sire," Hendrickson said.

"Good," Luke replied. He spun the chair around. Command Central had grown in his absence. The room was at least three times as large as he remembered. The screens that lined the walls now made a seamless moving picture of destruction. Hundreds of technicians worked on the main floor below, tending to the holy "3CI" of command, control, communication, and intelligence as they directed his ever-growing armies against the mindless fury of the invasion.

He shuddered as he watched graphic maps of the cancer that grew across his lands. The original infections were outlined in black. Around those empty spots, livid red growths spread tendrils ever outward.

Just like my own cancer, he thought.

His Empire was huge, but it had limits. He saw now that a full third of the total had succumbed to the barbarian invaders. Scenes of terrible carnage replayed themselves. Human waves of spear-waving warriors overwhelmed his own troops, ignoring their modern weapons, ignoring their armor, ignoring everything in their killing lust.

"Hendrickson, what do they do, after they win?"

The General said, "Nothing. They do nothing. They kill everything that lives, burn everything that remains, and move out. They never stop. We kill them by the millions, and millions more replace them. They leave nothing behind but fire and rock. Nothing."

Even the General looked shaken by the viciousness of the assaults. His face was tired, drawn, and wary. Perhaps, Luke thought, he's afraid I'll blame him. Once, he would have. Not so long ago, all the would have remained of General Hendrickson would have been flayed rags of bloody flesh on the floor. But that had been a time of certainty. Now, knowing how little he really knew, and finally beginning to understand the limits of his own power, Luke had learned humility. Ignorance had taught him. Ignorance was giving him knowledge, but of a new sort. He was not the center of the Empire—perhaps not the center of anything. It was a terrible thought, but not entirely unwelcome. It promised change, even growth. But only if he survived the present, and the catastrophe that grew around him like a fountain of death.

Luke remembered what he'd seen in the world beneath the World, where the tree of light lay burning. There was the real problem, not the failures or successes of his Generals. They were, after all, only his own failures and successes.

The Emperor can fail, he mused. I never knew that before. What else don't I know?

Stone arrived, face as calm as his name. "Sire? You wanted me?"

Luke gestured at the screens, at a particularly horrifying barbarian. "Can you bring me one of those? Alive?"

In the short time left to them, Luke would never know exactly what Stone had done to accomplish his feat—but two days later, Stone stood before him on the parade ground in front of the Main Command Center with a frothing, howling, snarling barbarian at his feet. The savage was so heavily manacled, he could hardly move.

The day was soft and warm and bright. The usual clouds had disappeared. On the parade ground beyond, ordered ranks of troops marched back and forth. The shouts of their Sergeants and the answering cries of the troopers made a pleasant, rhythmic counterpoint to the beautiful day.

"Here it is, Sire," Stone said.

Luke stared at his guardian. Even after the terrible battle in Ice, Stone had emerged unmarked. Now a dark, purplish bruise marred the right side of Stone's face. A livid gash snaked across his shoulder blade. There was a clear plastic cast around his lower left leg just above the ankle. The lacerated flesh beneath was plainly visible.

Luke couldn't imagine the forces necessary to injure Stone. Stone himself seemed unaware of his various wounds. He limped slightly as he shoved the squalling barbarian forward.

"Kneel before your Emperor, trash," Stone said.

The primitive spat, then spun quick as a snake, teeth gnashing, attempting to brutalize the Soldier's leg. Stone looked down on the beast-like figure. Then he smashed him in the face with his right fist. The savage fell back, blood staining his yellowed teeth and trickling from his mouth.

Luke gaped at this, aghast. His stomach churned. He couldn't tell if it was fear or disgust or hatred. Stone glanced up.

"Can I kill it for you, Sire?"

"No. Not yet."

Stone nodded and stepped back. Four troopers hauled the barbarian to his feet, dragged him within a couple of yards of Luke.

"No further," Stone said. The troopers stopped.

Except for his battered appearance, no doubt sustained in the process of capture, the marauder looked not much different than images Luke had watched on the screens. This one wore a strand of tarnished animal claws around his corded neck. Wild tufts of grease-smeared hair pushed up beneath a headband made of stinking, half-cured hide. Ragged braids tipped with crude clay beads extended from the top of the barbarian's head like a nest of rotten snakes.

Stone had taken away the invader's weapons. Only his belt and bizarre girdle or skirt remained. Even now, chained and beaten, the savage's erection twitched and jumped at his crotch. It was a monster, both the erection and the grotesque being who sported it.

Beneath the grime and blood, though, Luke's own green eyes gazed fiercely back at him—a glare of molten emerald. Luke knew what he had to do next. He didn't want to, but it had to be done.

"Hold him," he ordered. "Hold him tight."

Stone moved smoothly forward. He rammed his forearm beneath the invader's chin and jerked his head back in a painful choke hold. The savage mewled vacantly. Spittle mixed with blood at the edge of his mouth.

Luke ignored it all. He closed his eyes and reached out, seeking the heart of this rogue Icon, the kernel that must respond to his own power. For a moment in the dark, he saw nothing. Then a tiny crimson flame beckoned him. He surged forward and smothered the blaze, taking it into himself even as he let himself sink into it.

He screamed. His eyes flew open. He stood before himself, frozen, bug-eyed, and staring. Trapped! Somehow trapped in the mind pattern of the savage, caught inside its fevered skull. Watching himself watching himself watching himself.

Endless shocked mirrors.

He felt a wild, unfocused burst of joy. Bone-deep savagery flooded him. A single wave of bloodred lust erased memory, control, sense. Only the tiniest untouched part whimpered faint warnings.

It was too late. All he desired—all he *was*—was rape. Murder. Fire. Destruction.

*I am made Lucifer, destroyer of worlds.*

He reached out invisible hands and gathered all his power to him. Only a few feet away, his victim waited, unmoving. He felt lightnings roar up from his groin, through his belly, his heart, out to his hands. He thrust the troopers who pinioned his arms away. Only the terror on his back, around his neck, remained. He flexed his muscles once. The chains that fettered him burst in a shower of razored shrapnel. He spun to deal with the killer who had brought him here. This one would be short work. Then he could harvest the ultimate sacrifice.

Snarling, he heaved himself against the warrior. Stone showed no fear. The savage Luke leaped forward to grapple with Stone.

Stone's hands *moved*!

The motion was too quick for even his hyper-heated reflexes to follow. A crunching blow smashed across his face. Another just above the heart turned his chest to ice. He gasped. More blows thudded down. His knees sagged. Blinding pain exploded in his skull.

As he fell toward the dark, his final emotion was sadness. That, and a lingering taste of the fierce joy that was his only reason for being.

Luke came awake with a sudden rush. As soon as he opened his eyes, he remembered everything that had happened. Stretched out before him, the savage's battered frame, whose mind he'd inhabited for only a few short instants, lay bloody and torn. Pinkish yellow mucous oozed from his ear. A terrible stench arose. The barbarian had voided himself in his frenzy.

Stone stood astride him, his breath coming a bit faster than normal. "Sire? What happened? Did you see him break those chains? Where did he get power like that?"

"I saw," Luke replied.

Stone seemed shocked. "I've never seen anything like that. Almost like he—it—" He glanced at Luke. "Like it had *your* power." He paused and shook his head. "He sure as hell didn't have it before." Another pause, longer. "Do . . . you know what happened?"

Luke nodded. "yeah. I'm afraid I do."

"It's too dangerous," Stone muttered. "Let me kill him, Sire."

Luke shook his head. "No. I have to find out something."

Stone stepped back. "What do you want me to do?"

"Wake him up."

Comprehension began to dawn on Stone's features. He started to say something, changed his mind, and merely motioned toward the troopers who crowded around the supine form. Some left and returned with water buckets. They splashed chill liquid on the savage.

The invader shook his head once, twice. Propped himself groggily on skinned elbows. Then a terrible grin split his bloody lips. He stared straight at Luke.

"Sire!" Stone said. His voice was urgent.

"No." Then, to the primitive, who glared at him with a lizard's hungry gaze, "If you're coming, motherfucker, come ahead."

The beast-man came off the ground like a bolt from a crossbow. He launched himself directly at Luke's face. His fingers curled into claws. Arms straining. Muscles distended.

Luke had only an instant. It was long enough. Smooth as great tumblers shifting in mighty locks, he channeled his entire power and directed it at the apparition before him.

The nameless aborigine howled as the force took him. From out of nowhere, seen only by their action in the clear, warm, air—invisible knives began to hew away the savage's flesh. Gobbets of blood and gristle whipped out in a fine spray. Before their eyes the savage showed a thousand tiny lines on every inch of skin. Then a sheet of flowing crimson. Then, beneath it all, the chips of bone began to fly.

A moment later, nothing remained but tattered rags, bloody spatters, a queasy, nauseating pool on the white gravel of the parade ground.

In the background, Luke heard the sound of retching. He was surprised. Then he understood. These were only Soldiers. His courtiers would not have been upset. They'd seen the power of the Emperor a thousand times.

Luke sagged back, caught himself, stood straight. He glanced at Stone. "Now I know," he said.

Stone's head moved in agreement. "Yes. You can kill them."

Of course, Luke thought. He forced a final glimpse of the mess on the ground. Suicide *was* a traditional Imperial death.

## THE HEGEMONY: DEPARTMENT OF INFORMATION CONTROL AND ENCRYPTION

Colonel Arnold Hanestad floated silently in Reality Vee, that strange, complicated space created for the brotherhood of man and machine. He was a face dancer, one who danced upon the interface where minds of flesh and silicon merged in seamless communion.

In this space, he envisioned himself as a pair of hands whose fingers were attached to the strings of his desire. Neon threads flared from his fingertips in scintillant lines of green and blue and purple. Practiced fisherman that he was, he knew how to troll for his catch.

"Ah," he breathed. He felt the familiar tug that signaled his nets had found the particular piece of data he sought. He reeled it in. As he brought his find close, he made out its general shape. It resembled a flaccid tree with leaves made of dull silver and blue, almost like the scales of a fish—Reality Vee's representation of a hypertexted data bank.

"Good." He grunted softly, checked one final time to make sure nothing was amiss. Then he jacked out.

He opened his eyes. He sat in a small, dimly lit room, surrounded by banks of monitors. The colored screens rippled with movement. He imagined them as aquariums, each monitor displaying its own peculiar denizen of the very peculiar deeps where he angled for data.

It took long practice to extract the informational juice from so many displays, but Hanestad had been at his job thirty years. Reading the screens was second nature to him—no more difficult than face dancing or the other, more esoteric aspects of his job.

Subvocally he directed parts of the data he'd obtained to appropriate visuals on three different screens. A holo generator at his left swiftly built a three-color rendition of his subject, based on recent photos from various security desks around the Hall of the Web.

He glanced at the glowing statue, then said, "Kay Three enlarge."

Obediently, the holographic figure expanded until the pores of Charlie Seagrave's nose were clearly visible. Hanestad grinned. From this vantage point, Seagrave looked huge. He checked his figures to be sure. They said Seagrave was, if anything, a little smaller than the usual citizen of World.

"Kind of stupid-looking, too," he mumbled aloud. He turned back to the information that rolled across his monitors. Probably nothing to it, he decided. But the behavioral snoops had detected red-flag warning signs. Colonel Hanestad hadn't risen to his somewhat exalted position in the department of ICE by ignoring the machines. He was one of the few who had some idea of what slumbered in the hidden, dark rooms at the center of his domain.

His job was to protect those sleepers. He would do everything in his considerable power to see that such protection was accomplished. Part of his knowledge concerned the frightening tendencies of those dreamers, particularly the darkest and most hideous of them—who had not awakened in Hanestad's lifetime. Whom he most fervently hoped would continue to sleep. Unlike Charlie Seagrave, Colonel Hanestad knew a great deal of history and, by the nature of his job, much of what he knew was not a part of the usual educational process in World's schools. The history he understood was far too bloody for general consumption.

No, he had no wish to awaken the darkest dreamer. If learning everything there was to know about an insignificant Web technician named Charlie Seagrave would help assure the continued sleep of that one, then so be it.

He didn't intend to be gentle, either. Technicians like Charlie Seagrave were always expendable. Especially in the greater scheme of things.

# 10

## THE HEGEMONY: CITY ON WORLD

"You look terrible," Eileen said.

Charlie stared down at his cup of coffee. He knew she was right. The apparition that appeared in his morning mirror bore a rictus-grin that would have better fitted something newly released from a grave. There were bags under his reddened eyes. His skin had turned sallow and loose. His hairline looked even higher than before. His hand shook as he lifted his cup.

"I don't feel so hot, either," he told her. They had met in a small restaurant less than a mile from the Hall of the Web. It was a local hangout for techs of all stripes. The place was crowded at noon, but they managed to find a small table to themselves.

A soft tone chimed over the loud chatter of the crowd. Voices quieted. A large news screen slowly unrolled itself across the quaint chalkboard menu at the back of the room. The picture jittered, then brightened. Charlie found himself viewing a planet from deep space.

The shot rapidly pulled in tight, revealing the incredible destruction that had been wreaked on the hapless world. An unctuous voice over began: "A task force from the regional Hegemonic capital of Oranda arrived in the K'Mill system today to find scenes of vast devastation."

Now the camera began a split-screen pan of the world, showing the raw wounds of fresh volcanoes, the scars of new and blackened deserts, and here and there, the pitiful, broken remnants that had once been small but thriving cities.

"The planet, victim of a mysterious attack, has been destroyed. Rescue parties found only a single survivor, a computer technician who had been standing watch in a chamber miles beneath the surface.

"In the process of rescuing the survivor, brave crews disarmed a diabolical antimatter planet buster that had been placed above the sealed-over entrance to the hidden chamber."

The scene switched to a fuzzy view of a man, white-faced and blank-eyed, being half led, half carried aboard a landing craft. Ludicrously, the man waved at the cameras and flashed a skull-like grin.

"More on this fast-breaking story at the seventeen-hundred news hour," the announcer promised.

Charlie turned to Eileen. "That's bizarre."

Eileen shrugged. "All kinds of strange shit happens out on the frontier. Who gives a damn?"

But Charlie remembered the diorama he'd watched a moment in the Hall of the Web. Had that been K'Mill? He thought so. What a shame. He tried to reconcile the tiny, bright-eyed animal he'd seen scampering through the ancient trees with the picture of ruin he'd just watched. The effort made him uneasy. He said to Eileen, "I don't know. It's just—scary, that's all."

She pushed herself back in her chair and said, "You've got to buck up, Charlie. You look like you're falling apart on me."

"I'll be fine," he muttered, grudging her the reply. "If you just . . ."

"If I just what?"

"If you just quit riding me all the time," he said.

Her lips tightened. "I thought it was you who wanted to ride *me* all the time."

"Oh, fuck that shit. I mean—wait a minute, I don't mean that as an insult, understand—it's just that, Gods, Eileen, sex is the last thing I'm worried about right now."

"Hey. Tomorrow it will all be over. And don't forget, I'm behind you a thousand percent."

He sipped his coffee, wrinkling his lips in distaste at the bitter, cold liquid. "That's another thing. Behind me. What does that mean?"

"I can't come with you when you walk her in," she replied. Her patience seemed exaggerated to him. "Don't you think that would look kind of funny?"

"I hadn't thought about it," he said. "Why can't you come with us?"

She shook her head. "This is the best way, Charlie. My people tell me the security in the Hall responds to anomalies. We aren't known to be that friendly. If we show up with a third so-called technician, somebody might get suspicious. Just too many irregularities at one time."

He chewed on the thought. "Security? You mean, more than the guards and stuff?"

"Of course. Why do you think we're going to all this trouble? If it wasn't for security, we'd just parade your hooker right on by, right into the template room. By the way, she's a strange one, isn't she?"

"Who? Naomia?"

"Who did you think I meant?"

Charlie grinned faintly. He might be half out of it, but he knew jealousy when he heard it. "Naomia? She's great," he said, and grinned widely at her discomfiture. "You just have to know her better."

"Thanks. I'd just as soon not know anything about her at all. If it wasn't for—"

"If it wasn't for what?"

"Oh, nothing."

"Keeping secrets?" he asked.

"Of course I am." He had no need to know about Harrison Lever, or anything else for that matter. Mentally she gave herself a sharp, reminding shake. Charlie was a pawn. Best let him remain that way.

"Come on, Charlie. settle down. It's not going to be that big a thing. You bring her in, she does what she's paid to do, and that's it. No problems, right?"

Charlie drained the dregs of his coffee and placed the cup carefully on the table. It rattled faintly as he set it down. He stared at his still-quivering fingers. "Yeah, that's it," he sighed. "But what does that mean? Did you ever think how weird this all is? You, your people, all of this? Me? To get one hooker in to give one blow job to one thirteen-year-old blank brain?"

"Hey, Charlie. You're the one who keeps insisting that kid is real."

"Of course he's real, but he has no consciousness. He's just an empty bag. What is all this in aid of? I mean you talk about overthrowing the Hegemony. Yet what you're doing would be classified as child abuse on some worlds."

She snorted. "Charlie, your place isn't to worry about the reasons for things. Your job is just to do what you're told."

"Oh? So what happened to our partnership? You know, one for all and all for one?"

She said carefully, "We're together, all right. I promise you, when this is all over with, we'll be more together than we've ever been before. If you know what I mean."

He peered into his empty cup, as if seeking omens in the brown, milky patterns there. "Actually, Eileen," he said, "I think I'd prefer if we went back to the way things were before."

"What? You don't want to see me any more after this?"

"I could be in a whole lot of trouble. Even if this goes off without a hitch, some kind of alarm will go off somewhere. Maybe we can explain it away. But, like I said, I think that afterward we'd both be better off if we just cooled things. You know?"

Watch it, she told herself. He might mean it, or it might be some test his convoluted mind has dreamed up. She arranged her facial expression to reflect bravely suppressed hurt. "And I thought you liked me. I mean, really liked me. I know we didn't start off well, but—I thought our relationship had changed."

"Oh, it has," he assured her. "But I'm thinking of what's best for both of us. You're always telling me to trust you. You're gonna have to trust me on this."

Oh, right, she thought, suddenly tired of all the games. If truth were told, she knew, both of them hated the sight of each other. But the game had to be played to the very end. She said, "Charlie, I do trust you." She reached across the table and took one of his hands between her own. She squeezed lightly. He didn't respond much, merely looked up at her.

"Charlie, twenty-four more hours. Then it's over. And if you want us to be over, well—that can happen, too." *Bet your skinny ass*, she thought. "But let's not think about the future. Let's just concentrate on today. And tomorrow morning."

"Right," he said. "Tomorrow. The first day of the rest of my life. I hope."

"Yes," she told him. "That's it. That's beautiful."

And oh, so stupid, she thought, and smiled at him.

## THE WEB: EMPIRE

An errant breeze ruffled his hair. It was warmer here than in the capital. He purposely kept the weather good in the vast forest he'd created. He walked here a great deal now, alone with only the sighing of the wind and the rustle of leaves and the soft crunch of dry earth beneath his feet.

The infection had spread across half his body. His entire left leg had been consumed. He limped against the continuous pain that racked him with every motion.

Naomia had been no help. It had been weeks now, but she kept to her quarters and said little. When he visited her, she mostly danced. For some reason he found this soothing. There had been no repeat of the dream of sexual arousal, nor of the vision of destruction that had accompanied it. He paused and stared up at the boles of mighty forest giants. Then he sighed and squatted down, his back against the bark of a single ancient tree.

He'd never felt so hopeless. Even here, in the Empire, with all his powers intact, he saw no way to prevent the eventual destruction of both it and him. The terrible experience with the captured savage had shaken him to his core. Try as he might, he couldn't deny he'd slipped into the savage's pattern as easily as into a silken robe. They were the same. No matter what the outward appearance might be, the invaders were as much himself as Stone or Durward or any other Icon. The only difference was he couldn't control them. Even that had precedent—he couldn't entirely control Stone, either.

The barbarian had seized of him with appalling ease. It had seemed equally able to take advantage of his powers. He could destroy the Icons—but only with great effort. It was as if something held him back. He recalled his first thought, as he'd stared at the shattered hulk of the primitive Soldier, had been of suicide.

He stared at the towering forest growth around him. Tall and proud, the huge trees spiked into a giant green canopy. He wondered why they soothed him so much. Then, with a flash of insight, he understood: the great, pole-like edifices reminded him of his own erection at the time when Naomia had danced around it.

Somehow it was all tied up together—his erection, Naomia, Ice, the fire of the invasion, even the madness and the joy he'd felt when he'd become the invader himself. But there was no way out. The infection grew. The destruction grew. He couldn't see anything to stop it.

Blackness seized him. A chill darkness that squeezed his heart and turned his limbs to ice. Ice, he thought. Ice. Something . . . something there.

He closed his eyes and felt the wind on his heated cheeks. He tried not to think about anything. Let the problems fall like single stones into the great, quiet pool of his total knowledge. Something was wrong. Something he was missing.

He was bone certain there must be a way. He'd traveled to Ice, hoping to find information, and gotten Naomia instead. And what had she said?

*"There is a way out."* The certainty in her voice had been unmistakable. For a time it had heartened him, until he realized she would say no more. So what was

the reality of the situation? Perhaps that was the way to look at it, rather than view everything through the warped, cloudy prism of his own hopes and desires. What had *really* happened?

He began to tick off the events. The invasion had begun. He had requested help from other Empires, but none had given it. Only Ice had stood out, by virtue of its refusal to reply at all. So he'd gone to Ice, been nearly killed in a confrontation with something deadly that lived there, and been saved by Naomia. He'd fought and danced with her, and brought her back to his own Empire, where things were in even worse shape than before. Naomia was the only truly new element in the equation of his existence.

So what did she mean? Where had she come from? It was almost as if events had conspired at the final outcome—his new relationship with the woman.

He chewed his lower lip. There were two possibilities. She was either of the Web, or not of the Web. Yet beyond the Web was unthinkable. Beyond the Web didn't exist, except as a construct that framed the day-to-day work of the Empire. Or was that true?

A flash of blinding inspiration punched him in the gut. Yes! It would all make horrible sense if some agent beyond the Web itself was manipulating events. He gasped at the force of the sudden epiphany. The invaders came from the source of the tree—the Well of Light—but what was the root of the Well? Where did his Icons *come* from?

He summoned them, of course, but from where? Could it be that the Icons, Naomia, and the source of all his problems were one and the same? Then, like a sledgehammer, her wholly unconsidered words crashed through the walls of his preconceptions.

*"There is a way out."* Not "there is a way to solve your problem," but, "there is a way out."

Could that be the solution? He had no idea, but as he stood, then began jogging back along the forest path he'd already trod, he knew he had no other choice. It was the only possibility.

"Naomia," he muttered. "This time you give me *answers*."


## THE HEGEMONY: HALL OF THE WEB

A woman dressed in a plain brown uniform without insignia brought Colonel Hanestad another cup of coffee. She cleared away the debris of a late lunch, her face averted. Her face wore a perpetually frightened look. Tiny squint lines of fear had embedded themselves at the corners of her eyes. He ignored her.

He sat in his utilitarian office behind a wide metal desk. The only items on the desktop were two terminals, one with a monitor, the other with a jack cable dangling from it. Two simple metal chairs fronted the desk. A large, stylized portrait of the Hegemon in full ceremonial regalia hung on the wall behind Hanestad, smiling benignly down on him. Dust mottled the frame of the picture. Otherwise, the walls of the modest office were barren. A single window on his left looked out onto a completely enclosed courtyard. Three floors below, Hanestad could see a solitary tree, stunted and twisty in a concrete tub.

At times the surroundings in which he worked oppressed him. He didn't regard himself as an unreasonable or evil man. His wife had loved him until her death. His daughter, who still lived at home, thought the world of him. Of course, she had no idea what he did at work. Because he thought the world of her, he meant to keep it that way. It wasn't that he was ashamed of his profession. The world, particularly

World, was full of dirty jobs that somebody had to do. but one didn't advertise the details. It wasn't wise.

As for himself, he had no plans to remarry. He didn't particularly love his job. But he liked being good at it. Protecting the security of the Hall of the Web, particularly the data flows that were the life blood of the Hegemony, would seem on the face of it exciting and stimulating. He knew the truth. The workings of the templates and the vast processing arrays and data bases were of little interest to him. The charges he guarded in other parts of the Hall had not lived, in any real sense of the word, in his lifetime. From what he knew of those dire beings, he hoped that would remain the case.

He spent a great deal of his time at the interface, but even that work was boring—the never-ending task of monitoring all parts of the Hall, and making sure other, more physical segments of ICE that reported to him from beyond the Hall continued to function properly.

Occasionally, some dreary, stupid little plot would be uncovered. Then, neatly, surgically, he would crush it with no more emotion than he would an annoying insect. Just like this one, he thought. It had all the earmarks. He sighed, leaned back in his creaky, wooden chair, stared at the ceiling, then closed his eyes.

He reviewed what little he knew. Sparse though it was, it was enough for him to act. He was neither judge nor jury, nor did he need one. His authority derived from a greater power than the mundane institutions of City on World. In the Hegemony, his brief went unquestioned.

Still, he liked to be certain in his own mind before taking final steps. This technician, Eileen Michelson, seemed to be the key. He knew more about her than she did herself. Somebody was manipulating her, just as she manipulated the hapless Charlie Seagrave who had led him to her. It was obvious. He didn't know who yet, nor did he know to what end—but he doubted it would be hard to find out. She herself would tell him, and gladly.

As for Charlie Seagrave, his situation would be funny if it wasn't so ludicrous. What did the two of them think they were doing? Obviously, the Michelson woman was the brains of the inside operation. Charlie Seagrave, equally obviously, was being blackmailed somehow. He sighed again. He wasn't particularly happy with what he would do next. But he would do it. There was a routine to such things.

He leaned forward and said, "Pick up the Michelson woman. Carry out the usual routine."

Then, efficient civil servant that he was, he completely forgot her. He turned to handle the next item on his busy afternoon schedule. He had two years till retirement. He wondered just when it was he'd begun to start counting the days.

They came for Eileen at 1600 hours. They took her from the small cubicle where she had been checking the daily log just prior to leaving.

She looked up when the man and the woman entered. They didn't knock. As soon as she saw their blank faces and cold, empty eyes, a great fear seized her. She knew it was all over. Her lips moved silently, then stopped.

"Eileen Michelson?" the man said.

"Yes," she replied. She was astonished at how firm her voice sounded.

"Come with us, please," the woman said.

"Who are you?"

"Come with us, please," the woman repeated. She

leaned forward and inserted a chip into the reader on Eileen's small desk. The sigil of the department of Information Control and Encryption flashed there, then gave way to several pages of a warrant of detainment. Eileen tried to read the convoluted, legalistic language, but only a few words stood out, like rotten raisins in a deadly pudding. Subversion. Arrest. Conspiracy.

"Just routine," the man said.

"Yes," Eileen replied. Her voice was flat, dull. "Just routine."

By 1700 hours, she sat in a tiny, white-tiled cell. The nightmare had begun.

After a time they took her clothes away. Then they walked her down a short hallway that led from her cell to another room. Her guards were two women, short, heavyset, void-faced. They handled her like meat. Their thick, calloused fingers bit into the soft flesh of her upper arm as they seated her on a metal chair. She shivered at the cold caress of the steel, and goose bumps suddenly broke out on her skin. They stood on either side of her. They seemed to ignore her, but they exuded a sense of quiet watchfulness.

"Wh-what . . . is this?" she whispered. "What's going on? Why am I here? I've done nothing."

One of the women leaned forward and punched her in the face. The blow was stunning. She felt cartilage crunch in her nose, heard the celery crackle of it as it broke. Nausea swirled in her gut.

"Shut up," the woman said.

She faced a gray, scarred, metal desk. Behind the desk was a single empty wooden chair. She heard the door behind her open softly, then click shut. A shuffle of footsteps. A short, kindly, fatherly looking man walked behind the desk and sat down. He smiled at her.

In his arms he held a small, white furry animal. A pet of some kind, she guessed. She was so distraught, she didn't see anything odd in this. He placed the animal on the desktop in front of him. He held its front paws with one hand, and petted its soft back with the other.

A flicker of hope burned faintly. He seemed like a gentle man. Kind. She fastened on small detail. The man was elderly. His hair was full but completely white. Not the dull, tarnished white that often came with old age, but hair the color and sheen of snow. Like the pet, almost. The collar of his plain blue shirt was unbuttoned. There was a small brown food stain on one lapel of his casual jacket. Dark purplish veins covered the back of his gnarled hand as he stroked the animal.

She focused on the little pet. It had long, floppy ears. Its black eyes darted wildly. Its pink nose twitched constantly. It seemed frightened. That was odd. Why would a pet be afraid of its master?

The man spoke in a soft, whispery voice. "My name is Arnold Hanestad," he said. "I have to ask you some questions. I want you to answer me truthfully. Can you do that?"

She nodded. The entire front of her face had gone numb.

"You'll have to speak up," he said. "I can't hear you."

The woman on her right slapped her heavily on the side of her head. Pain whipped through her skull.

"Stop that!" Hanestad said sharply. "Miss Michelson will be cooperative. I'm sure. Isn't that correct, miss?"

"Y . . . yes," she replied. She wanted to vomit.

The man nodded. "Fine. If you are truthful with me, everything will be fine. I'm sure there is just some misunderstanding here."

He paused, glanced down at the tiny animal on his desktop. Then he looked up, his expression quizzical. "Are you interested in pets, Miss Michelson?"

She started to nod. Then she remembered. "Yes."

"This is a rabbit," he said. "It comes from the planet Ancient. Ancient is, as its name implies, an old planet. Some say the first, but we have no evidence of that."

She remained silent. He hadn't asked her a question.

"Rabbits are reputed to be very timid creatures. They're not generally regarded as pets. Most often the citizens of Ancient eat them." He looked down at the rabbit. "Of course, a rabbit must be properly prepared." A strange light came into his eyes. At that moment she thought they resembled some kind of metal. Lead, perhaps. Or dull steel.

Still holding the shivering animal by its front paws, he reached with his other hand into his coat pocket. He brought out a small silvery instrument maybe three inches long. He looked up. "This is a monomole vibroblade," he informed her. His thumb did something to one side of it. A faint, whirring sound filled the room.

"There is a blade here of monomolecular crystal," he told her. "It is so thin, it's essentially invisible. A mechanism inside the butt causes the blade to vibrate back and forth in a small arc very rapidly."

She stared at him, totally confused. What was he talking about?

His meaningless, vacant smile flickered on, then off again. "In order to prepare a rabbit, you must first skin it," he said. "The fur and skin aren't considered edible."

He nodded to himself. A low, dull knot of horror began to rise from her stomach, fill her chest, choke her throat.

"Let me show you," he said conversationally.

A moment later, the rabbit began to scream. It was a high-pitched, whistling sound, and it easily overrode the sound of her own vomiting.

After a time he said, "These are guts." After a further time, he said, "That's how you clean a rabbit. Are you hungry, Miss Michelson?"

His fatherly manner dropped away then, and burnished-steel edged his voice. "No? Then are you feeling talkative? Do you feel like talking now?"

She did.

## THE WEB: EMPIRE

He told Naomia what he'd been thinking. As he spoke, she watched silently, her eyes slightly narrowed. She seemed to absorb each word individually.

"Connections," he said. "Too many connections. Too strange. The invaders have erections. Now I get erections. I get erections around you. In dreams, here. The invaders come from the outside. You come from the outside. You said there was a way out."

His last words came in a rush, leaving him breathless. He stopped. He realized he had nothing more to say.

"What do you want me to do?" she said.

"Answer my question."

"You haven't asked a question," she told him.

She was right, he realized. He hadn't asked her anything, unless his entire monologue had been a question. What was the question he wanted to ask her?

"Do you know the way out?" he said at last.

She regarded him for one long, green instant. Then, slowly, she nodded. "Yes, I do."

"Can you show me?"

Once again, she nodded.

"Good," he told her. "Then show me."

\*     \*     \*

Time was dancing its sly two-step again. It seemed he'd been suspended for ages with his problems, like strange ornaments hung in the wind, crashing against each other. He couldn't remember when his flesh had not been rotten, peeling, and inflamed. The time before, that long time long gone, had stretched without end. Then the barbarians had come, and time had become all present, no past or future. His recollections of childhood, when the Empire had been smaller, less complicated, had gone faded with age. He'd never had much concept of a future. Now everything seemed to converge on the moment.

"That's it?" he asked her. "Nothing more, that's all?"

She nodded. "This is all"—she gestured widely, encompassing the lavish room, the walls, the palace, the Empire—"it's only a construct, you know. You *know* that, right?"

He thought about the Web, and the deep Well beneath the Web, and how his Empire, and all the Empires, floated like glittering bubbles on that darkness. "Yeah. I know."

"But you never thought about it otherwise. You never took it down the next step. What it all means."

He shook his head. "No."

"That strike you odd at all?"

It hadn't. Now it did. Now that he thought about it. Why had he never thought about it before?

"You never thought about it because you're not built to think about it," she told him. Once again, he wondered if she could read his mind. He had no idea what she could do. Anything was possible.

"Not built? What does that mean?" he asked.

She shrugged, a sharp, awkward movement. "You're not a construct," she said. "Not precisely. More like an operating system."

The words were meaningless. "Operating system? What does that mean?"

She didn't answer his question. Instead, she said, "The septal region. In the human brain."

Unbidden knowledge rose in his mind. He saw pictures, diagrams, heard droning, explanatory words. The words in his mind played a counterpoint to the words from her mouth.

"And the hypothalamus. It controls the release of certain hormones, and is stimulated by them." Her voice was measured, dreamy. "At puberty, the septal region may become stimulated and produce lust. Also certain regions of the hypothalamus, creating rage. An interesting combination. The old sex and war thing. Men have known it for eons. Ever since the climb from slime. It all makes puberty so . . . interesting."

He listened to the replay, more detailed, inside his skull. Amazing the amount of knowledge he had squirreled away there, never accessed. He knew more than he knew. Was it enough? What did it have to do with him?

"You are a little boy," she told him. "But not for long. You have a destiny. First you had to be a little boy." She paused. "And now you have to stop. You have to . . . take control."

He winced. Somehow her words were painful, cutting him. Telling him things he didn't want to hear. Things he knew were true. Painful things he couldn't escape.

"There is a wider world," she intoned. Her voice was like a slow-beating drum. "You have a place in that, too. There is a way out."

He shook his head. "Who are you? How do you know these things?"

She stared at him. "You called me. Didn't you know? I only came because you wanted me to."

"That's crazy. I don't even know you. How could I call you?"

"You don't know me? Are you sure?" She faced him, arms spread slightly, palms out. She waited.

He watched her breasts, the shadows of her ribs, the dark outline of hair above her genitals. His penis began to harden, to rise up, and as it did so, he stood.

"I . . . don't know," he said. It was an ultimate confession. He revealed his ignorance to her as a reluctant gift. All things soft and vulnerable, upon a silver plate. An offering.

She nodded. "But you will, little boy. You will." She stepped forward and took his erection in her hands. Her lips came forward and brushed his. "Soon."

He turned away for one final moment. "Is this the way out?" he whispered, his heartbeat loud in his ears, warm in the cup of her fingers.

"One of them," she told him.

## THE HEGEMONY: HALL OF THE WEB

Colonel Hanestad didn't think about the sight of Eileen Michelson being led, broken and shuddering, from the interrogation room. It wasn't that he didn't let himself think about her, or that he wiped the memory from his mind. It simply had no meaning for him. It was part of the job.

He didn't know what would happen to her now, nor did he care. She was no longer a factor in this little plot. She had told him everything she knew. Unfortunately, it had not been nearly as much as he'd hoped for. Her answers only created questions, and the questions were larger than she understood.

Still, as he sat in his own office and replayed a video of the interview, he couldn't help but laugh.

The sound of his involuntary chuckle was thin and disbelieving. A prostitute? A blow job?

Near the end she'd screamed, "It's only a *joke*. A Gods damned *joke!*" As if she'd really believed it. He knew better, and so did she. What she didn't know was that her understanding of the situation was as flawed as the pitiful lie she tried to pass off at the end.

He watched the final scenes, then switched off the replay. "Harrison Lever," he said aloud. There was a problem. His preliminary check showed that Harrison Lever didn't exist. His preliminary check procedure was more thorough than other department's full-scale investigations.

He grunted, reached forward, and picked up one end of the jack cable. He glanced at a time readout glowing redly on one corner of his small monitor screen: 2000 hours. This insanity was supposed to take place the next morning at 0900 hours. Naomia the hooker didn't seem to exist either.

He had thirteen hours to unravel the puzzle. Absently he inserted the jack plug into the socket beneath his ear. The room winked out, and he stood upon the face.

It wasn't enough to simply stop the plot. He had to know why. That was what his job was really about. Knowing why.

He was amazed. This might actually be something. And there was not much time. It would be a long night. But not as long as the night for Eileen Michelson. For her, the night was endless.

He extended his nets and began to dance.

Face dancer, he thought, and, as much as he could be, was in his own way content.

## THE HEGEMONY: SCARLET SECTOR

Naomia and Zero walked briskly down a wide corridor. The parlors that lined this way were blank-faced, encrusted with neon, their doorways like empty mouths emitting a smog of beckoning holograms. The pleasures here were more esoteric. Chemicals and hormones and machines. The denizens of City who walked here looked dazed. Their eyes were full of stunned bemusement.

Naomia strode in front of Zero. The ghostly pleasure seekers slipped past her like water past the bow of a ship.

"Somebody knows," Naomia said. "Somebody tried to break my safeguards."

"Who?" Zero's voice was calm. "Why?"

She shook her head. "Somebody with ICE. A honcho, working out of the Hall of the Web."

Zero's eyes flickered. "That's bad."

"They tried for you, too. Luckily, you don't exist."

"Did they get through?"

"No."

"What did you do?"

"I broke the fucker's own shields. I corrupted his own banks without his knowledge. He was good, but I'm better."

"Face dancer?" he asked.

"Yeah. Yes. Nasty one, too."

"So where does that leave us?"

"Still on," she told him. She glanced at the nailtale on her left pinkie finger. "In an hour and a half, I walk through the front door of the Hall of the Web with that poor stupid boy. Thirty minutes later, you come get us out of there."

Zero wrapped big fingers around her arm, tugged her to a halt. "wait a minute. They know?"

She turned and faced him. "Yes, they know. It doesn't matter. They're going to let us in." She paused, then laughed bitterly. "Can you imagine? All this trouble, and now they're going to let us walk right in."

"Why?" Zero asked.

"Because he strained that Michelson woman's brains and found out about our little plot. But she didn't know anything. So he's gonna let us stumble right into his trap. He figures it's the easiest way to unravel the whole mess. It made him nervous, not being able to find either of us with his precious machines. He's not used to that. It raised his hackles. Now he's a little worried, and a lot curious."

Zero's eyes were thoughtful. "I'm going to need a bigger diversion, if they're waiting for us."

She nodded grimly. "You'll have it."

He pursed his lips. "Twisten?"

"I didn't want to, but—"

He exhaled slowly. "That should be big enough. And it'll make getting off-planet easy." He chuckled. "*Real* easy."

"I hope so," she said.

He thought he heard a tinge of worry in her reply. But the promise she'd just made had taken him by surprise. He knew what was involved. Zero felt a slow flush of awe. He said. "That kid's really important. Isn't he?"

She began to walk away from him. He caught up in time to hear her mutter, "You better fucking believe it."

They walked a few steps further. "We could die in there, something goes wrong. All of us. The kid, too."

"It's not the dying that worries me," she replied. "I've done that. It's the living that's a problem. But then, it always is."


## THE WEB: EMPIRE


They fell through the glittering interstices of the deep beneath the Empire like leaves through a storm.

Around them swirled the diamond motes of other Empires, a galaxy both strange and beautiful. For one instant, he thought he saw something else: a place where serene blue globes floated like ornaments among gigantic green shapes, all interconnected by innumerable silver cords. But that vision passed almost as soon as he saw it, leaving a faint sense of loss. He blinked.

"Soon . . ." Naomia whispered.

They dropped together, arms intertwined, her fingers a long caress on his aching body. His penis surged against her belly, and she laughed.

Now the false galaxy vanished, and he beheld the tree as a distant flame upon ebony, growing larger. He didn't find it odd that he had to travel through the universes to reach the source of his own Empire. The structure here was plastic. He thought he saw only one face of reality, as he understood it.

Swiftly the flame in the distance grew into a mighty fire. The outlines of the flames became visible. He saw the golden spread of the tree growing endlessly from the Well of Light. As before, a part of the tree lay burning upon the darkness—the true source of his infection.

He felt a twinge of identity. Somehow the tree and himself were one. He had a sense of the tree being greater than the part he saw. Each one who penetrated here, to the heart of things, would see his own source of creation.

Now the bones and bark and leaves of the tree rolled beneath them growing ever more vast, until they floated over an endless landscape of gold and black and fire.

Naomia's hands were a symphony upon his flesh. His body throbbed in time with hidden drums. Her breath was warm on his ear, her words soft yet full or urgency.

"Soon, my Lord. Soon we come to the place."

He could see for himself the focus of the infection, rushing closer. Pressure like a wind grew against them. Naomia laughed aloud. The sound became thunder that rode against the wind. They moved forward.

Suddenly the entire scene vanished. They stood on a vast and empty plain that stretched to a mountain range shrunk to the size of a toy in the distant vista— but he knew the mountains were huge.

"Now," she said. A rough bliss growled like magma in her throat. "Now we will fight. Now, Lord, *you* will fight."

An answering thrill of wild joy seethed in his own veins. His erection stood out in front of him like a battle flag. he turned toward the distance and waited for the assault he knew would come.

The sky above them turned the hard blue of burning summer. A great light began to glow beyond the mountains. Then, like honey, the light spilled forth upon the plain.

Luke saw a savage army flow like water across the stone toward him. Millions—billions—of screaming, jeering savages armed with clubs, knives, swords, bows, and spears rushed forth in a tidal wave of destruction. They shouted maddened cries of battle lust and clashed their weapons together.

He and Naomia stood alone, facing them. "Your armies, my Lord. Summon your own host," she said. She stamped her right foot. Great cracks grew in the blasted rock beneath her.

He rocked against the earthquake she'd unleashed. His own armies? But what—? Then he understood. He faced himself here—those raving barbarians were himself. It was *himself* he must conquer in order to survive. So he must bring all of himself to the battle.

"Stone," he said. "To me."

And Stone was there. "Here, Sire," he said.

"Durward."

And Durward said, "I'm with you, Sire."

"Hendrickson."

"Right here, Lord. And your armies, too."

It was so. Now Stone, glowing with a molten red light, stood on his right hand, and beyond him Durward, glittering like a diamond. Spreading out behind were hosts of Soldiers. Tanks and gunships and planes overhead. The rumble of vast metal. Hendrickson looked down on him from the turret of a gigantic main battle tank.

"Ready, Sire," he barked, and saluted.

Stone moved slightly, and things of shining steel appeared in his hands. He was made a mighty hero then. "Ready, Sire," he said.

Durward raised his arms, and the sharp crackle of electricity sparked before his face. "Ready, Sire," he said.

Now music began to sound, harsh trumpets, long, booming drums. The wild skirl of flutes.

Naomia's voice was a terrible blend of scream and laughter. *"Your weapons, Lord!"*

And in one hand he grasped the three-tined trident. Another held the sharpened ax whose brightness was greater than the sun. Another wielded the great discus made of human faces and arms. And finally he brandished a mighty bow, whose curve and string glowed with the colors of the rainbow.

Naomia laughed wildly, her aspect suddenly terror. Her teeth, sharpened points, mirrored the gnashing jaws of the skulls around her neck. Her tongue became a lolling red ribbon of lust between those teeth. She wielded the fan and the noose, the sword and the skull-topped club, and from her lips came a long sound of wailing and despair. She breathed death.

Luke tasted her breath, and was borne up, and faced the golden horde of demons that was himself.

Strode to the center of the stone and brandished his arms. A huge fire burned in his loins. His penis ached with red fire that choked his veins, swelled his muscles, burned his mind.

He screamed his defiance and rage at them. At his back, the sound of his hosts was thunder. At his face, the sight of his enemy was lightning.

They came together.

Holocaust.

## THE HEGEMONY: HALL OF THE WEB

Charlie Seagrave met Naomia on the plaza in front of the Hall of the Web. It was a few minutes before 0900. Overhead the sky was blue and clear. The foot traffic here was sparse, only a few tourists wandering aimlessly. A slow, warm breeze ruffled their odd, off-World costumes.

Naomia wore a plain white smock over trim white slacks. Her dark hair was bound back neatly. Her face was scrubbed clean. Now he thought she looked younger than before. Even in the bright sunlight, he couldn't see any trace of the wrinkles and lines he'd noticed before.

He saw this in passing. His mind was in turmoil, sludgy with fear. He came up to her and took her hand. She glanced at him in surprise.

"I didn't see you," she said.

He pulled her toward the long, broad steps leading up to the pillars that fronted the massive building. "Come on," he said. "Let's get this shit done with."

She allowed him to tug her forward. Her long, muscular legs moved in parody of a womanly walk. He didn't notice, but she adjusted her gait. It had been a long time since she'd cared about such things.

"What's the matter?" she asked.

He didn't look back. "I tried to call Eileen this morning. There was no answer. She was supposed to talk to me before we went in." Worry thrummed in his voice.

"Is that a problem?"

"I don't know. Maybe something happened to her. It isn't like her. This is what—" He stopped. He remembered that Naomia knew nothing of the larger ramifications of the plot. Had he gone crazy? About to tell a common whore details of a bizarre cabal to overthrow the Hegemon? It sounded insane even to him. Gods only knew what she would think. He still couldn't imagine how what he was about to do would in any way accomplish that grandiose aim.

In fact, he couldn't imagine much of anything anymore. His entire existence had shrunk down to this tiny nubbin of time. He kept telling himself that if he could only get through this madness, then it would be over, and he'd at last be free.

A part of him knew this was folly. He was in too deep. He couldn't get out so easily. But he didn't want to think about that either. He focused instead on the act. He'd become existential without having any knowledge of that long dead philosophy. The act was all, and all that he cared about.

He dragged her up the steps and into the darker shadows beneath the main entrance. Only a few more minutes. Then he could rest.

Colonel Hanestad had gone schizophrenic. It was a difficult technique, but one he'd mastered long before. His ability to dance on the face and at the same time reserve a part of his mind to keep watch on true Reality was a talent that had aided him greatly in his rise to the top of ICE's hierarchy. Now, while large sections of his awareness tugged and pulled on the blue strings of his desire within the interfacial chasms, one of his eyes remained open, stolidly watching Seagrave and Naomia's progress as they entered the museum in the front part of the Hall.

He spoke aloud. "Let them in. Nobody interfere."

The other part of his mind, dancing on the face, checked to make sure the arcane mechanical and electronic devices that guarded the hall were equally muzzled.

He had brought great weapons to bear. In his hours of searching, he'd been unable to discover anything about Harrison Lever, or the prostitute Naomia. He didn't even know what she looked like, although he supposed the woman with Seagrave was she. Even with a solid confirmation of body structure and features, he still wasn't able to come up with a match.

A hooker and a revolutionary, both enigmas to his searching. It frightened him. Therefore augmented battalions of troopers, well hidden, now guarded the Hall. New machines had been brought, new weapons, new spies. Nothing could move inside the Hall without his knowledge. Nothing these two could carry inside would be weapon enough to cause damage. The whole ridiculous scenario of a blow job to be performed on a template must be a ruse. But a ruse concealing what?

If they carried a bomb of some kind, he would know. If they carried other weapons, he would counter them. He had made the Hall of the Web into a gigantic trap. Now all that remained was to spring it.

All his senses, both hidden and mundane, flickered on the naked edge of vigilance. Whoever these bastards were, whatever they planned, he was prepared for them.

He watched them hurry among the dioramas and spoke directly to the watchers who guarded the door through which Seagrave usually passed.

"Here they come," he said. "Get ready."

## THE HEGEMONY: NEAR SPACE; SYSTEM/WORLD

The farthest alarms began to sound long, sonorous warnings as the ever-seeking machines noted the disturbance.

Disturbances. Hundreds of them.

Something approached the boundaries of System/World through Twistor Space.

Something enormous.

# 11

## THE HEGEMONY: HALL OF THE WEB

"Come on," Charlie said.

Naomia plodded sullenly past the diorama of now-lost K'Mill. "That's pretty," she said.

"We don't have time for you to gawk at tourist displays," he told her. He had let go of her hand. Now he reclaimed it and pulled her forward again. Some of the terrible fear he'd felt had dissipated. They hadn't been stopped, hardly even questioned at the innocuous main gate. The guard on duty had barely glanced at them. Nor had any machine offered them question.

Reluctantly, she allowed him to lead her on. Her white smock flapped loosely about her slender limbs. Charlie didn't think she looked much like a tech, but nobody else had raised an eyebrow. Yet.

He guided her up to the inner gateway. "Do just like me," he whispered. He placed his palm on the reader, then presented his retinas for inspection. As she did the same, he held his breath. But the only thing that happened was that the armored door, as usual, slid wide to admit them to the smaller chamber beyond. The killing box, he thought of it, remembering half-forgotten science classes.

Again, they passed without incident. On the far side of the door, he realized he was sweating. The worst was over now. It was a straight, unguarded walk to his own work space and the template room, which housed the object of a practical joke he wished he'd never heard of now.

Naomia walked behind him, hiding a smile. His thoughts were as transparent as glass. How could he know his innocence? He'd dreamed up the joke, certainly. But the dreams had come through machines, pleasure machines he'd used before he met her. The manipulation of the human mind was a subtle process, but a simple one, as well. She'd been doing it forever—or so it seemed.

She watched with interest as he led her down halls, some empty, some peopled with ambling technicians who looked much like Charlie or Eileen. Pasty-faced, smug people, secure and insular in their careers, completely oblivious of the long fall into decadence that shadowed their culture, even their species.

Something had gone wrong with man, a long time before. She thought she knew what it was. Now, at long last, she would begin the task of rectifying the mistake. She called it the Original Sin. The sin wasn't entirely hers, but she'd played a part in it. The atonement would be of her making, though. She hoped it wouldn't be a mistake as well—but it would take eons to know the truth. She was willing to wait. But first, there had to be a beginning.

Here, now, the beginning began.

"This is it," Charlie said.

On the far side of the room, the template rested in endless sleep. She walked over to the steel slab. The massive shape that hid the template's head concealed his features. She remembered a face from long ago, still bright and sharp in memory. Had the universe truly been remade? Some thought so. In her occasional moments of uncertainty, she thought so, too.

Yet it seemed fitting that if this template—she glanced at the tiny silver plaque attached to the side of the slab—this Lucifer Angelus—and wasn't that a name to conjure with?—if this template was the one she remembered, returned, and was about to reborn—then it was fitting that his face remained hidden while she committed the act.

The act was fitting, too. She would spill his seed, and from that seed would grow a new epoch for humanity. Would grow. She hoped. If she was right.

Too many questions, she thought, and thrust them away. In this moment was the act. The act was all.

"Him?" she said.

Charlie nodded. "That's him." He paused. "Well? Go ahead. Do it. Do what you're paid for."

Some color had returned to his face. Poor thing, she thought. How little you know.

Then she corrected herself. How little we all know. She moved to the table. She bent forward. Her lips touched the template's penis. Then her tongue. Slowly, the organ began to rise.

Charlie watched with jumbled feelings. Jealousy, but how could he be jealous of this bag of empty meat? He couldn't imagine that the template actually *enjoyed* the act of fellatio. That blank brian, its pattern duplicated thousands of times each second by incredibly tiny machines nestled inside cells like marbles inside cathedrals, had never known this world.

Only for a moment did he wonder what the blow job might do to those basic patterns. It was a fleeting thought, and soon gone. His imagination allowed him to conceive the patterns might have existence elsewhere, in the electronic interstices of the Web itself, but he could carry the image no further.

His thoughts, as he watched, were filled with relief. *It's almost over*, he thought. *And nothing has happened to us. No arrests, no torture, nothing. Maybe Eileen just fucked up again. She was like that. A true fuck-up.*

Soft, wet sounds came from the slab where Naomia worked. Work—all in a day's work, he thought inanely. *I'm gonna make it*, he thought. *I'm gonna be okay!*

Colonel Hanestad watched the scene in the template room with a mixture of disbelief, stunned humor, and trepidation. He couldn't quite decide which emotion was paramount.

"Would you fucking look at that?" he breathed. He was alone in his office, so nobody heard him. He watched his monitor screens, and with his deep mind he watched the electronic approaches. Nothing stirred. Only a hooker giving a template a blow job.

He laughed again, loud and high, trailing down to a series of guttural barks, almost coughs. But beneath his laughter, the fear wouldn't go away. He had not yet found any trace of Harrison Lever. That was unheard of. And though he watched the hooker called Naomia, all he knew of her was what he saw with his own eyes. As with Lever, the prostitute was unknown to every data bank he could access—and he could access them all.

So what was the meaning of this ludicrous scenario? *That* was what worried him the most, its very meaninglessness. It made no sense—but it had to make sense. What had happened meant organization, talent, wealth. Power. It took all those things to create invisible people. Lever and Naomia were invisible. Therefore all the rest followed, and organization, talent, wealth, and power never combined forces in something as simple as joke. He didn't know the meaning of this, but there was meaning. He was absolutely certain of it.

Soon he would discover the meaning. He was equally certain of that, as well.

## THE WEB: THE DEEP BENEATH

Lucifer Angelus Imperator rose up on wings of fire. The battle screamed around him in tones of brass and terrible winds. He slew by the thousand. He harvested heads by the basket full with his ax sharp as sunlight. He threw his discus made of arms and faces into the onrushing horde. It spun like a great saw blade and struck fountains of blood wherever it touched. With his bow he cast a thousand arrows, and each arrow found the heart of an enemy and pierced it. But his trident was terror. From each of its three tines came black fire, and whatever that fire rested on, even for an instant, became nothing. With his trident he carved a swath of chaos in the very fabric of the True Deep, so that where that terrible force went, nothing at all remained.

On his right, Stone fought with flashing silver blades, and tiny shining things that exploded, and other, more arcane forces that tore and wrenched and dissolved. Beyond, Durward hurled lightnings at the savage barbarians, and they withered before him. But the most fearsome of all was Naomia.

Her aspect had changed. She had become black as night all over. Her pointed teeth were long yellow fangs, between which dangled her long red tongue. She howled constantly, a rising and falling sound that was appalling. Even the barbarians were terrified of it, and some threw down their weapons and ran from her.

Her fan was edged with steel, and when she waved it, vast winds smashed into the horde. With her noose she snared them in great clots of screaming flesh. The skull atop her blackened club opened jaws and tore limbs from bodies while its weight pulverized bone and sinew. From her sword dripped a force similar to the chaos of the trident, a dark and slashing power that left void in its wake.

Behind and above and beyond, the rest of his host bombed the savages, shot them, crushed them, roasted them as in a gigantic oven.

The sound of the carnage could not be described. It was storm and eruption and holocaust. And still the savages came on, dying by thousands, millions, endlessly.

After a time Lucifer looked and realized he would lose. The source of his enemy was himself, and he was inexhaustible. More and more of them poured from the mountains. Now he noticed the newer ones were larger, and in the shattered distance beyond, he could see giants with erections as large as mighty trees clambering down to join the battle.

He paused in his slaying a moment and shouted at Naomia. "I can't hold them! They are too strong!"

She didn't seem to notice what he said, but then he watched her begin to change. Like the emerging giants in the distance, she also began to grow. Her stature became an elephant. A great tree. Finally she bestrode the battlefield as a monstrous peak, its head in the clouds, its roots in the bowels of the earth. Where she put her foot, stone cracked and ran like honey. Her bellows of rage tore the fabric of the sky. Her weapons became the elemental power of earth, wind, fire, water.

He was seized with the joy of her, and rose to meet her, and together they began the dance.

"I am Death, the Shatterer of Worlds," he shrieked, and slew millions.

Her formless laughter was answer enough, as millions fell before her. And then she opened her mouth and began to feed.

It seemed the sky itself cracked, revealing emptiness rimed and edged with teeth. With four hands she scooped in the squirming, raging savages. Giants stormed up and were swallowed. She swept the battlefield with a plague of yearning chaos, and in the end she engulfed them all.

She ate the savages. She ate his hosts. She ate Durward, who disappeared into her maw screaming. In the end she swallowed Stone himself who, at the final moment, lay down his weapons and bowed to her. Then he was gone, and they faced each other on the plain of stone in the Deep Beneath.

"Death and destruction," she howled.

"The shattered worlds," he agreed.

They danced a final time, closer and closer, his erection between them as prize, weapon, gift.

She swallowed him, he ate her, and darkness covered the Deep Beneath.

At last they were one.

He slept.

## THE HEGEMONY: HALL OF THE WEB

Naomia raised her head. The template's penis lay flaccid against his naked belly. Strewn out in a glittering fan across his skin was a necklace of semen, bright as pearls. Naomia stepped back.

"Finished," she said. There was wonder in her voice.

Charlie had watched. It hadn't taken long. Near the climax, the template had arched his back, curled his toes, thrashed his arms about.

Charlie had never seen the template move like that. Hadn't even known it was possible. The maintenance of the template's body was too complicated and delicate a task for mere humans, or even gross machines. Everything was carried out by incredibly tiny molecular devices, trillions of them, that tended the template on a cellular level.

He shook his head. Naomia stared at him, her dusky face bright. Her green eyes glittered. She seemed to be waiting for something.

"Now what?" Charlie asked.

Colonel Hanestad had monitored the act on every level, including the levels of the Web he was allowed to reach. Something very strange was beginning to happen. He felt a thrill of fear, stronger than anything he'd felt before.

"Get them," he breathed. "Get them out of there. Now!"

He rose from his desk, tore the jack cable from his skull, and rushed out.

Things were going very wrong.

## THE HEGEMONY: DEEP SPACE; SYSTEM/WORLD

The fabric of the void burst wide open like a rotten apple, and ships boiled forth. Later, the machines would note over three hundred violations out of Twistor Space. That was later. Now there was no time for thought, for counting.

Unbelievably, World itself was under attack.

The heart of the Hegemony convulsed.

## THE WEB: CHAINS OF LIGHT

Luke was climbing. He didn't know how long he'd been trudging through these cold, vaulted chambers, but the road led up. All around him great, gray figures labored unceasingly. The sound of their hammers as they worked the stuff upon their anvils was a continuous avalanche of sound. He barely spared them a glance. The stuff they shaped writhed golden and glowing. Chains, he thought, chains of light.

The battle had stunned him. He remembered none of the details, not consciously. Only a feeling of fullness. Naomia had eaten the savages, and then himself. He'd eaten her. He was full of death and light and need. Somewhere up ahead in the dull distance was the source of the chains that the automatons so assiduously shaped.

He walked on, and after a time he found the Well. Here the empty-faced men of metal dipped tirelessly, ladling light stuff out for others to mold and cast. He walked to the edge of the pool and looked down. The light was bright as stars, but to him it only seemed a window.

In there, he thought. *Through there.*

Naomia hadn't lied. There was a way out.

He took it.

## THE HEGEMONY: HALL OF THE WEB

Harrison Lever—Zero—checked the time readout and nodded to himself. He spoke aloud.

"Now," he said. "Do it."

Three attack craft equipped with lethally illegal Twistor Field generators leaped forward as one. The entire front of the Hall of the Web disintegrated.

Colonel Hanestad, approaching the template chamber at the head of a squad of Hegemonic Guards, halted. The massive, ancient building shuddered beneath Zero's irresistible blow. The force of it threw Hanestad against one wall of the corridor, bruising his shoulder painfully. Up ahead he could see the door to the chamber, slightly ajar.

He knew he'd miscalculated badly. Now he wondered if he would survive his own mistakes. He examined that thought briefly, then ignored it. There was only so much he could do. He would do it, then.

"What's the matter with you?" he snarled at the squad, now unsteadily climbing to its collective feet. "It's right there. Get moving!"

Naomia said, "I want to see his face."

"You're crazy. Don't touch that—!"

But Charlie was too late. She bent forward and with a single motion tilted back the round enclosure that housed the neuro-nanotechnological transfer chains.

Charlie squeaked in terror, but at the same time paused, fascinated. The template's eyes were closed. From his skull, instead of hair, grew an uncountable web of incalculably tiny strands. Monomole optical fiber, a part of his mind told him. But the fibers were so tiny, the entire nest of them resembled a cloud of golden light, a halo around the sleeping boy's head.

There was unutterable beauty to the boy's face, unmarked by any human experience, unlined, without flaw.

"Perfect . . ." Naomia breathed. "He's perfect."

Luke fell through light, faster and faster, gathering strands of it to himself as he fell. He felt a flash of sadness. What he was doing now was irreversible. He didn't know how he knew it, but it was true nonetheless. The Empire was gone, and with it Durward, Stone, even the savage destroyers.

Yet still they were with him. He'd eaten them all in the end, and now all were one. If he could return to the Empire, he would find his wounds healed. But he couldn't go back. Not now. Not ever.

He had come to the end, but he thought perhaps it was only the end of the beginning. He held that thought as the light exploded around him, and he flowed forth through a trillion chains into a world for which he'd never been made.

Charlie made a choking sound. The template's eyelids flickered. A long, slow shudder ran through soft muscles. The flaccid penis twitched slightly.

Then the template named Lucifer opened its eyes.

They were green as the sea after a storm.

He tried to raise his head, but the transfer housing restrained him. HIs lips slipped together, fell apart. A pink tongue darted out, retreated.

Naomia put her hands out and held that beautiful head. Charlie had never seen her expression on any human face. The dread, longing, and hope there seared him to his bones.

"Who are you?" she whispered.

The body of Lucifer Angelus spoke its first human words.

"I am born," he said.

"Get away from there," Colonel Hanestad said.

The wall beyond the template dissolved in a silent cloud of dust. Zero stepped through, garbed in reflective battle armor that glittered like a thousand mirrors. He raised a strange, hammer-shaped weapon that made a sound like a gigantic zipper when he fired it.

Hanestad was lifted off his feet and flung backward

against his squad. He crumpled bonelessly. More of Zero's troops rushed through the gap, weapons chattering.

Zero stepped up to the table and raised his visor. His battered features were merry, but his gray eyes looked a little crazy. "Let's get a move on," he said. "We've got a plane to catch."

Charlie Seagrave's head swiveled back and forth from Zero to Naomia to Luke. His mouth hung loose and open. His eyes bulged slightly. His Adam's apple jigged up and down. He was trying to speak, but nothing came out except a choked gargle.

Naomia turned to Zero. "Take him, too." She pointed one long finger at Charlie. Her face was concentrated, intent. She looked as if she was trying to remember something.

"Him? Why, in Gods name?" Another wave of troopers flooded the hole at his rear and took up protective positions, their weapons focused on the door. "We've got a tight schedule, Naomia."

Luke's face was blank as an empty plate, but when Zero spoke her name, his green eyes flickered. Charlie saw it clearly. It was as if something very deep and hidden had swum up to the surface of those eyes.

"Naomia?" Luke said. His voice was soft, clumsy. Disused.

His head slowly turned. She looked down on him. "Hi, Luke," she said. "Welcome back."

The first spatter of blood—a tiny, magical dot, suddenly appearing—splashed across Luke's naked chest. Then another.

The sound of a million tiny whips filled the room. Her flesh exploded from her bones in a welter of crimson. Then the hidden knives chattered at her skeleton like microscopic teeth. The stench of charred calcium filled the room. It stank of burning stone.

"Noooooo . . ." Luke screamed. His eyes snapped shut. His head fell back, nothing left to support it.

Zero lurched forward. His right foot slid on the red, viscous puddle that had been a woman only a few seconds before. He caught himself and scooped Luke's deadweight under one brawny arm. His other hand flashed across the web of fiber optics that connected Luke's skull to the machines. The net parted with a crackling flash. Luke's body convulsed once, then went limp again.

Zero glared at Charlie. "You," he said. "She says take you. So I take you. Come on."

"I—I'm." Charlie shook his head once, then bent over and vomited, short, hard streams. It was over in a moment. He looked up, his face pale. "I'm not going anywhere."

A kindly look came across Zero's features. "Sorry," he said gently. "You don't get a choice." He stepped forward.

# INTERLUDE

## THE HEGEMONY: DEEP SPACE; SYSTEM/WORLD

The small armored cruiser darted with two of its fellows deep among the welter of gigantic battle platforms, which even now were turning the fabric of space-time into an impenetrable maelstrom as they dived back into the safety of Twistor Space. Zero had shed his armor. Now he sat in his small stateroom and chugged down half a martini.

"Gin," he said. "Comes from Ancient. Good World. Good booze. Want some?"

Charlie had no idea what a martini might be, but he nodded. Some kind of drug, he hoped. He still shook, long, racking shudders that made his jaws ache. But the seizures were lessening and numbness was setting in. He was grateful for that.

Zero handed him a glass, and he sipped. The fiery liquid stung his throat and made his eyes water, but a moment later warmth filled his stomach, and he sighed.

Luke slept like a dead man on Zero's bed. The

monomole fibers that had coated his head were gone.
Charlie had no idea where. Naked skin glistened
there, yet even bald, Luke seemed incredibly young.
And helpless, Charlie thought.

"What's going to happen to us?" Charlie said.

Zero grunted, then shrugged. "You, I haven't figured out yet. But that one"—he tilted his big, grizzled
head in the direction of the sleeping boy—"is going
to Ancient. He's gonna be a Soldier. Not a bad life.
I've liked it, at least." He seemed pleased with
himself.

"A Soldier?" Charlie wondered. He drained the
rest of his drink.

"He's gotta learn sometime," Zero said. "He can't
sleep forever."

"No," Charlie Seagrave said thoughtfully. "I suppose not." He paused. "What happened to Naomia?"

A flicker of unease crossed Zero's broad, battered
features. "I don't know," he said. "Nothing I knew
about. Maybe she made a mistake."

Charlie looked over at the sleeping template—the
sleeping boy, he amended himself. Maybe that had
been her mistake. but Eileen had been right. Somehow, the universe had been changed by Naomia's act.
He wasn't exactly sure how, or why, but he could
feel the change himself, when he looked at Luke's
beautiful, unsullied face.

Had Naomia expected to die? And what weapon
had harvested her life? He suspected he knew already,
but it would take some getting used to. The Hegemony had been ruptured in its deepest, most secret
heart to extract one sleeping boy. Who knew what
powers the template might hold? He suspected he
would eventually find out. His old life was over, that
was certain.

"A Soldier?" he remarked again. "That might be

interesting. Since, as you say, he can't sleep forever."

The two men stared at each other, silent, while they
waited for Lucifer to wake.

THUS ENDS THE FIRST OF THE LUCIFERIAN CHRONICLES